Lost Identity

Also by Ray Green
Buyout – A Roy Groves Thriller (Book 1)

For five ordinary guys and one rather extraordinary woman, the only escape from the corporate rat-race is to buy the company they're working for: take it all to a new level, save hundreds of jobs and make some serious money.

But it quickly becomes clear that nothing is as easy as it seems. The bid is quickly undercut as twisted corporate politics and personal vendettas take over.

When the buyout becomes *all or nothing* for the management buyout team, it all spins out of control: marriages fall apart, lurid secrets are discovered, life savings are spent on the stock market, illegal insider dealing becomes a matter of fact and blackmail, theft, betrayal and manipulation are the new rules of the game.

A once-in-a-life-time opportunity turns into a lurid nightmare.

BUYOUT is a gripping and compulsive page-turner about the power of money to unveil the deepest in human nature. It's also a story about chasing one extraordinary dream. At an extraordinary price.

Also by Ray Green
Payback – A Roy Groves Thriller (Book 2)

Roy Groves is Operations Director of a successful company manufacturing dashboard instruments for luxury cars.

A fatal motorway fire is traced back to a fault in the product supplied by Roy's company. Was it a tragic accident or something more sinister? As Roy and his colleagues battle to establish the cause of the fire, and save the company from bankruptcy, they discover that they have been the victims of sabotage.

Eventually, it emerges that an old enemy of Roy and the rest of the team has reappeared and is intent on destroying the company and every member of its management team. Once just a business adversary, their nemesis is now so consumed with hatred that he is on the edge of insanity; he resorts to blackmail and even murder in the pursuit of his goal.

PAYBACK is a chilling tale of how hatred can twist and corrupt the human soul.

Also by Ray Green
Chinese Whispers – A Roy Groves Thriller (Book 3)

Chuck Kabel is on a business trip to China, visiting the factory to which his UK-based company subcontracts the manufacture of its products. He unexpectedly collapses and dies at the airport before he is able to report on his visit. When the Chinese authorities are evasive about the exact cause of death, the suspicions of his boss, Roy Groves, are raised.

Roy decides to investigate further; it soon becomes clear that there are serious financial irregularities within the Chinese company, and that dark forces are in play, intent on ensuring that these do not come to light. When Roy edges closer to uncovering the truth, he is warned off but refuses to back down, unaware that he is about to confront the Chinese Mafia, who will stop at nothing to achieve their objectives.

When his own family are targeted by his opponents, Roy embarks on a desperate battle to protect them, now well aware that if he should turn to the police their lives will be in even greater danger.

CHINESE WHISPERS is a frightening tale of organised crime and the way in which it uses and abuses legitimate business for its own illegal purposes, relentlessly destroying the lives of anyone who stands in the way.

Also by Ray Green
Horizontal Living: A Tale of Expats Abroad - A Roy Groves Thriller (Book4)

Roy Groves has led a colourful career in business, during which he battled with corporate politics, deception, and even vicious criminals. But now Roy has retired and he is looking forward to a quieter life. He and his wife, Donna, have bought an apartment in an exclusive development on Spain's Costa del Sol.

He soon learns, however, that there are financial problems: the community is, in effect, bankrupt. Roy is persuaded to take on the role of president of the community, confident that, with his extensive business experience, he should easily be able to sort things out. It soon becomes clear, however, that nothing is as simple as it seems.

As he tries to come up with a rescue plan, Roy discovers that a poorly-constructed retaining wall has begun to collapse, threatening the development with a landslide. And this is just the start ...

As the problems mount up, one after the other, Roy becomes entangled with an astonishingly diverse cast of characters: the devious building developer; the vengeful former President; the Russian prostitute, and her mafia minders; the deranged Middle-Eastern doctor; the devastatingly glamorous French girl who moves in next door; and many more ...

HORIZONTAL LIVING is an illuminating insight into the shenanigans which pervade an ex-pat community abroad: sometimes hilarious, sometimes hard to believe, but sometimes darkly disturbing.

Also by Ray Green
Identity Found – The Identity Thrillers (Book 2)

Stephen Lewis and Carla Fernandez fled from Miami, Florida a year ago, to escape a terrifying battle with drug trafficking cartels and professional assassins. Now they are living a quiet life in Canada, under false identities.

But when a young female journalist is murdered in New York City, Stephen recognises that the killing has all the hallmarks of one of the world's most highly paid and notorious assassins. Why should this man, who can command a fee of millions of dollars for a single hit, be hired for such a seemingly insignificant contract? He concludes that the journalist must have been investigating something big – very big – and had been murdered to shut her up.

The police seem not to have made this link, and Stephen cannot approach them directly, as he is wanted in connection with the events in Miami. Fearful that there may be some terrible plot underway, possibly with many lives at stake, he decides to investigate. Carla insists on helping him.

Before long, Stephen and Carla find themselves battling for their lives once again.

Also by Ray Green
New Identity – The Identity Thrillers (Book 3)

Jason Hardwick and Gabriela Suarez have been on the run for almost three years – pursued by a network of professional assassins. Now they are living under false identities in the Market town of Chichester, in England.

Mark Bowman was the detective who helped the couple escape from a terrifying confrontation with their pursuers in New York City some fifteen months ago. Now he has been murdered. His killer is Jade Lacroix: a beautiful, highly intelligent, bisexual assassin. Jason and Gabriela are her next targets.

When Jason and Gabriela learn of Mark's death, they realise that these people will never give up. What can they do to fight back?

Alexis Miller – also an NYC detective – was Mark's girlfriend. She has vowed to bring his killer, and those she works for, to justice.

Will Alexis track down the assassin before she gets to Jason and Gabriela? Will she become a target herself? Who is the shadowy figure behind this murderous network?

'New Identity' is the thrilling, shocking conclusion to the 'Identity Thrillers' trilogy.

Lost Identity

Lost Identity

The Identity Thrillers – Book 1

By Ray Green

Lost Identity

Published in Great Britain by Mainsail Books in 2017

First Edition

ISBN 978-1-9999406-0-7

Published by Mainsail Books
www.mainsailbooks.co.uk

Cover design by Ana Grigoriu-Voicu
ana@books-design.com

Prologue

Downtown Miami – Thursday March 2nd

Sergio Lopez and Jorge Arteaga hurried along the darkened alley, Sergio still carrying the briefcase, which he had refused to leave behind. As they approached the brightly-lit street which crossed the end of the alley, the sound of a distant police siren, somewhere behind them, made them stop dead in their tracks.

'You gotta ditch the case,' urged Jorge.

'But it might have some money inside,' protested his partner. 'Once we get outta here we can easily force it open.'

The siren sounded as though it was getting closer.

'Christ, just look at yourself, man,' growled Jorge, eying his partner's ripped denim jeans and faded, brown tee-shirt. 'You just ain't the type to have a fancy briefcase like that ... and you got blood all over you. If the cops stop us, we're screwed.'

The fear and indecision in Sergio's eyes were obvious, but he was clearly reluctant to abandon the case, which he clutched tightly to his chest. 'I ain't leaving it 'til I've got it open and checked what's inside,' he insisted.

The sound of the siren grew louder. Jorge wasn't in the mood to debate the issue any longer; he wrenched the case from his partner's grasp and flung it to the ground. 'Come on! Let's split ... NOW!' He emphasised the point by grabbing Sergio's sleeve, dragging him away from the case and towards the end of the alley.

'What the fuck you doing, man?' hissed Sergio, wrenching himself free, ripping the sleeve of his tee-shirt in the process.

He made as if to turn back and retrieve the case, but froze as the flashing blue and red lights of a squad car came to a halt at the far end of the alley, some hundred or so yards away.

'Shit!' he muttered, abandoning his lunge for the briefcase and flattening himself against the wall just behind his partner.

1

There was clearly no turning back now. Hugging the wall closely, they began edging their way away from the squad car and towards the main street, less than twenty yards away. As they reached the street, Jorge crept forward and stole tentative glances to left and right. There was no sign of the cops, nor any sound of a siren, other than the one which wailed insistently from behind them.

'All clear,' he whispered. 'Let's go!'

They turned to the left and began making their way along the street, trying to look as inconspicuous as possible. Within a minute they picked up the sound of a second siren, which seemed to be coming from somewhere ahead of them. They stopped, looking anxiously at one another, unsure whether to turn around or press ahead. When a third siren joined the cacophony it became impossible to determine where each individual sound was coming from.

'Fuck!' muttered Sergio. 'The place is crawling with cops ... what are we gonna do?'

'Just keep going,' replied Jorge. 'They won't be looking for us yet.' He was nowhere near as confident as he tried to sound, but Sergio was already on the brink of panic and needed to be kept as calm as possible; the last thing they needed was for him to do anything stupid which might attract attention to them.

They pressed on, Jorge doing his best to make them blend in with the general flow of human traffic in the street. Every time they passed through the pool of light cast by an overhead street lamp, though, Sergio quickened his step as he sought the relative anonymity provided by the more dimly-lit areas between the lamps.

'Hey, slow down man,' urged Jorge, grabbing the other man's arm. 'You're just gonna make us look even more fucking obvious.'

Sergio shook his arm free, whirling to face his partner. 'I ain't hanging about just waiting to—'

He was cut short by the wail of yet another siren – much closer this time. Seconds later, the flashing lights of an approaching squad car came into view as it rounded a corner, around two hundred yards ahead, and headed directly towards them.

'Shit!' hissed Sergio, 'what the hell do we do now?'

'Go down there,' hissed Jorge, indicating a darkened alley just a few yards ahead and to their left.

As they turned into the alley, they could see that it connected with another brightly-lit street, around a hundred yards ahead, which ran parallel with the one they had come from. They hurried forward, making for the sanctuary of the darkest point, midway between the two streets.

Behind them, the sound of the siren was getting louder; they looked back to see the squad car draw to a halt right at the end of the alley.

'Goddam it!' muttered Sergio. 'They're bound to spot us now.'

Jorge grabbed his shoulder and dragged him back until they were both flattened with their backs against the wall. 'Just keep going ... slowly. If we stay close to the wall, we can make it to the other end without them spotting us.'

Sergio nodded, nervously. 'OK ... let's go.'

They edged forward, occasionally looking back; the car was still there, but now they were within about twenty yards of the other end of the alley. With a bit of luck—

Another squad car screeched to a halt right in front of them. They both dived into a doorway just to their left, huddling behind a garbage dumpster which was parked outside. Seconds later, the alley was flooded with light as one of the officers switched on a powerful flashlight.

'That's it,' whispered Sergio, 'we're trapped now ... we gotta give ourselves up.'

As the beam from the flashlight swung away and played up and down the wall opposite, they were afforded a brief moment of darkness. Jorge clamped his hand across his partner's mouth and dragged him further back into the doorway alongside the dumpster. 'Listen,' he hissed, hand still pressed against Sergio's mouth, 'I don't intend to go down for no murder rap, so just stay calm and don't panic. They ain't spotted us yet.'

Sergio wrenched himself free of his partner's grip, his eyes flaring with anger. 'I didn't do no murder ... that's your fucking problem.' He reached behind his waist, and withdrew from his belt a wicked-looking knife with perhaps a nine-inch blade, holding it up in front of his partner's face. 'Now you do what you like, but I'm going out there, hands in the air.'

He lowered the knife, preparing to throw it to the ground in front of him when he stepped out from the shadows. In that brief moment, Jorge grabbed the hand holding the knife, and once again clamped a hand over his partner's mouth. The other man tried to turn the knife back, but Jorge was the stronger of the two.

Their faces were just inches apart as the tip of the knife was forced, ever so slowly, closer to Sergio's body. His eyes widened in abject terror as he felt the cold steel penetrate the thin fabric of his tee-shirt and press against his skin. Jorge brought to bear his full body weight and, millimetre by millimetre, the knife sank into the other man's flesh. Sergio's eyes bulged in terror and pain as he made a last, superhuman effort to resist, but his strength was failing. Jorge gave one final thrust, angling the knife upward beneath the other man's rib cage. His expression changed to one of surprised shock. Jorge twisted the knife to left and right before withdrawing it and plunging it deep into the other man's body for a second time. The life drained from his eyes and Jorge felt his body go slack, its dead weight dragging downward. He removed his hand from the dead man's mouth, and slid it under his arm and around his back, taking the weight of the body as he withdrew the knife. He allowed the limp form to slide slowly to the ground, dragging it as far into the doorway as possible.

Panting from the exertion, he stole a glance back down the alley, in the direction from which they had come. One of the cops had got out of the squad car and was playing the beam of another flashlight up and down the alley. Jorge pressed himself back into the doorway.

'Anything up that end?' came the distant voice.

'Nah, nothing here,' replied the man at the nearer end of the alley, switching off his flashlight.

Jorge heard the sound of the nearer car making off, emitting a brief chirrup from its tyres. Seconds later, he heard a car door slam and the other squad car also moved off.

He remained stock-still for around thirty seconds, allowing his pounding heart to settle a little, before bending down to remove the wallet from Sergio's back pocket. *No sense in leaving that behind*, he thought. He slipped the wallet into his own pocket, before cautiously, emerging from the doorway, stepping over the body, taking care to avoid the rapidly spreading pool of blood.

Stealing another couple of glances up and down the alley, he stripped off his bloodstained tee-shirt and used it to wipe his fingerprints from the handle of the knife before dropping it into the dumpster. He then used the ruined tee-shirt to wipe the worst of the blood off his hands before dropping that, too, into the dumpster.

Finally, he set off down the alley, hoping that his bare-chested appearance would not attract too much attention. It was a risk, but not as bad a risk as being seen covered in blood. On a warm evening like this, he wouldn't be the only young guy roaming around without a shirt on.

Shame about Sergio, he thought, *but the crazy bastard always did panic too easily.* He just hoped his bosses wouldn't be too hard on him for the way he had dealt with his partner …

Chapter 1

Sunday March 5th

She was on top of him, straddling him, moving gently to and fro, her long, blonde hair brushing his cheek as it swayed with her movement. Her deep blue eyes, intense with desire, locked onto his as she leaned forward, the ghost of a smile playing around her generous lips. She lowered her lips to his, allowing the hard buds of her nipples to brush tantalisingly against his chest for a few seconds before pressing the full, soft warmth of her breasts against him. Her tongue curled into his mouth, probing, exploring every corner. He closed his eyes, savouring the exquisite kiss as much as the sensation burgeoning in his loins.

All too soon, their lips parted; she moved to a more upright position and began a sinuous, undulating motion, which became more urgent as every second passed. Instinctively, he slid his hands behind her hips, pulling her to him, his desire to prolong the delicious experience gradually becoming overwhelmed by the burning need to move to a climax. He sensed that she, too, was almost ready.

He opened his eyes, wanting, above all else, to watch the changing expression on her beautiful face as their lovemaking moved towards its zenith. But as he opened his eyes, he found his vision was blurry, wavering; he couldn't see her clearly. What was going on? He closed his eyes tight shut and opened them again, trying to shake free of the trance-like veil which had enveloped him. As his vision began to clear, his heart skipped a beat. In an instant, the heat of sexual desire had vanished, to be replaced by a whirlwind of shattering confusion.

Where were those beautiful, azure blue eyes? The eyes which now locked onto his were a deep brown colour. And her long, blonde hair was now jet black. Her skin tone was no longer pale and porcelain-like: it was the colour of mahogany. What the hell was happening?

Her face moved closer to his once more. Through a swirling haze, he saw her lips move. Everything seemed to be in slow motion as he heard the words, distant and echoing, as though through a long tunnel.

'Are you OK? Can you hear me?' The accent sounded South American or, perhaps, Spanish.

But as he struggled to make sense of what was happening, the vision of her face began to fade, gradually becoming subsumed in a grey mist.

Her voice became fainter. 'Stay with me ... wake up ... they'll be here soon ... try to ...'

But she was gone.

***

Beep ... beep ... beep ...

The regular, insistent sound was gradually becoming louder, intruding into the warm, private cocoon which he occupied.

Beep ... beep ... beep ...

Go away, will you?

Beep ... BEEP ... BEEP ... BEEP ...

He could ignore it no longer. He tried to open his eyes, but his eyelids refused to respond to his brain's instruction – they were resolutely glued shut.

He tried to call for help, but his parched tongue clung to the roof of his mouth.

He tried again. 'P-please ... c-c-can somebody help me?'

A few seconds later, he felt a hand on his cheek.

A female voice intruded. 'Sir ... are you awake? Can you hear me?'

'Y-yes ... I c-can hear you.'

He tried once more to open his eyes; finally, his eyelids freed themselves and flickered open. At first, all he could see were blurry shapes of light and dark but, as he blinked to try to clear his vision, the female face which he dimly remembered from his dream began to materialise once more.

Except it wasn't the same face ...

This face was more rounded and the complexion paler. Her hair was short and dark, styled in a bob. When she spoke, the accent was different, too – now it sounded American Deep South.

'Doctor Holt … Doctor Holt … he's coming around!' she cried, rushing away, leaving him dazed and bewildered.

He tried to lift his head, but the stabbing pain which shot through it made him slump back into the pillow. As he raised his hand to try to determine the source of the pain he could feel the texture of some kind of fabric, realising, eventually, that his head had been bandaged. With a considerable effort, he managed to turn his head to one side, wincing as the pain lanced through his skull once more. Alongside him was a screen showing several green, glowing, horizontal lines punctuated by sharp peaks pulsing at regular intervals.

He felt a hand on his shoulder and heard another voice – male this time.

'Sir, can you see me … and hear me?'

Tentatively, he swivelled his head towards the sound. The man leaning over him was middle-aged, thin-faced, with a neatly-trimmed beard. His pale grey eyes radiated kindness and warmth.

'Yes … where am I?'

'You're in hospital. I'm a doctor … my name is Alan Holt.'

'But why am I here? What happened?'

'You have suffered a severe head wound. You have been in a coma for three days.'

As he tried to sit up, the spear of pain in the back of his head forced him back down; the man laid a gentle restraining hand on his chest.

'Don't try to move just yet … you have a minor skull fracture.'

'A skull fracture? Oh my God ... is it … well … am I going to be alright?'

The doctor removed his hand. 'There is no need to worry unduly. As far as we can ascertain it is not severe enough to have impinged on your brain, and we do not believe surgery will be necessary. Nevertheless, it will take some time to heal. We can give you something for the pain, but you must rest.'

'But what happened to me? Was it an accident, or …?' His words tailed off.

'We don't know for sure what happened,' said the doctor. 'It wasn't an accident, though. We were rather hoping you would be able to tell us what happened.'

'Well, I was just …' As he struggled to recall what had happened he felt a sickening emptiness inside – he had absolutely no recollection of whatever had happened to put him in hospital.

'Now, what do you remember about the incident?' prompted the doctor.

'I … I don't remember anything.'

The doctor's face creased with concern. 'Do you remember why you were in that alley?'

'An alley … what alley? I don't remember anything about any alley.' He clutched at the doctor's sleeve. 'What's happened to me? I can't remember anything.'

'OK …OK,' soothed the doctor, 'don't worry – you're going to be fine. It seems that the blow to your head has caused some memory loss, but it's probably temporary. Having been in a coma for three days, you can't expect everything to get back to normal immediately.'

He let go of the doctor's sleeve and sank back into the pillow as the enormity of the situation began to register. 'But what *did* happen to me in this alley?'

'As far as we can ascertain, you were the victim of an attack, in which you received a severe blow to the head. As for the motive, we have no idea. Do you know if anything was stolen from you?'

He screwed his eyes tight shut, concentrating intensely as he tried to recall what had happened, but it was no use. 'I don't know,' he muttered.

'Alright, don't stress about it. Hopefully the police will come up with something.'

He shook his head in frustration. 'How did I end up here … in hospital?'

'The emergency services received a 911 call … fortunately very soon after the attack. If that hadn't happened, the outcome might have been far worse – you were losing a lot of blood. Do you know who made the 911 call?'

Once again, he trawled the depths of his brain for an answer but, once again, came up blank. He shook his head. 'No … I don't remember *anything*.'

'Apparently the caller was a woman. Were you perhaps travelling with your wife ... or a female business colleague ... or—'

'I told you,' he snapped, exasperated, 'I can't remember *anything*.' He immediately regretted the tone he had adopted with the doctor who, after all, was only trying to help him. 'I ... I'm sorry Doctor. It's just so ... well, frightening ... being unable to remember *anything*.'

'Don't worry,' said the doctor, his voice calm and reassuring, 'I completely understand. Now then, let's just take it step by step.'

He nodded, breathing deeply as he tried to calm and compose himself. 'OK, but sorry, anyway ... for the outburst.'

'No apology necessary,' soothed the doctor. 'Now then, when they brought you to us you had no I.D. on you. Can you tell me your name?'

'My name? Yes, it's ... it's ...' He groped for the words that should have tripped so easily from his tongue, but they eluded him.

'Yes?' prompted the doctor.

But he wasn't listening – he was concentrating on a superhuman effort to probe the deepest recesses of his own mind, searching, grasping. And then, at last, it came to him ...

'Stephen,' he gasped. 'Yes ... definitely Stephen'.

'Good,' said the doctor, his face relaxing a little.

'And what about your surname?'

He closed his eyes as he tried to revisit that elusive corner of his brain which had just given up this first shred of information.

'Lewis ... my name is Stephen Lewis.'

It was the tiniest of steps forward, but a step forward nevertheless. Stephen Lewis allowed himself a small smile.

'You see? Your memory is starting to return already. Now, from your accent, I assume you are English. Do you remember why you are in Miami?'

'Miami? I'm in Miami ... Florida?'

The doctor nodded.

The realisation that he didn't even know what country he was in quickly dashed the brief sense of euphoria resulting from the recollection of his name. He screwed his eyes tight shut as he tried to recall what he was doing in Miami, but it was no use; he let out a noisy sigh of exasperation. 'No ... I'm sorry ... I can't remember.'

'OK, don't worry – it will probably come back to you soon. Anyway, at least we know your name now. We can check with the police whether anyone has been asking after you. Meanwhile, you need to rest. We'll give you something for the pain, and a mild sedative to help you sleep. We'll talk again tomorrow morning.'

With that, the doctor left the room, leaving the nurse to administer the medication. She gave him a small plastic beaker with four capsules in it. She helped him raise his head a little and, one by one, he swallowed the capsules, taking sips of water from the cup she held to his lips.

As he settled back and closed his eyes, he tried to make sense of his situation. Who was he? Why was he in Miami? Why would anyone want to attack him? His head swirled with a tangled maelstrom of disconnected thoughts. But none of it made any sense.

Before long, he gave up; sleep overtook him.

Chapter 2

The distant drone of the engines suddenly changed in tone and he sensed the pace of the aircraft slacken slightly as he experienced the familiar weightlessness in his stomach: they were starting their gradual descent.

He glanced across at his wife; she was still fast asleep, a strand of long, blonde hair draped carelessly across her cheek and over the corner of her mouth, where it fluttered rhythmically each time she exhaled. He leaned over and gently pulled the hair away from her finely-sculpted cheek. Her pretty, slightly-upturned nose twitched, and she emitted a sigh but did not wake. She looked so much younger than her thirty-seven years and, even after four years of marriage, he could still hardly believe that such a beautiful woman would have chosen him, an average-looking guy, five years her senior, to be her husband. There was no need to wake her just yet, so he set about gathering together the papers he had been studying and packing them away in his briefcase.

'Can I take that for you sir?' said a flight attendant, reaching out for the briefcase.

'Thank you. I didn't want to disturb my wife.'

'Of course,' she said, smiling. 'But we'll be arriving soon anyway. I'll put your case in the overhead locker, right here.'

As he reached over her to pass the case to the flight attendant, his wife shifted position, pulling her blanket up around her shoulders and letting out a sort of contented snuffling noise, but still she did not wake.

He turned to gaze out of the window, where they were just about to descend into a cloud layer so dense that it looked more like a snow-covered field, gleaming in the bright sunshine. It was easy to imagine you could just get out and walk on it, kicking up the icy crystals as you passed.

As they entered the cloud layer, the change in outlook was as abrupt as if someone had flipped an invisible light switch. All that could be seen, now, was an impenetrable, greyish-white miasma, rapidly flickering as the aircraft sped through areas of differing cloud density. And then, suddenly, they were through, and the vista laid out below could be clearly seen. Gone was the splendid isolation of the open skies, to be replaced by the expansive vista of southern Florida. The highways were choked with traffic, barely moving as it snaked between the swathes of concrete and glass and across the vast bridges which crossed the sparkling waters of Biscayne Bay. The intra-coastal waterway, with its many inlets and backwaters, was packed with boats, small and large.

This network of inland waterways, and the substantial pockets of green space which had been preserved, lifted the whole scene from potentially depressing urban sprawl to inviting, semi-tropical retreat. He had never been to Miami before and was looking forward immensely to his stay.

Having been awake for practically the whole journey, perversely, now that they were on their final approach, the desire to sleep became almost irresistible. He leant his head back and closed his eyes, just for a few moments …

***

He heard distant voices: a man and a woman … no, perhaps two men and a woman. He was no longer in the aeroplane; he was back in his hospital bed. He tried to re-enter the pleasant world of his dream, which seemed a far more inviting place than the harsh reality which now threatened to intrude.

It was no use: the harder he tried to drift back to that cosy place, sitting alongside his beautiful wife, the more he—

Suddenly he was wide awake. He opened his eyes, blinking against the harsh glare of the overhead light.

'Doctor! Nurse!' he cried. Within seconds Doctor Holt appeared in the doorway.

'What is it, Mr Lewis?'

'My wife … I'm here with my wife.'

'Your wife?'

'Yes … I remember now.'

'This is excellent news,' declared the doctor.

But Stephen Lewis didn't share the doctor's assessment. 'Oh, my God! She'll be worried sick. If she hasn't heard from me in over three days, she'll be—'

The doctor raised a calming hand. 'OK, OK. Just tell me what you remember.'

'I was with her on a plane. She was asleep right beside me.'

'And you think that plane was headed here ... for Miami?'

'I ... yes, the view out of the window ... the waterways. Yes, I think we were coming in to land in Miami.'

'OK, very good. Now, can you tell me your wife's name?'

'Of course. It's ... it's ...' But her name just wouldn't come. He clenched his fists in frustration. 'I ... I can't remember.' He sighed, heavily.

The doctor moved to calm him, making a sort of slow, downward, patting gesture in the air with his hand. 'Please ... don't stress about that right now ... I'm sure it will come back to you in due course.'

'But I can describe her,' breathed Stephen.

'Go ahead,' encouraged the doctor.

'She's tall; slim; blue eyes; long, blonde hair; and beautiful ... she really is beautiful.'

'Perhaps it was your wife who placed the 911 call,' suggested the doctor.

He considered this possibility for a moment but quickly rejected it. 'No ... if that were the case, surely she'd be here.' He fixed the doctor with a penetrating stare. 'What if she was with me when I was attacked? I have to find her ... she may be hurt.'

The doctor's reply was delivered in a soft, calming tone. 'Please don't worry, Mr Lewis. I'm sure there's no reason to suppose she's hurt.'

He tried to sit up, a spear of pain lancing through his skull. 'But if she was with me when I was attacked, she could be—'

The doctor placed a gentle restraining hand on his shoulder, easing him back down in his bed. 'Look, let's take it one step at a time. We can give your wife's description to the police and they can check whether a lady matching that description has reported you missing.'

'But what if she's—'

'Calm yourself, Mr Lewis. If she's here in Miami, I'm sure the police will be able to find her.'

Stephen's head slumped back into the pillow. 'I suppose so.'

'Look, there are actually two police officers here right now. They're waiting to interview you just as soon as you are able to answer questions. Do you feel up to it, or shall I tell them to come back tomorrow?'

'No,' he sighed, 'let's get it over with ... though I'm not sure I can really tell them anything useful.'

'Just tell them everything you can remember,' said the doctor. 'No-one can ask any more of you.' He gave his patient a reassuring pat on the shoulder before leaving the room.

Stephen closed his eyes and, as he did so, that delicious vision of his lovemaking, with the woman who he now realised was his wife, came flooding back. As he gazed into those deep blue eyes, it suddenly came to him ...

'Emma!' he blurted, his eyes wide open now. 'Her name is Emma.' But there was no-one there to hear his cry.

A few seconds later, however, the nurse from the previous day entered the room, followed by two police officers.

'Ah, Stephen ... these two gentlemen—'

He sat bolt upright, interrupting her in his haste to share this latest flash of insight. 'I remember her name: it's Emma. My wife's name is Emma. She'll be trying to find out what's happened to me. We have to find her.'

'OK ... that's fantastic,' said the nurse. 'Your memory is gradually coming back. Now that we have a name and a description of your wife, I'm sure we can—'

'Ahem ...' She was interrupted by one of the police officers reminding her of their presence.

'Er, Stephen ... these two gentlemen are police officers. They would like to ask you a few questions.'

'And then we'll get right on the case with finding your wife, sir,' said the taller of the two.

'OK,' said Stephen, anxious to get this over with so that they could get on with the much more important business of locating Emma, 'but I don't think I'll be able to tell you much.'

'Twenty minutes maximum,' scolded the nurse. 'He's still very weak.'

'Officer Brooks,' said the taller guy, stepping forward. 'And this is Officer Rodriguez. Mind if we sit down?'

They didn't wait for a reply, both pulling up chairs alongside the bed. Rodriguez pulled out a notebook and pen, looking expectantly at his partner, who was evidently going to do the talking.

'Now sir, I understand that you are suffering a degree of memory loss, resulting from your head injury.'

Stephen nodded. 'It's the weirdest sensation – trying to remember anything at all is like trying to recall the elusive details of a dream you've just had. You know it's there, tantalisingly close, but you just can't quite reach out and grasp it.'

Looking at the expressions on the two police officers' faces did little to convince him that his attempt to convey the turmoil which beset him had struck any kind of chord.

'Yeah,' said Brooks, 'must be kinda tough.'

You got that right, thought Stephen.

'So,' the police officer continued, 'just what *can* you tell us about what happened on Thursday?'

'Well, not much, I'm afraid. I can remember hardly anything that happened before I woke up here, in hospital. I don't even know what I do … did … for a living or what the hell I'm doing here in Miami.'

'So nothing about the assault?' prompted Brooks.

'No … nothing. The only things I can remember are my name – and now my wife's name, and what she looks like. I can see her in my mind's eye in perfect detail. She's tall – about five-nine, slim, long blonde hair, thirty-seven years old and …' His heart leapt with the realisation that he had just remembered her age. Snippets of his memory *were* starting to return.

'Let's see if any of this helps,' said the police officer turning to his partner who passed him a plastic zip-lock bag. 'Apparently these were the only things you had with you when you were admitted.' He withdrew from the bag a gold ring with three small diamonds embedded in its surface. 'You were wearing this.'

As he gazed at the ring, a dim and distant memory began to stir. He saw an image of a hand … no, *two* hands. A small, feminine hand, with elegantly-manicured nails, dwarfed by the much larger, man's hand which held it. Both wore matching rings – gold, embellished with three diamonds. It was a photograph: he and Emma, on their wedding day, holding clasped hands towards the camera, displaying their identical rings.

16

'My wedding ring,' gasped Stephen. 'My wife has one exactly the same.'

'OK, good,' said Brooks, 'that's one more thing which will help to identify your wife if—'

'What do you mean?' demanded Stephen. 'Why would you need to "identify" her? Has something happened to her?'

'No, sir – nothing like that. It's just that the more information we have, the easier it will be for us to find her. So now we have her name, her description, and a precise description of her ring. That gives us a good starting point.'

'Wait a minute,' said Stephen, as another memory came back to him. Somehow, answering these questions, forcing him to trawl the muddled depths of his brain, seemed to be stimulating more and more fragments of recall. 'My wallet ... I keep a photograph of the two of us in my wallet. If you have an actual photograph of my wife then surely it will help you to—'

The police officer shook his head. 'I'm afraid you had no wallet on you when they brought you in. I guess the lowlifes who attacked you must have taken it, along with anything else you had on you.'

Stephen's heart sank as quickly as it had lifted.

'By the way,' continued the police officer, 'can you remember if you *did* have anything else in your possession when you were attacked?'

'I already told you,' sighed Stephen, 'I can't remember anything about it.'

The policeman shrugged. 'I'm surprised they didn't take off with the ring too,' he continued. 'Looks like it could be worth a fair few dollars.'

'They probably didn't spot it,' added the other police officer – the first words he had uttered since arriving.

Stephen didn't respond; he had no desire to prolong this conversation any longer than necessary.

'OK,' said Brooks, 'what about this?' He took from the bag a small leather-bound book and passed it to Stephen. 'Apparently, it was lying on the ground right beside you. The paramedics picked it up.'

Stephen took the book and turned it in his hands – a diary; he didn't recognise it. He looked up at the two police officers and shook his head.

'Take a look inside,' said Brooks.

Stephen flipped through the pages; his brow wrinkled in puzzlement.

'But … there's nothing written in it. Why would I be carrying a diary without any—?'

'Look again,' interrupted the police officer. 'Check out this week.'

Stephen went to turn to the relevant pages, but stopped dead when he was hit by a dawning realisation. 'I'm afraid I don't know which *is* this week.'

A slight shadow flitted across the police officer's eyes. Disbelief? Irritation? Could be almost anything. Anyway, the moment passed, and Brooks's countenance resumed its previous neutral, detached look.

'Today is Monday March 6th.'

Stephen turned to the relevant page: nothing. He looked up, puzzled and gave a slight shake of his head.

'Go forward a few pages,' prompted Brooks.

The date Thursday March 9th was ringed in black ink. What did it mean? He gazed at the page for several long seconds but the date triggered nothing in his brain.

'Well?' prompted Brooks.

'It's … this Thursday. Just a few days' time.'

'I know what day it is' – Stephen thought he detected a hint of annoyance in the police officer's voice – 'but does it mean anything to you?'

'I'm afraid not,' sighed Stephen.

'OK, now turn to Sunday July 23rd.'

'But that's months away … what could that have to do with my current situation?'

'Just take a look will you?' muttered Brooks, his tone now clearly betraying his growing impatience.

Stephen found the page; this date was also ringed in black ink. He shrugged, helplessly.

'So I guess *that* date doesn't mean anything either.' It was more of a statement than a question.

'Sorry, no.'

Brooks rolled his eyes; Stephen was starting to take a real dislike to this guy.

'OK, well those were the only things you actually had with you when they brought you here, but we had a good look round the scene of the attack. There was all kinds of garbage on the ground, but we did pick up a couple of things that might be relevant.' He delved into the bag and withdrew the next item. 'What about this?'

He held up a small gold-coloured cylinder: a lipstick.

Stephen's heart stuttered. 'Oh my God! Is it Emma's?'

The police officer gave him a stony stare. 'I was hoping *you* might be able to tell *us* … What colour does she wear?'

Stephen conjured in his mind that vivid image which had dominated his dreams these last hours. 'Most of the time it's a sort of pink colour … yes, she nearly always wears pink lipstick.'

'Yeah, well so do most dames,' muttered Brooks.

By now, Stephen felt an overwhelming urge to plant a punch squarely on the man's already-crooked nose. He resisted.

The police officer took the lipstick back, removed the cap, and twirled the base to expose the contents. 'Does she wear *this* shade of pink?'

Stephen's eyes narrowed as he concentrated intently, trying to match the colour in front of him to his mental image. After a few seconds his shoulders slumped in defeat.

'It … it could be … but … I just can't be sure.'

'OK, I've got one last thing to show you.'

He took the final item from the bag and passed it to Stephen. It was a business card: pale blue background with an image of a leaping swordfish. It bore the words 'Eduardo's Restaurant'.

'I'm afraid I've never heard of this place,' said Stephen.

'Well, there was all kinds of shit on the ground where you were attacked but this card looked kinda cleaner and newer than all the other stuff so we figured you might have dropped it during the struggle. And if you turn it over, you can see there are a few spots of blood on it, which also suggests—'

'Blood?' he gasped. With trembling fingers, he turned the card over; the three dark stains seemed to portend something terrible. 'Oh God! Maybe something's happened to Emma.'

'No … we already checked the blood group: it matches yours. You left a hell of a pool of the stuff on the ground after you got whacked on the head.'

A wave of relief coursed through his body – only to be replaced, moments later, by a renewed spear of dread. 'But what if she's the same blood group as me?'

Brooks extended his hand, palm-outward, in a calming gesture. 'Relax ... we did a DNA check too, and it's definitely *your* blood.'

Relief flooded through him once more. He took a few moments to compose himself before speaking again.

'OK, well have you checked out this' – he glanced at the card again – '"Eduardo's Restaurant"?'

Brooks gave a derisory snort. 'Hardly a "restaurant" – more of a scruffy diner really. Full of damned Latinos.'

Rodriquez visibly stiffened at this pejorative remark; he might be second or third generation, but he clearly had some Latino blood in him. Nevertheless he said nothing, instead lowering his gaze and resuming his note-taking duty.

'But did you check it out?' insisted Stephen.

'Yeah, we went there ... talked to the owner and a couple of his waitresses, but they don't remember a tall, white guy like you in the joint recently. We even showed them a photo, but the fact you were flat-out unconscious, with a bandaged head, in the photo probably wouldn't have helped, even if they *had* seen you before.'

'So, you don't really have *any* leads right now?'

'I guess not. We were hoping you might be able to help, but as you can't remember anything at all about the attack' – once again that slight tone of annoyance or scepticism revealed itself – 'we really don't have much to go on. Anyway, if you do recall anything which might help us, just give me a call.'

Stephen was only too pleased to terminate the interview and see the back of this unpleasant policeman and his superfluous sidekick but whatever he thought of them, he *needed* their help.

'Please,' he said, as the two men stood up to leave, 'you have to find my wife.'

'We'll do our best, sir,' said Brooks. 'We now have a name, a description, and we know she wears pink lipstick.' The sarcasm in his voice was only thinly veiled. 'Of course, we don't even know for sure that she's actually *in* Miami at all.'

Stephen fought to control the anger which surged within him. 'Look, I'm sure she *is* here. I remember her sitting alongside me on the plane.'

'Oh, so now you remember something you neglected to tell us earlier.'

'What? What do you mean?'

You never mentioned anything about a plane ... or about your wife being with you on it.'

'Didn't I? Well ... oh, I'm sorry ... I told Doctor Holt about it, and I assumed—'

The police officer silenced him with a raised hand. 'So was this plane coming into Miami?'

'I ... I think so.'

'You think so ... but you don't actually know?'

'No,' he admitted. 'I can't be absolutely sure, but ... can't you check immigration records? Won't they show whether a Stephen and Emma Lewis came into Miami recently?'

'We'll take a look,' said Brooks.

'Don't worry,' piped up his usually-silent partner, 'if your wife is here in Miami, we'll find her.' Somehow, Stephen was less than convinced.

Moments later they were gone, leaving Stephen to ponder the handful of items they had left with him – the only clues to a life which was now a closed book. A wedding ring; a diary with nothing in it, other than two highlighted dates; a lipstick; and a business card for a seedy diner.

What the hell did it all mean?

<u>Chapter 3</u>

The following day he awoke feeling rather better – at least physically. The nagging ache in his head had finally dissipated, and he felt much stronger. He noted that the drip, which had been connected to his wrist, had now been removed, and he was able to sit properly upright. His mental state was, however, a different matter entirely: in spite of all his best efforts, he could make no sense of the discussion with the two policemen, or of the various items they had presented him with.

He decided to test his legs, swinging them over the side of the bed and tentatively attempting to stand. He felt a little unsteady on his feet, but he *could* stand up. He tried taking a few steps; his balance was a little off, but overall, not too bad. Even though his life was in turmoil, it felt good to experience the simple sense of independence engendered by the ability to stand, literally, on his own two feet.

The nurse appeared in the doorway. 'Well, I can see that *you* are feeling much better,' she said, a warm smile creasing her friendly countenance.

'I am,' he confirmed. 'The headache's faded away and,' he said, spreading his arms wide and looking down at his own feet, 'I can finally get up and walk.'

'That's very good,' she said, fussing and trying to shepherd him back towards his bed, 'but, please don't try to do too much too soon.'

'OK,' he said. 'You're the boss.'

She smiled. 'You're dead right – around here at least, that's exactly what I am.'

Stephen was immediately drawn to this woman; he liked her no-nonsense manner, which he sensed belied a genuinely caring individual.

'What time is it?' he said, skilfully evading her attempts to encourage him back into bed.

'It's almost 3 p.m. You've been asleep for around fourteen hours straight.'

'Fourteen hours?' he gasped. 'I need to get up and dressed ... try to figure out what's happening to me.'

'Not just yet,' she replied firmly, placing her hands on his shoulders, gently but insistently guiding him towards the armchair alongside the bed. 'Your body obviously needed the rest, and you're still too weak to be up and about.'

'OK,' said Stephen, sinking obediently into the chair. 'I guess I need to do as I'm told.'

'You do,' she said, smiling.

'By the way,' he said, accepting, for now, his temporary confinement to the armchair, 'you never told me your name.'

'Kelly.'

'Well, thank you Kelly, for everything you've done.'

'Oh, just doing my job,' she said, dipping her head a little and raising a hand to sweep away a stray lock of hair from her cheek.

He didn't for one moment believe that, for this likeable woman, it was 'just a job'. She was clearly one of those people for whom helping others was second nature.

'Well, thanks anyway. I owe you.'

She batted her eyelids, but did not respond directly. 'By the way, I've brought you a local newspaper. As you're here in Miami, you might as well know a little about what's going on around here. Who knows ... it might even help you recall something about why you're here.'

'Thanks,' he said, smiling.

'Would you like a cup of coffee before I bring your breakfast?'

'Do you have tea?'

Her face broke into a broad smile. 'How very British,' she laughed.

'Actually,' he replied, frowning slightly, 'I don't know *what* nationality I am.'

'From your accent, you couldn't be anything else ... well, maybe Australian at a stretch, but I'd say British. Anyway, of course we can do tea ... how do you take it?'

'Milk, no sugar,' he replied, without hesitation.

'See?' she said, smiling, you didn't have to even think about that – you *know* how you take your tea. Your memory hasn't been stolen from you completely – it's just … well … muddled. I'm sure that many more things will start coming back to you soon.'

He fervently hoped she was right.

'Anyway,' she continued, 'I'll go and make that tea.'

When she had left the room, he picked up the newspaper. He read the headline on the front page.

Can this maverick businessman really make the White House?

Although the newspaper was a local journal, this was a national news story which, apparently, was gripping the nation. Campaigning for US presidential elections was well underway, and it seemed that a flamboyant, multi-billionaire businessman was threatening to completely overturn the political establishment and, potentially, sweep to power against all the previous predictions of political analysts.

It was all fresh news to Stephen. He had previously been completely unaware that the USA was even in the throes of an election campaign, and the names of the key players set out on the page in front of him meant absolutely nothing to him. He sighed in frustration at his own total ignorance of these obviously-important events.

When he turned the page, however, the headline he saw immediately triggered a jolt within him.

Breakthrough in Treatment of Drug Addiction to be Announced This Week?

He read on …

The fourteenth annual Drug Addiction Conference will be held on Monday March 13th at the luxurious Palm Grove Hotel in Miami Beach. As always, it will attract experts in the field of addiction treatment from all over the world, but the attendance, this year, of Bob Gench, multi-billionaire tech giant and renowned philanthropist, has fuelled rumours that a breakthrough is to be announced.

The keynote speech is to be given by Professor Richard Mandelson, whose research in the field of drug addiction has been sponsored by Bob Gench. The fact that Gench has decided to attend in person has only added to speculation that a ground-breaking discovery is going to be unveiled.

He had no idea why this story had provoked such a strong reaction within him but, somehow, he felt sure that it held the key to why he was in Miami.

He laid the newspaper down on his lap and rested his head back, closing his eyes as he struggled to make the connection. Drug addiction … research … Gench … Mandelson. Why were those names so familiar?

And then he realised …

I'm supposed to attend that conference – that's why I'm here in Florida.

He could not fathom just *why* he should be attending such a conference, but somehow he knew it was true. He felt a surge of elation as this realisation came to him – it was another small, but significant piece of the jigsaw puzzle.

But why would he have arrived in Miami more than a week before the conference, and why would he have been passing through a narrow, unlit alley? Try as he might, he could make no sense of it. And, what about Emma? He was sure, now, that Emma had come to Miami with him, but had she been with him when he was attacked? He screwed his eyes tight shut and clenched his fists as he strained every sinew with the effort of trying to retrieve more snippets from the morass swirling just beyond his reach. Maybe she had—

A familiar voice intruded. 'I have your tea here Stephen. I'll just … what's the matter? Are you OK?'

With the interruption, the moment had passed and the further details, which had seemed so tantalisingly close, slipped away into some faraway, murky gloom. He gave up and opened his eyes to see the nurse setting down the cup and moving towards him, concern etched across her face.

He was desperate to share with her this latest flash of insight. 'I know why I'm here, Kelly,' he declared, jumping to his feet, adrenaline now smothering the pain and weakness which had previously afflicted him. He picked up the newspaper and thrust it towards her, pointing at the headline which had caught his eye just a few moments earlier. 'See this article? That's the reason I'm here in Miami … it's for this conference. And this Palm Grove Hotel … I think I'd already heard of it. Maybe that's where—'

'Whoa!' she cried, placing her hands on his shoulders and gently encouraging him to sit back down. 'You need to slow down. Let me get Doctor Holt, and then you can take us through what you remember.'

She hurried from the room, leaving Stephen still struggling to piece together the disjointed pockets of information which had come back to him in the previous few minutes.

Half an hour later, Stephen had recounted everything he could remember, in the process recalling a few more scant details. The nurse and Doctor Holt had sat in silence as he disgorged absolutely everything he could recall.

Finally, Doctor Holt spoke. 'But you still don't remember anything about the attack itself?'

He closed his eyes as he tried once more to grasp those elusive memories. There was nothing … but then, just for a moment, a woman's face materialised in his mind. Dark skin; fine cheekbones; dark brown eyes; aquiline nose; strong, straight black hair. She moved her face towards his and … The image faded as quickly as it had appeared.

'There was a woman,' he whispered. 'Latina I think … she …' He clenched his fists in frustration, unable to grasp any link between the face he had glimpsed through the swirling mists in his mind, and what had happened to him in that darkened alley.

As he opened his eyes to see the expectant expressions on the two faces opposite, he exhaled heavily. 'I'm sorry … I just can't remember.'

'Do you think your attacker was a woman, then?' prompted the doctor.

'No … I don't think so. I think she may have been trying to help me, but…' The effort of recall was just too much now. 'I just don't know.' He slumped back into his pillow, exhausted by the sheer effort of trying to remember.

'OK … don't worry' said the doctor, 'you are making excellent progress. With just a few more days' rest and recuperation, hopefully, you will recall much more.'

Stephen shook his head. 'No ... I have to get out of here ... right now.'

'Out of the question,' said the doctor. 'You need to rest now. With trauma of this nature there could be all kinds of after-effects. We need to keep you under observation for a few more days at least.'

'I'm sorry Doctor, but Emma may be hurt, and even if she's not, she'll be worried sick. I have to find her.'

'Can't you leave that to the police?'

Stephen sighed. 'I already told you what they were like – they really didn't seem that interested. Hell, I'm not sure they believed I even *have* a wife. Look, at least I now know where we were headed: the conference is being held at the Palm Grove Hotel, and I think that's where Emma and I would probably have been staying. I can start by going there.'

'But you have no money, no I.D. ... nothing.'

'I'll manage,' Stephen insisted. Actually, he wasn't at all sure how he would, but he *had* to find Emma.

The doctor sighed. 'If you insist, then of course I cannot keep you here. However, I need to raise the unfortunate question of payment. Do you know if you have insurance?'

The last thing Stephen needed, at this stage, was a hold-up over money. He had no idea whether he was insured.

'Absolutely,' he lied. 'That's one thing I *do* remember.'

The doctor inclined his head, ever so slightly, and his eyes narrowed a little. 'I'm sure you appreciate that I'm not supposed to allow you to leave the hospital until you have furnished proof of insurance or ability to pay.'

Stephen spread his hands, helplessly. 'Doctor ... you know full well that I was admitted with practically nothing on me. As soon as I find Emma I'll be able to give you the details.'

The doctor lowered his head and began stroking his chin. 'Where will we be able to contact you?'

'For now, I don't have a mobile phone, a computer, or anything. Can't you trust *me* to contact *you*?'

The doctor looked up at him. 'And if you leave the country?'

'Look, I don't even have a passport right now, so there's no way I can leave the country. You have my word that I will contact you to arrange payment just as soon as I have sorted out this mess and got my life back.'

27

Doctor Holt gave a deep sigh, eventually appearing to relent. 'Nurse, if you can sort out Stephen's clothes for him, I'll prepare the necessary discharge papers.'

'Thank you … thank you both. For everything.'

Around thirty minutes later, the nurse returned carrying a pile of clothes.

'Thank you, Kelly. I really appreciate everything you've done for me.'

'Oh, it's nothing really,' she said, laying the clothes on the bed. 'I'm afraid your jacket and shirt are ruined … the blood wouldn't come out. But I've found you these from our lost property store.' She held up first, a shirt; and second, a long, leather jacket. 'The jacket might be a bit warm for the local climate but it's the only one I could find which looks like it might be big enough. I hope they fit OK.'

'Thank you,' said Stephen, smiling. 'I'm sure they'll be fine.'

'And … er, well, you'll need some money. You know … for food, cabs, and stuff … just until you find your wife and, hopefully, get your wallet back.'

'Oh, don't worry … I'll just—'

'I've just been out to the ATM around the corner. I'm afraid this is all I can lay hands on today,' she said, reaching into the front pocket of her uniform dress. 'Two hundred dollars.'

'No,' protested Stephen, 'you don't have to—'

'Please … take it. You'll need it. You can pay me back once you've sorted everything out.'

He was overwhelmed by the kindness and generosity shown by this caring and compassionate woman. It went against all his instincts to accept her offer but, inside, he knew she was right: he *would* need cash to get through the next day or two.

'We-ell, if you're sure.'

'I am.'

'Well, give me your contact details then. I promise you'll get it all back, and more, just as soon I can send it to you.'

She pulled out a business card from her pocket and scribbled something on the back. 'That's my home phone number and email.'

'Thank you again,' said Stephen, leaning forward to kiss her on both cheeks.

Her cheeks flushed; she turned her head momentarily to one side before turning back to look at him, a warm smile lighting up her pleasant features. 'I'll leave you to get dressed. Doctor Holt will be here shortly.'

It was more than an hour later when the doctor finally appeared. 'OK Stephen, please sign these papers, which release you from my care.'

Stephen was surprised at the way his signature flowed from his fingertips as naturally as if nothing had happened to him at all.

'But,' continued the doctor, 'if you have any further adverse symptoms, call me immediately.' He handed Stephen his card. 'And in any case,' he added, 'those stitches will need to be removed between next Thursday and next Sunday, so why don't you come back then? After the nurse has removed the stitches I can give you another check over … just in case.'

Thirty minutes later, Stephen stepped out of the main entrance to be greeted by a stifling blanket of hot, humid air, contrasting starkly with the air-conditioned environment of the hospital.

Time to go and get my life back.

Chapter 4

'So … you in Miami for long?' said the cab driver, swivelling his head towards Stephen, who was seated in the back of the car.

'Uh … not sure at the moment.'

'Oh, why's that then?'

'I just need to … uh, sort a few things out. I'm not sure how long it will take.'

'Oh, not on vacation then?'

'No.'

'Business then?'

'Kind of.'

'What kind of business you in then?'

Stephen couldn't have actually answered that question even if he had wanted to – which he didn't. He was in no mood to engage in idle chatter with this man: his brain was too busy grappling with the significance of the conference and his own involvement with it.

'It's … complicated,' was his cryptic reply.

'Oh … how's that then?' persisted the driver, once again looking over his shoulder.

'Look out!' cried Stephen, pointing ahead as a black Chevy swerved to avoid them.

'Whoa! Sorry about that. Guess I need to keep my eyes on the road.'

'Yes, I think that'd be a good idea,' said Stephen. 'And by the way, I'm trying to read something here,' he added, picking up the newspaper from his lap and holding it up where it could be seen in the rear-view mirror.

'OK, pal … just trying to be sociable,' muttered the driver.

Stephen did not reply; the other man fell into a sullen silence.

Stephen read the article about the conference again, this time continuing right to the end in the hope that it might shed more light on his situation. It didn't.

He turned the page back to the beginning of the article and looked again at the photograph alongside the headline. There were two men standing together: according to the caption, Professor Richard Mandelson and his sponsor, Bob Gench. The one on the left looked very familiar: narrow face; dark brown hair, slightly unkempt; round-rimmed spectacles. He assumed that the multi-billionaire tech giant and philanthropist Bob Gench must be a very well-known figure. He had probably seen the man's photograph many times in the past, so it was no surprise that he recognised the image.

But then he spotted something which sent a jolt right through him: according to the caption, Bob Gench was the man on the *right*. So the face which had seemed so familiar was actually that of Professor Mandelson. Why on earth should Stephen know *that* face so well?

And then it came to him ...

With a blinding flash of insight, Stephen realised that *he* worked in the field of medical research, himself – at Oxford University in the UK. That was why he had come to Miami Beach to attend the conference. Of *course* he would have known of Professor Mandelson's work, and he would probably also have seen his photograph before. Perhaps he and Mandelson were even working in related fields. Yes! That was it: they *were* working on parallel lines of research. More than that – they had even been exchanging research findings via email. No wonder the professor's name and photograph seemed so familiar. He tried to recall more about his relationship with Professor Mandelson. Was it restricted to exchange of research data, or had he actually met Mandelson in person? He didn't think so, but in his current, confused state of mind he couldn't be one hundred percent sure.

These recollections had come in a giddying rush, but now his head ached with the effort of trying to tease more vital slivers of information from the most heavily-shrouded corners of his brain. For now, though, he could retrieve nothing more.

But a picture *was*, slowly and painfully, starting to come together. Now if he could just find Emma, then—

His thoughts were interrupted as the car lurched to a halt – rather more abruptly than necessary.

'OK – we're here. Thirty - two bucks.' The man's tone was distinctly frosty.

Stephen paid the driver, offering a silent thank you to Kelly for her generosity as he counted out the exact money; he did not intend to waste any of his very limited resources on tips. As he stepped out of the car, he heard the driver mutter something under his breath. He didn't stop to ask him to repeat it.

***

The Palm Grove Hotel was an imposing sight: manicured lawns, punctuated by artfully-placed palm trees and fountains, framing a wide, curving driveway, which led to the smoked glass main entrance.

He walked up to the main entrance where a uniformed bellboy greeted him with an effusive smile. He stood aside, dipping his head slightly as he ushered Stephen towards the door, which slid silently aside at his approach. Since the man didn't even have to open the door for guests, Stephen wondered what, indeed, was the point of him being there at all. Hardly the most pressing question of the moment, he reminded himself.

As he stepped into the entrance lobby, Stephen was enveloped in the freezing embrace of the over-zealous air conditioning. *Too hot outside, and too bloody cold inside*, he mused. The space was vast, with fluted columns extending towards a high, vaulted ceiling, and the marble floor polished to a dazzling sheen.

He crossed the open floor and took his place behind a couple of other people standing at the reception desk. As he glanced to his left he saw a large banner, mounted on a metal stand.

Welcome to the fourteenth annual Drug Addiction Conference – Monday, March 13th – Palm Grove Hotel Banqueting Hall.

He looked all around, taking in the surroundings. Had he been here before? Nothing looked familiar. And yet, the more he trawled the ravaged ruins of his mind, the more he was convinced that he and Emma must have booked into the very same hotel, where the conference was to be held. Maybe they had just—

'Can I help you sir?'

The two people who had been standing in front of him were now both being attended to, and a third receptionist gestured for him to approach. She was an attractive thirty-something with olive-coloured eyes and dark hair, scraped back from her face and pinned firmly in place at the back. Her makeup was immaculate, as befitted front-of-house staff in an upmarket hotel such as this.

'Are you checking in, sir?' Her well-rehearsed smile revealed two rows of dazzling, white teeth.

She did a pretty good job of pretending not to notice the bandage which Stephen still wore around his head, with only an almost-imperceptible flicker of the eyes betraying her. He resolved to get rid of the damned thing as soon as he could find Emma and get to his room; the bleeding had long since stopped. There would still be the matter of the shaved patch and the ugly stitches, but he still had most of his abundant shock of hair, which he wore quite long. A bit of artful rearrangement with a brush and comb would go some way towards disguising the site of the injury.

'No, I believe my wife and I have already checked in.'

A slight flicker of uncertainty flitted across her eyes.

'Doctor and Mrs Stephen Lewis,' he said, smiling.

'So ... how exactly can I help you, Doctor Lewis?'

'I need a room key.'

'Oh, you've lost your entry card?

'Not exactly ... well, yes, I suppose so. I've had a ... well, an accident ... and now I don't have my card.'

Her brow furrowed. 'Oh, I'm sorry to hear that, sir. Just hold on a moment while I check ...' She tapped a few keys on her computer. 'Ah yes, Doctor and Mrs. Lewis. Checked in on Thursday March 2nd.'

His heart leapt: they *were* staying in the hotel. At last he would be able to find out if Emma was safe and well.

'Now,' continued the receptionist, 'if you can just confirm your room number ...'

He sighed. 'I'm afraid I can't.' He pointed to the bandage around his head. 'I've suffered a head injury and ... well I can't remember everything properly.'

'I see,' she replied, her lips forming a lopsided pout as she tried to process this explanation, which he had to admit sounded rather lame, even though it was true. 'Er, well, do you have some I.D. on you?'

'No, I don't,' he muttered, spreading his hands in a helpless shrug. 'My passport and wallet are missing.'

The receptionist was now looking distinctly unsettled, glancing to left and right as though searching for someone to come to her aid.

'I lost them in the accident,' he added. Judging by the expression on the girl's face, he guessed that his attempts to expand on his explanation weren't really helping.

She looked at him with eyes that now looked distinctly unsettled. 'I think I'm going to have to—'

'Look, Kirsty' – he read the name from the gold-coloured badge she was wearing – 'I'm in a spot of trouble here. I've been missing for over four days; my wife will be worried sick. I need your help.'

Her expression softened a little.

'Can you just call her in our room and ask her to come down? She'll identify me and confirm everything I've told you.'

'We-ll,' she mused, her head tilting to one side and her brow puckering in a thoughtful frown, her lips forming a slight pout, 'I guess that would be OK.' After a second or two, her pensive expression gave way to the professionally-honed smile once more. 'Sure – just give me a moment.'

She dialled the number, while Stephen anxiously waited. After about twenty seconds she placed the handset back in its rest.

'I'm sorry, there's no answer.'

'Dammit!' he hissed, under his breath, slamming his hand down on the counter in an involuntary gesture which made a surprisingly loud bang.

Her male colleague, standing a few feet to her right, turned towards the sound. 'Everything alright, Kirsty?'

'Sorry,' sighed Stephen. I just—'

'It's OK, Rod,' she said, 'everything's fine.'

The man stared at Stephen for a few seconds, before warily turning back to face the guest he had been dealing with.

She placed a reassuring hand on Stephen's arm. 'Look, I think I'd better call the manager. Maybe he can help you.'

She moved away from Stephen and picked up another phone from a desk by the back wall. She dialled a number, turning away so that her back was towards him. When she began speaking she had lowered her voice; he could only make out brief snatches over the general background noise in the hotel lobby.

'... this guy ... claims he's a ... yeah, his wife. No ... says he lost it ... an accident ... Well, yeah ... his head's all ...'

Stephen gave up trying to discern what she was saying. He gazed, once more, at the banner advertising the conference, this time noticing some open double doors just behind it, flanked by two men in dark suits. As Stephen looked beyond the doors he could see that there was some kind of black-tie function going on in the room, with men in tuxes and women in elegant evening gowns gathered in small groups, chatting and sipping cocktails.

A memory stirred. *The pre-conference party*! It was a gathering to allow conference attendees to meet and mingle before the conference proper.

The cogs churned for a few seconds, before a dawning realisation settled: *I'm supposed to be in there!*

The two gatekeepers were ushering a few more guests into the room. Stephen's gaze remained fixed on the scene, but his brain was only dimly registering what his eyes were seeing: all his mental faculties were now fully occupied with trying to process these new memories which were coming back to him.

But then, suddenly, the sight in front of him shook him back to full consciousness with a jolt. The woman waiting to be admitted to the room looked instantly familiar. The long, slightly wavy, blonde hair tumbling down her lightly-tanned back, laid bare by the deeply plunging cut of the back of her long, black evening gown; the willowy figure; the elegant walk, as the man on the door ushered her through.

'That's her!' he gasped, but the receptionist, still intent on her phone conversation, seemed not to hear him.

Without further thought, he rushed over towards the double doors. One of the men at the door raised a restraining hand.

'Excuse me,' said Stephen, 'I'm supposed to be in there.'

'Do you have your ticket?' enquired the man.

'I ... er, well, no ... I've lost it.'

The man eyed Stephen up and down. The borrowed, slightly ill-fitting jacket and open-necked shirt were hardly in keeping with the general dress code in the gathering beyond the doors. The bandage binding his head probably didn't help, either.

'Well, can you tell me you name, sir?'

'Yes, of course ... Stephen Lewis ... Doctor Stephen Lewis, Oxford University. I'm here with my wife. I've just seen her go in.'

'OK ... let me just check the guest list.' He raised the clipboard he was holding and ran his finger slowly down the sheet of paper attached to it. 'Yes, I have it here … Doctor and Mrs Stephen Lewis.'

'Thank you,' sighed Stephen. 'Now if you can just—'

His path was blocked by the other man, a shorter, stouter figure, probably in his fifties, and almost completely bald. He wore round, wire-rimmed spectacles. 'Could you perhaps, show us some I.D. Doctor Lewis?'

'I don't have any,' snapped Stephen, his exasperation now starting to bubble over. 'And perhaps you can tell me who *you* are?'

'Derek Schultz, Head of Hotel Security,' he replied, his voice calm and level, in contrast to Stephen's rather agitated tone.

He was a good eight inches shorter than Stephen but appeared anything but intimidated as he looked up at him through the thick lenses of his spectacles. The name suggested German heritage, but the accent was pure Floridian.

'Look, I'm sorry to have raised my voice like that. I've been involved in … an incident. I was attacked by some thugs in the street. That's how I got this injury' – he pointed to the bandage around his head – 'and it's how I lost all my papers. My wife's in there somewhere. She doesn't know what's happened … I have to speak to her.'

The man regarded him through narrowed eyes for several long seconds. 'You will appreciate, Doctor Lewis, that we have to be extremely careful about ensuring we check carefully that—'

'Wait!' cried Stephen. 'Look, there she is: the tall woman with her back to us in the black evening gown.'

The man's gaze followed Stephen's pointing finger, turning back to face him again once he had also seen her. 'That is your wife?'

'Yes, and she hasn't seen me for four days. I've been in hospital … she'll be worried sick.'

Schultz's round face puckered in a sceptical frown, his lips pursed as he appeared to weigh up what Stephen was saying.

'Look, why don't you just take me to her? She'll be able to identify me and we can clear all this up.'

Schultz exchanged a brief glance with the man on the other side of the door. Some sort of unspoken signal seemed to pass between them before the shorter man's expression softened.

He released a weary-sounding sigh. 'OK, Doctor Lewis, let's go and see your wife.'

'Thank you,' breathed Stephen.

The other man laid down his clipboard on the table alongside him. 'Shall I come with you?'

Schultz waved a dismissive hand. 'No, stay here on the door. I'll take Doctor Lewis over to his wife.'

Emma still had her back to them as she chatted to two other women. As Stephen and Schultz approached them, Schultz cleared his throat, noisily, to attract her attention. 'Excuse me, Mrs Lewis …'

She turned around, looking expectantly into the security chief's face.

'I have someone here to see you.'

She turned her gaze towards Stephen. The relief he felt at seeing her beautiful face once again, and finding that she was unharmed, was almost overwhelming. Tears sprang, unbidden, from the corners of his eyes as he stepped forward and placed his hands on her shoulders.

'Emma, thank God you're safe.'

She recoiled, shaking herself free from his hands. 'I'm sorry … do I know you?'

The words hit him in the solar plexus like a pile driver.

Chapter 5

'Emma,' he gasped, wracked by confusion, 'what's the matter? Is this some kind of joke?'

Her brow furrowed as she inclined her head to one side. 'A joke?' she said. 'I ... er ... I'm sorry, but I don't quite understand. I think there must be some mistake here.'

He couldn't quite process what he was hearing; it was unreal – like some sort of weird dream. 'Emma ... please don't do this. You're scaring me.'

She looked enquiringly at the security chief, whose expression was a bizarre mix of concern and bewilderment. 'I'm sorry, but I'm afraid I don't know this man.'

'Emma ... I'm your husband, for Christ's sake. Why are you doing this?'

Her eyes widened in surprise. 'My husband?' She shook her head. 'I'm afraid I really don't know what you are talking about. My husband is right here.'

She turned and took a few paces towards a group of four men who were engaged in their own conversation, apparently oblivious of the drama playing out just a few yards away. She tugged at the sleeve of one of the men.

'Stephen, I think you'd better come over here.'

He excused himself and came over, facing Stephen directly. He was tall and of muscular build, his physique not unlike Stephen's own. He was probably about the same age, too.

'What's going on here?' he said, glancing alternately from Stephen to Schultz, his expression wary. The accent was English.

Stephen's head was spinning wildly now. He grabbed Emma's shoulders. 'Emma what the hell is this all about? Who is this guy?'

'Hey back off, mister,' the newcomer growled, grabbing Stephen's arm and lifting it from Emma's shoulder, forcing himself between the two of them. 'I'm her husband. Who the hell are *you*?'

Schultz placed the flat of his hand against Stephen's chest, gently pushing him back. He raised his other hand high in the air and made a rapid beckoning gesture. Two very large men in black suits materialised from somewhere at the back of the room and began weaving their way between the other guests.

'He's lying,' protested Stephen. 'He must be forcing her to say these things.' He pointed an accusing finger at the stranger. 'Who are you ... really?'

'I'm her husband, Doctor Stephen Lewis.'

'This is crazy ... *I'm* Doctor Stephen Lewis.' He looked in desperation at Schultz. The two heavies were now right behind him, waiting for instructions. 'Look, I can prove it.' He held up his left hand. 'We have matching wedding rings, see?' He turned to face Emma. 'Show him ... show him your ring.'

She sighed, raising her eyebrows and giving a small shake of her head. She held out her hand to display ... a two-tone band of white and yellow gold ... with no inset stones.

'But that's impossible ... we both had matching rings. That's not your wedding ring. It must be ... I ... What's happening here?'

The imposter placed his own left hand on Emma's wrist, revealing that he, too, was wearing a two-tone band, identical to that which graced her ring finger.

Stephen felt a wave of nausea sweep over him. He pressed the heels of his hands against his temples, squeezing hard as he struggled to process what was happening.

Schultz gave a brief nod, and the two heavies stepped forward, each taking one of Stephen's arms.

'No!' cried Stephen. 'I don't know what this guy's game is, or how he's forcing Emma to say these things, but he's *not* Stephen Lewis.'

'I'm so sorry to have bothered you Mrs Lewis. It won't happen again,' said Schultz.

'No ... Emma, you have to tell them,' cried Stephen. But she merely took a step backwards, sending him a pitying look.

They led Stephen away.

***

One hour later, he was ensconced in the hotel security office. Schultz was sitting, arms folded, on the edge of a desk looking down upon

Stephen, who was slumped in a low armchair. Behind the other desk in the room sat one of Schultz's minions, evidently waiting for instructions. More ominously, in the corner, sat a police officer – thankfully, not the unhelpful bastard who had interviewed Stephen in the hospital.

'Look,' murmured Stephen, still reeling from the deeply unsettling and totally inexplicable encounter he had just experienced, 'I don't know what the hell is going on out there, but that guy is not me.'

'Well, self-evidently he is not *you*,' replied Schultz, his voice heavy with sarcasm, 'but the question is, who exactly *are* you?'

A spear of anger lanced through the fog of fear and confusion which had gripped him. 'I *am* Doctor Stephen Lewis,' he insisted. His head was now pounding with an overwhelming ache.

'So why does the lady—'

'My *wife*,' he interrupted.

'Of course,' replied Schultz, his voice dripping with ill-concealed scepticism, '… so why does your *wife* not recognise you? Why does she insist that the other man – the man you say is an imposter – is actually her husband, Doctor Stephen Lewis?'

Stephen hung his head, shaking it despondently.

'Come on, help me here … help me understand,' pressed Schultz.

Stephen lifted his head, making eye contact with the security chief. 'They ... they must be somehow forcing her to do this.'

'Forcing her … hmm … and why, exactly, would they be doing that?'

'I … I don't know,' he admitted.

'And who, in any case, are "they"?'

Stephen shook his head, helplessly; he had no answers.

'Well?' prompted Schultz, evidently losing patience fast now.

'Look,' pleaded Stephen, 'I don't know what's going on here, but if I could just have a few minutes alone with her, maybe I could find out what—'

Schultz shook his head, firmly. 'Out of the question, I'm afraid. I can't risk another scene like the one we just had.'

Suddenly, an idea came to Stephen. 'Do you have CCTV covering your reception desk?'

'Well, yes … of course we do.'

'Then go back and check the footage for last Thursday ... March 2nd. You should be able to see Emma and me checking in. That will prove who I am.'

Schultz's lips formed into a thoughtful pout as he stroked his chin for a few seconds. At length he turned to his colleague seated at the computer on the other desk. 'OK Leyton, just check it will you? Last Thursday.'

'Sure ... just give me a minute or two.'

'Thank you,' sighed Stephen.

The police officer, who had said very little so far, was evidently getting restless. 'Look, do you still need me here? Has anything criminal actually taken place?'

'Just bear with us for a little longer if you don't mind,' said Schultz. Stephen thought he could detect a hint of irritation in the security chief's voice; whether it was directed towards him or the police officer wasn't entirely clear.

Several minutes passed in silence while his colleague located and examined the relevant recordings. 'OK, got it,' he eventually announced.

Stephen and Schultz moved over and crowded round the laptop; the police officer didn't bother.

'It's right here,' continued the security guy. 'Mrs Lewis checked in at 8.05 p.m.'

Sure enough, there was Emma at the counter, smiling as she chatted to the receptionist. But she appeared to be on her own, apart from the bell boy hovering behind her with her luggage. Where the hell was *he*?

'Looks like she checked in on her own,' added the security guy, somewhat superfluously.

'No, I have to be there somewhere,' insisted Stephen. 'Just wind back and forward a little.'

Schultz gave a weary nod.

They searched the footage from ten minutes before Emma approached the desk to ten minutes after she took her key card and headed for the elevator. There was no sign of Stephen.

'OK,' began Schultz, 'I think we've seen enough—'

'No, wait ... look, maybe I arrived later. I already told you my memory's all screwed up. Maybe Emma got here ahead of me.'

'Look, I think we've done everything we possibly can. Maybe your head injury has caused more severe effects than you realise.'

'Please ...' pleaded Stephen, 'just check it will you? I know I'm pretty mixed up right now, but I do know who I am, and I know my wife ... and I'm afraid that she's in some kind of trouble. I don't know who that other guy is, but he's *not* Stephen Lewis.'

Schultz fixed him with a steady gaze, his eyes narrowed and head tilted slightly to one side. He said nothing for several seconds, but eventually relented. 'OK,' he said, turning to the man at the laptop, 'fast forward through as far as midnight on Thursday.'

'On it,' he replied, shuffling closer to the screen as he set about his new task.

The policeman had evidently had enough by now. 'Look, I got other work to do, so are you gonna press any charges here or not?'

Schultz turned to Stephen. 'Can you assure me that you won't cause any more trouble once we've finished these checks?'

'You have my word,' said Stephen.

'Then I think we can deal with this without any further help from the police.'

'Thank you,' breathed Stephen, a wave of relief washing over him.

The police officer huffed and puffed, clearly irritated that his time had been wasted, but he left without further comment.

As the two of them sat in silence, waiting for the other man to complete his checks, Stephen experienced a weird flashback. He was back in his lab at Oxford, deep in conversation with another man, bespectacled, and round-faced, his bald pate flanked by dense strips of grey hair either side. *Of course!*

He jumped to his feet. 'Yes, that's it!' he cried.

'What? What is it?' responded a startled Schultz.

'There's another way I can prove who I am. Call the University of Oxford Medical Sciences Division. I have a colleague and good friend based there: Doctor Henry Parker. Let me talk to him; he'll vouch for me.'

Schultz looked at his watch. 'It's almost 9 p.m. now: it'll be the middle of the night in England.'

Stephen's shoulders slumped in defeat.

'Hey, boss,' interjected the other security guy, 'I think I've got something here. A Doctor Stephen Lewis arrived just before midnight, to join his wife who had already checked in earlier.'

'Thank God,' breathed Stephen.

He and Schultz both moved over to look at the computer screen. The freeze-frame clearly showed the face of the man at the counter. It wasn't Stephen: it was the same man who had been with Emma earlier that evening – the man claiming to be *him*.

Chapter 6

'This is impossible,' Stephen cried, pressing his palms against his temples. 'That guy is *not* Stephen Lewis. You have to let me talk to Emma alone and find out what's happening.'

'You know I can't do that, Doctor … well, whatever your name is.'

Stephen whirled on Schultz, towering over him; the other security man rose to his feet. Schultz took a step backwards, clearly unsettled by the invasion of his personal space, but at the same time indicating, with a hand gesture, that no intervention from his colleague was necessary.

'Please sit down,' said Schultz, calmly, '… unless you want me to call the police again.'

Stephen exhaled loudly, struggling to keep his frustration in check, but he did as the other man asked. Losing it with Schultz was going to get him absolutely nowhere. He decided to adopt a more conciliatory approach.

'I'm sorry. Look … maybe you're right. The attack … everything that's happened. Maybe I really am more screwed up in my head than I realised.'

'So,' said Schultz, regarding him through narrowed eyes, 'are you now saying you are *not* Doctor Stephen Lewis?'

'I … I don't know.' His head was spinning from overload, and he just couldn't figure out what to say or do next. At length, he pulled from his pocket the card which Dr Holt had given him. 'This is the doctor who was treating me … he warned me that I could suffer all sorts of unexpected after effects. I think I need to go and see him again.'

He raised his gaze to meet that of Schultz, whose expression had softened somewhat.

'I think that would be a very wise course of action. Would you like us to call you a cab to take you back to the hospital to see your doctor?'

Stephen nodded, dumbly. 'Yes … that would be good … thank you.'

'We'll cover the fare,' added the security chief, who now appeared to have some sympathy for Stephen's befuddled state of mind.

'Thank you,' repeated Stephen.

Fifteen minutes later, the taxi pulled away from the main entrance of the hotel with Stephen seated in the back. His mind was in turmoil as he tried to decide what to do next. He had no intention of actually returning to the hospital – to do so would just waste valuable time. But what should he actually *do*? It was clear that he wasn't going to get any further with Schultz, and the police obviously weren't going to be of any help. No, he was going to have to rely on his own resources to try to figure out what was going on. As the car left Miami Beach and set off across one of the huge bridges which crossed Biscayne Bay en route to Downtown Miami, he made his decision.

Shortly after the taxi had entered the streets of Miami, Stephen leaned forward to speak to the driver.

'Stop!'

'What? But we're still a couple of miles away from—'

'I've changed my mind … please let me off here.' He had spotted an internet café on the left-hand side of the road.

'Your choice, buddy … I've already been paid, so it don't matter to me.'

The driver pulled over, and Stephen stepped out. As the cab pulled away, he looked left and right, waiting for a gap in the traffic so that he could cross the street. Annoyingly, his view of the oncoming traffic to his left was obscured by a silver SUV which had pulled up, right on a yellow line, about twenty yards back. The combination of the heavy traffic and his restricted view down the road made it just about impossible to judge when he could make a dash for it. In the end, he gave up and walked back down the street, past the parked car which had been obscuring his view and on about another fifty yards until he reached a pedestrian crossing, controlled by traffic lights. As he waited for the lights to change, he heard a car horn sound to his right. He turned towards the sound and saw the silver SUV executing a hazardous U-turn, cutting right across two lanes of traffic.

When the lights changed, and Stephen was able to cross to the other side of the road, he turned back towards the internet café, walking right past the silver SUV which was now in the queue at the lights. The driver of the car behind had his head and left arm out of the window as he gave the middle finger to the guy in the SUV, shouting something which Stephen couldn't make out over the general hubbub in the street. In spite of his desperate situation, Stephen couldn't help but smile at just how easily a minor traffic altercation could provoke such rage.

When he reached the internet café, he purchased thirty minutes of browsing time, which was the minimum amount on offer. Upon logging on, the first thing he did was check the website of the University of Oxford Medical Sciences Division, searching for the number of Doctor Henry Parker's direct line. He quickly found Henry's profile, with a brief biography, and information about his field of research. Frustratingly, though, there was no direct phone number listed.

He backed up to the site's homepage to see if that would guide him to a list of phone numbers. All it provided, however, was a general number for the Medical Sciences Division. But as he gazed at the number he immediately recognized the area code and the first three digits of the number itself – another fragment of his memory was returning.

He realised that the direct line numbers differed only in the final three digits. He closed his eyes as he tried to reach out for the elusive numbers. Yes, his own direct line ended in '276' and Henry's in ... *come on, think* ... *yes* ... *'279'*. He pulled from his pocket a notepad and pen, which he had picked up at the hotel, and scribbled down both the general number and that of Henry's direct line, in case the fragile memories should desert him once more. As soon as he could find a payphone, he'd give Henry a call. Even though it would be the middle of the night the UK, he could, at least, leave a message.

But then a thought struck him: how would Henry be able to make contact once he had received the message? Stephen had no fixed place of residence and, right now, he didn't even have a mobile phone.

What had happened to his damned phone anyway? Surely he must have had one before the attack, but what had happened to it? Had he lost it? Had it been taken by whomever it was who attacked him? He closed his eyes, trying desperately to recall the events of that fateful evening …

***

The take-off of the plane had been delayed by almost three hours due to heavy fog at Heathrow and the pilot had only been able to make up about half an hour of that time.

As they waited in line to get through immigration, Stephen turned to Emma. 'By the time we get through here and pick up our luggage, there's no way I'll have time to go to the hotel and freshen up before my dinner date with Richard.'

She gave a small frown, cradling her chin between thumb and forefinger. 'That's OK – I can take the luggage, get a cab to the hotel, and check us in, while you go straight to your date with Professor Mandelson.'

'You OK with that?' he said.

'Yes – sure. You go ahead.'

'OK – I'll join you at the hotel as soon as I can.'

Thanks to an interminable wait to get through immigration, it was around an hour and a half later when the cab driver finally loaded their luggage into the back of the car.

'OK,' said Stephen, giving Emma a brief kiss on the cheek, 'I'll see you in a few hours' time.'

As the cab pulled away, he looked at his watch again: 7.25 p.m. Would he be able to get to the restaurant by eight? He approached the next cab in the line; the driver looked him up and down before moving his head a little to one side, as though trying to see what was behind Stephen.

'No luggage, buddy?'

'No, just this briefcase.' He held up the case. 'My wife's gone ahead to our hotel with the rest of our luggage. Look, I'm in a bit of a hurry; how long will it take to get to Downtown Miami?'

'Depends which part. Where d'ya wanna go?'

'Do you know a restaurant called "La Mariposa"?'

'Sure – we should get there in about twenty minutes if the traffic's OK.'

Stephen sighed with relief – they should make it in time.

The traffic *wasn't* OK, though. At 7.50 p.m. they were completely stationary, hemmed in front and rear with no means of escape.

'Is it usually like this?' enquired Stephen.

'Nah – must be an accident or sump'n. Look, we're almost there, actually, but God knows when this shit is gonna clear.'

'Dammit!' muttered Stephen. 'I'm supposed to meet someone there at eight.'

'Well, we're real close. If you want to jump out and walk, you could be there in about five or ten minutes.'

'OK,' said Stephen, seizing on the opportunity that the driver had offered, 'which way?'

'See that alley up there on the right?'

Stephen nodded.

'Cut through there, then hang a left when you come out in the next street. Carry on for about three blocks and it's on yer left. Nice place, I've heard.'

'OK. How much do I owe you?'

'Oh, I guess forty bucks'd cover it.'

Stephen thrust a fifty-dollar bill into the man's hand. He jumped out of the car without waiting for his change.

'Hey, buddy ... don't you want ...' called out the driver, but Stephen was already striding purposefully away from the car and didn't bother to turn around.

As he turned onto the alley, he heard what sounded like a woman's voice. It sounded as though she was in distress – he thought he heard her—

***

His train of thought was rudely interrupted.

'Hey, excuse me pal, but are you intending to actually use that computer, or are you just gonna sit in front of it staring into space. It's kinda busy in here and I ain't got all night to wait.'

Stephen looked up to see a tall, skinny white guy, probably in his early twenties, with long, greasy, black hair protruding from under a grubby, grey baseball cap, worn back-to front.

'I … I'm sorry. I just got sort of … well, distracted. Give me just a few more minutes to finish what I'm doing, and then I'll be out of here.'

'Hey, you Australian?'

'English.'

'No kidding? I've always wanted to visit England. I've got a buddy who lives in London. He says it's a great place to live. You from London?'

'No – Oxford'

'Oh yeah, I've heard of that – it's where you got that Oxford and Cambridge college place.'

Stephen just nodded: he had no desire to prolong this conversation by giving an impromptu geography lesson.

'Hey, what'd ya do to your head?'

'Er, it's kind of a long story. Look, if you're in a hurry, maybe it'd be best if you just let me get on and finish up here. I only need about ten minutes.'

'Oh, sure. I'll just sit over there' – he pointed to a threadbare couch in front of the window – 'until you're done.'

Stephen was more than a little irritated that his train of thought had been interrupted – if it had not been, perhaps he would have remembered even more about what had happened in that darkened alley. Nevertheless, this was a massive step forward. He now knew that not only were he and Professor Mandelson professional associates, but that they were actually due to meet for dinner that evening. Furthermore, he now understood how he had come to be in the alley where he was subsequently attacked.

But there were still so many questions …

Who was the woman crying out in distress? What had been happening to her? Did that have something to do with the attack on *him*? Who was his attacker anyway? The briefcase … what had happened to the briefcase? And where was his wallet … his passport …?

Maybe it would all come back to him in time, but right now he wanted to check one more thing on the Medical Sciences Division website, before the young guy in the baseball cap began hassling him again. From the homepage, he clicked on the tab labelled 'Academic Staff' and scrolled down the list of names. He soon found what he was looking for.

Dr Stephen Lewis

Dr Stephen Lewis is a Research Fellow specialising in the field of treatments for drug addiction. He has over twenty years' experience in this area and has contributed to the development of several important new therapies.

He is currently conducting research into cocaine addiction, liaising closely with Professor Richard Mandelson at the University of Miami, in Florida.

That was it: cocaine addiction. This was the field of research in which he and Professor Mandelson had been sharing and comparing their findings. And now, Mandelson had made a major breakthrough, which he intended to unveil at the forthcoming conference. He had invited Stephen to meet with him before the conference itself so that he could preview what was to be announced.

Stephen returned his attention to the computer screen, scrolling down to see if he could learn any more. Rolling up from the bottom of the screen emerged a portrait photograph of Dr Stephen Lewis ...

It wasn't him.

The face staring at him from the screen was that of the man he had seen with Emma at the hotel: his nemesis.

Chapter 7

'Hey, you OK man? You look like you've seen a ghost.'

The voice came from somewhere close behind him, but Stephen barely registered it; his eyes were fixed on the screen – staring at the image of the man who had stolen his identity.

He felt a hand on his shoulder; finally, he managed to tear his eyes away from the screen and gaze up at the young guy with the back-to-front baseball cap.

'I ... uh, yes ... I ... I have to go,' muttered Stephen, finally shaking himself free of the trance which had gripped him. He clicked the 'back' button a couple of times to exit the website and logged out. 'It's all yours,' he said.

With that, he stood up, grabbed his jacket from where it hung over the back of the chair, and made for the door.

'Hey, you sure you're OK, buddy?' came the voice from behind him. You sure don't look—'

But Stephen was already halfway through the door. As the warm, humid air hit his face he suddenly broke out in a cold sweat. His head was swirling with a maelstrom of disconnected thoughts. Could it be that this other man really *was* Dr Stephen Lewis? *And if so,* he thought, *who the hell am I? And how come I know so much about him ... and about Professor Mandelson? And what about Emma?* None of it made any sense.

He began walking along the street, completely oblivious to his surroundings as he grappled with the chaos that was overwhelming his brain. *Perhaps I really am going mad.*

Suddenly, he felt a wave of exhaustion sweep over him. He needed to rest, to think, to try to unravel this crazy situation. He looked all around, and spotted a small coffee shop, just across the street; that would do. He crossed at a pedestrian crossing, just a few yards ahead, and stepped inside the coffee shop, taking a seat by the window. They didn't serve tea, so he ordered a coffee in an attempt to wake himself up while he tried to figure out what to do next. As he sipped the scalding hot liquid, he glanced through the window to see, on the opposite side of the street, a silver SUV parked at the kerb. Was it the same one he'd seen earlier making that hazardous U-turn? No, probably just coincidence. After all, silver SUVs weren't exactly a rare sight around Miami, and he couldn't even remember what make the other car was. Nevertheless, he did take the trouble to check this one out: it was a big Ford. He noticed that it had a bad scrape along the left hand side.

He turned his attention back to his current situation. However much he tried, he could find no rational explanation for the bizarre sequence of events which had beset him. He was tired and confused; he needed somewhere to spend the night. Maybe after a good night's sleep, he might be able to glean some kind of order from the chaotic jumble which filled his addled brain. He pulled out the wad of banknotes which the nurse, Kelly, had so generously lent him. He swiftly counted them: there was still a hundred and fifty-one dollars left. He could probably just about afford a cheap hotel for the night while still leaving himself enough cash for the next day or so.

He left the exact money for the coffee on the table – still conscious of the need to conserve his precious resources – and headed for the door.

'Thanks a bunch, pal,' muttered the scruffy-looking attendant who cleared the table, mouthing something else – probably uncomplimentary – under his breath as Stephen stepped outside.

He began walking along the street, looking for somewhere to spend the night. After walking for a few hundred yards he hadn't found anywhere. Maybe he should ask someone?

He stopped a randomly-chosen, but respectable-looking middle-aged man. 'Excuse me sir, but do you know of a reasonably-priced hotel or motel around here?'

'Say ... you Australian?' said the man, smiling.

Oh no, not that routine again.

'No ... English,' replied Stephen. 'Look, I need somewhere to spend the night, but I don't want to spend much. Do you know of anywhere around here?'

The man thought for a few moments before replying. 'I think if you head back that way' – he pointed back in the direction from which Stephen had just come – 'there's a little place called ... oh, I can't remember exactly. Some sort of Spanish-sounding name.'

Stephen couldn't recall seeing anywhere as he had passed that way earlier, but maybe he had missed it, given his current preoccupied state of mind.

'OK – thanks.'

'Sure,' said the other man, as he went on his way.

Stephen was about to start retracing his steps when he saw it … A silver SUV had pulled over on the opposite side of the street about thirty yards back. As Stephen registered the scrape along the side of the car, he realised it was the same car he had noticed earlier. Surely, this could no longer be mere coincidence. Was this car actually *following* him? A shiver of apprehension shot through him.

He abandoned the idea of heading back in the direction which would take him closer to the car and instead carried on in the direction in which he had been walking, stealing an occasional glance over his shoulder. There was no sign that the car was moving after him; maybe his imagination was just working overtime.

He came to a Metrorail station and, still feeling a little nervous, made his way inside, taking the escalator up to the main concourse. It was getting late now, and the station was pretty quiet. He wandered aimlessly for a few minutes before coming across a payphone. He decided to give Henry Parker a call.

Although he obviously didn't expect Henry to be in his office at this hour, he was nevertheless relieved to hear his familiar voice; at least he had remembered the number correctly.

'You've reached the office of Doctor Henry Parker. I'm afraid I can't take your call right now, but if you'd like to leave your name and number, I'll get back to you as soon as possible.'

'Henry, I'm in trouble. I'm in Miami for the conference but I got attacked in the street. I've lost all my belongings, and Emma doesn't even seem to …'

His voice tailed off as he noticed a tall man in a black leather jacket leaning against the wall of the concourse, about thirty yards away. He was, ostensibly, reading a newspaper, but when he looked up, over the top of the newspaper, he made brief eye contact. In that moment, Stephen *knew* he was being followed.

'Henry, I have to go. I'll call again when I have a contact number I can give you.'

He hung up and, trying to look as casual as possible, walked across the concourse towards an entry gate which led to the platforms. As he approached the gate, he glanced over his shoulder to see the man in the leather jacket walking straight towards him.

He had no idea why this guy was following him, but he had no intention of hanging around to find out. He vaulted over the gate and broke into a run, dashing along a corridor towards one of the platforms. He glanced back to see the other man scrambling over the gate before elbowing a dawdling couple out of the way in his haste.

A train had just pulled up. Stephen sprinted along the platform, swerving to avoid the handful of passengers exiting the train and trying to put as much distance as possible between himself and his pursuer. At the last moment, he dived into one of the carriages. It was clear that the other man wouldn't be able to catch up with him before the doors closed, but, to Stephen's alarm, he jumped into another carriage on the same train – two back from his own.

His heart pounding, Stephen waited … waited … and then, as the doors began to close he stuck his foot in the way, causing the doors to retract. He jumped out and immediately flattened himself behind a pillar, hoping his pursuer had not seen him.

He hadn't. A few seconds later the train pulled away and he stepped out from behind the pillar. He watched his own carriage roll by, followed by the next, and then he saw him. The man in the leather jacket had a thin, craggy face, and dark, penetrating eyes. His black hair was slicked back in something of the style of a fifties rocker. As he made eye contact with Stephen, he slammed his fist against the window in frustration, mouthing something which Stephen couldn't make out.

**

Having evaded his pursuer, Stephen made his way back out onto the street, climbing over the barrier gate when it was quiet enough to avoid being seen by too many other passengers. He retraced his steps until, eventually, he found the motel which the passer-by had told him about. 'El Refugio' was a pretty down-at-heel joint, the neon sign outside flickering on and off erratically, and the cracked glass alongside the main entrance held together with black duct tape. By now, though, Stephen was ready to crash just about anywhere and, as the sign read 'Rooms $50', it wouldn't consume too much of his meagre cash reserve.

'You got I.D.?' enquired the grossly overweight guy behind the counter.

'I'm afraid I don't ... I had an accident and, well ... I've lost all my stuff.'

The other man shook his head. 'Can't give you a room without I.D. More than my job's worth.'

'Will this help?' said Stephen, peeling off another ten dollars from his wad of cash and adding it to the fifty he had already laid on the counter.

The man pursed his lips and shook his head once again, the sharp intake of breath signalling the impossibility of Stephen's request. Nevertheless, as Stephen made to retrieve the banknotes the man swiftly relented.

'OK, room eleven,' he said, grabbing the money and stuffing it into his shirt pocket.

'Does the room have a phone?'

'Afraid not ... if you want a room with a phone, that'll be another ten.'

Stephen exhaled noisily. He handed over another ten-dollar bill which joined the rest of the cash in the man's shirt pocket.

'Room fifteen,' said the fat man, smiling.

Once safely ensconced in his room, Stephen tried calling Dr Henry Parker once more. Once again, he got through to Henry's answering machine. 'Henry, its's Stephen again. Sorry I had to ring off earlier but there was this guy following me and ... well ... it's a long and complicated story, but ... Henry, I'm in real trouble. Can you call me back on this number as soon as you get this? It doesn't matter what time of day or night ... just call me as soon as possible.' He read out the number and hung up.

Having undressed and showered, he sat on the edge of the bed and laid out on the bedside table the few items which the police had given him while he was in hospital: his wedding ring, which should have matched Emma's, but didn't; a lipstick which might, or might not, have been Emma's; a card for Eduardo's Restaurant; and a diary with just two dates highlighted. What did any of it mean?

One of the dates highlighted in the diary was Thursday March 9th – just two days away. What was the significance of that date? It wasn't the date of the conference – that was on Monday 13th March. So what was so special about Thursday 9th? And what about the other date: Sunday July 23rd? That was months away. None of it made any sense.

What should he do now? The police had previously seemed disinterested in his plight, but things had now got a lot worse. Surely, now that he was able to tell them that he was being followed, they would take him seriously and do something about it? But then again, what actual proof did he have that he *was* being followed? Should he go to them anyway?

In his current state, exhausted and confused, he just couldn't process it all. He needed to sleep …

Chapter 8

Something was pressing repeatedly on his chest, several pulses of crushing pressure and then a few seconds of relief. The cycle repeated again and again – relentless, irresistible. He tried to open his eyes, but his eyelids refused to respond to the signals his brain was sending. The unrelenting blackness which enveloped him was punctuated only by the regular cycle of insistent pulses of pressure followed by occasional respite. He didn't know where he was, or what was happening to him. All he knew was that he was powerless to do anything other than submit to whoever, or whatever, was doing this to him.

Finally, though, the persistent rhythm stopped, but now he couldn't breathe – something was covering his nose and mouth. But then, the strangest sensation: his lungs were filling with air of their own accord. Suddenly, his mouth and nose were freed from whatever had covered them, allowing him to exhale. As he did so, he felt a choking sensation, coughing and gagging as he fought to breathe properly. Finally, with one last spluttering gasp, he succeeded in clearing his windpipe and sucking in a delicious lungful of cool, life-giving air. Moments later, he managed to open his eyes. His vision was blurry, but, as the mists began to clear, he found he could just make out a woman's face.

'Emma?' he croaked.

But it wasn't Emma. The deep brown eyes, dark skin, and black hair belonged to another woman entirely – a woman he didn't know, yet who, somehow, seemed strangely familiar. Where had he seen her before? She seemed to be straddling his body, leaning over him, her face just inches from his, her expression filled with concern.

As she moved her face away from his and raised herself to a more upright position his eyes fixed on an image on the front of her shirt; it looked like a badge or logo of some type. As he struggled to focus on the image, he was finally able to discern that it depicted some sort of fish, leaping and twisting in the air—

***

Suddenly, he was wide awake. He switched on the lamp and rummaged through the items lying on the bedside table. After a few moments, he found what he was looking for: the business card which the two police officers had brought to him when he was in hospital. As his eyes gradually adjusted to the light, the link which his half-asleep brain had just made was confirmed. There it was: the swordfish logo, just as he had seen in his dream. There had to be some connection between the dark-skinned girl in the dream, and Eduardo's restaurant.

He dragged himself to his feet and stumbled over to the window. As he opened the grubby blackout blind, his eyes were assaulted with a blinding shaft of sunlight. How long had he slept? He glanced at the clock on the wall: 10.07 a.m. He had been asleep for around nine hours.

Henry hadn't returned his call, so he tried again, but again he only got through to the answering machine. He left another message.

By the time he had washed and dressed he was feeling more or less human once more. Henry still hadn't called back, but at least Stephen now had a plan ... of sorts.

The fat man was still there on reception, still wearing the same clothes as he had the previous evening; he was now fast asleep, slumped in his chair. The faint whiff of body odour which assaulted Stephen's nostrils as he stepped past the crumpled figure confirmed his suspicion that the man had probably spent the entire night right there behind the desk.

Stephen stepped out of the front door of the motel into the bright sunshine; he screwed his eyes half-shut, shading them with his hand to give them time to adjust. He made his way back to a drug store which he remembered passing on his way to the motel the previous night. He used another seventeen dollars of his rapidly dwindling resources to purchase some large Band-Aids, antiseptic spray, and a small bottle of mineral water – he had drunk a little water from the tap in the motel that morning but he wasn't keen on risking any more of the slightly brown-tinted liquid.

When he returned to his room, he discarded the – now, frayed and grubby – bandage. Once he had cleaned up the area of the wound, with the aid of a hand-held mirror opposing the wall mirror in the bathroom, he was pleasantly surprised to see that most of the swelling had subsided and he could detect no sign of infection. A thin layer of stubble had regrown in the area that had been shaved and he soon realised that this would prevent a Band-Aid from sticking properly. *Damn!* he thought. *I could have saved myself six dollars on those.* He wasn't sure just how money-conscious he had been in his previous life, but having to rely solely on a limited cash reserve, with no prospect of its replenishment, certainly concentrated the mind.

He sprayed the wound site with antiseptic and carefully rearranged his hair – which was, fortunately, quite long and very thick – so that it more or less covered the shaved area. Now, at least, he would no longer be attracting curious looks wherever he went. He headed down to the motel reception and checked out, keeping conversation with the malodorous figure behind the desk to a minimum.

Now it was time to find out what had happened.

***

He gazed at the leaping swordfish logo above the frontage of Eduardo's Restaurant – just the same as that on the card, and on the front of the shirt of the woman he had seen in his dream. As the police officer had said, the restaurant – more like a diner really – didn't look up to much, but maybe … just maybe, it might provide some answers.

As the aroma of cooking bacon wafted past his nostrils he realised that he was ravenously hungry. When had he last eaten? Not since he had left the hospital. He stepped through the door to find that the place was packed solid; it must be very good or very cheap … or both. As the police officer had observed, most of the clientele, and staff, appeared to be Latinos.

A couple stood up, vacating a table right by the window; he dived in before anyone had even cleared the table. No-one came to attend to him immediately, but there was a menu on the table so he set about making his selection. He was gratified to see that the prices were, indeed, very reasonable. He would eat first, and ask questions afterwards.

'Yes sir, what can I get you?' The accent sounded familiar.

He looked up at the waitress. The front of her shirt bore the leaping swordfish logo. As their eyes met, he recognised her immediately. The dark eyes, distinctively shaped nose, and well-defined cheekbones: it was the girl he'd seen in his uneasy dreams. Her welcoming smile evaporated in an instant, to be replaced by an anxious, haunted expression. In an instant, he knew ...

'You recognise me, don't you?' whispered Stephen.

'I ... er ... I'm sorry sir. I don't believe we've met before.'

'Please ... Carla' – he had read her name from the badge she was wearing – 'I know you were there when I was attacked. I'm in big trouble ... I need your help.'

Her eyes darted from side to side. 'I'm really sorry, sir ... There must be some mistake.'

He grabbed her wrist and, with his other hand, withdrew the lipstick from his pocket and laid it on the table. 'Look ... it's yours, isn't it?'

She tried to pull away from him, glancing anxiously from left to right, but Stephen's grip on her wrist was relentless.

'Please ... let go of my wrist. You're hurting me,' cried the girl, panic now starting to rise in her voice.

'Look at it,' insisted Stephen. 'I know it's yours ... you must have dropped it when—'

'Hey, Carla ... everything alright over there?' The big Latino guy in a greasy white apron, standing just behind the counter, had evidently detected the altercation.

Stephen ignored him, still not relinquishing his grip on the girl's wrist. 'Please,' he implored, 'you have to help me.' Her eyes were filled with a mixture of fear and confusion.

The big guy came striding over. 'OK, pal ... you'd better take it easy now.'

Stephen relaxed his grip on her wrist. 'I'm sorry ... I just ...'

'I think you'd better leave.'

'Yes ... I'm sorry.' He turned to Carla. 'I don't know quite what happened ... back in that alley. But I think that you helped me, so ... well ... thank you.'

As he turned to leave, he took one last look into her dark eyes; the fear seemed to have gone, to be replaced by a look which could have been regret or compassion ... or both. The big guy's countenance, however, wore a menacing scowl. This was definitely not the moment to pursue things any further.

He was still desperately hungry, so he decided to go into a rival diner on the opposite side of the street – it looked barely any more salubrious than Eduardo's, but by now he was ready to eat just about anywhere. He wasted little time perusing the menu before placing his order.

Having devoured a mountainous portion of eggs, bacon, hash browns, and mushrooms, he ordered a cup of tea while he considered his next steps. He really needed to talk to Carla. He just *knew* that she had recognised him; if he could persuade her to talk to him she might have some of the answers which he sought. Maybe she would be more forthcoming if he could catch her outside of her workplace. Should he wait here and try to intercept her when she finished her shift? But he had no idea when that would be. Nevertheless, he decided to give it a try. He settled down to wait.

As he sipped his tea, he began mulling over what he knew so far. He realised that he was now able to piece together much of what he was supposed to have been doing during his trip to Florida. He pulled from his pocket the pen and notepad and jotted down as much as he could remember of his planned schedule.

Thursday March 2nd – Dinner with Professor Mandelson

Tuesday March 7th – Party at Palm Grove Hotel

Friday March 10th – Pre-conference reception at the Palm Grove

Monday March 13th – Conference proper, also at the Palm Grove

Was there anything else? And what was the significance of the date highlighted in the diary, Thursday March 9th – the very next day? He closed his eyes and concentrated all his mental energy on trying to recall anything else ... any tiny detail which might help him unravel this mess. Try as he might, he couldn't remember anything which might make the following day significant.

But then he did remember something – something very important. Wednesday March 8th, that very day, he was due to meet with Professor Mandelson at his lab to go over the details of his discovery. Although, as far as he knew, he had never actually met Mandelson face to face, they had been exchanging research notes for months. Surely the professor would vouch for him.

What time was he supposed to be there for the meeting? However hard he tried, he just couldn't remember. He decided to just go there straightaway. He would have to come back another time to try to talk with Carla.

He called for the bill and settled it – again without any tip – and headed for the door.

***

The revelations about Stephen's relationship with Professor Mandelson triggered a flood of further memories, which came back in a giddying rush. By the time he reached the Marsden Medical School at the University of Miami he had recalled quite a bit of what he and Professor Mandelson had been working on. He felt sure that a face-to-face meeting with Mandelson would further help him to untangle what the hell was going on.

The campus was extensive, but the site map posted near the entrance enabled Stephen to find the right building without difficulty. Inside, seated behind a desk at the back of the foyer was a round-faced, bespectacled woman, who looked up and smiled at Stephen's approach.

'How can I help you, sir?'

'Doctor Stephen Lewis – I have an appointment with Professor Mandelson.'

A puzzled frown creased her face. 'Doctor Lewis?' She looked at her watch and consulted the computer screen in front of her.

'Yes, I'm afraid I'm not actually sure what time I was supposed to be here – I've lost my diary you see.'

Her frown deepened. 'But you are Doctor Stephen Lewis?'

'Yes,' he said. 'Look, Professor Mandelson and I know each other very well. Even if I'm not here at quite the right time, I'm sure Richard will see me now.' Stephen hoped that the casual dropping of Mandelson's Christian name would ease his passage past this determined gatekeeper.

Her eyes narrowed slightly, her lips forming a pout. 'I … I'll have to call him,' she said.

Ignoring the phone which was right in front of her on the desk, she got up and stepped into a small room just behind her chair. She spoke in hushed tones which Stephen could not distinguish. As he was standing at the desk he noticed, alongside it, a layout map of the building. Stepping closer to study it, he observed that each room was marked with the name of the academic staff located therein. It took him but a few seconds to find Professor Mandelson's lab, located on the second floor. He decided not to wait for the receptionist to finish her call, instead striding swiftly towards the stairs, taking them two at a time.

The second floor appeared to be entirely taken up with medical laboratories. As he made his way down the long corridor he checked the names on each door he passed. Most of them he didn't recognise, but one or two names stirred some distant, elusive memory. Finally, he found the one he was looking for; it was open. He tapped his knuckles on the door and stepped inside. He immediately recognised the man just putting his phone down as Professor Mandelson: his face was now completely familiar. There was also another man in the room, with his back to Stephen.

'Professor Mandelson ... it's Doctor Stephen Lewis. I'm so sorry to have—'

As the other man turned around, a leaden boulder descended in Stephen's gut. It was the same man, claiming to be him, who had been with Emma at the reception in the Palm Grove Hotel: the man who now seemed to frustrate Stephen's every move.

Chapter 9

'What's going on here?' demanded Professor Mandelson, glancing from one man to the other, his forehead wrinkled in puzzlement as he tried to process what he was seeing and hearing.

'Richard, it's me ... Stephen Lewis. I was supposed to meet you for dinner last week, but there was an ... incident. I just couldn't make it.'

Mandelson's face was a mask of confusion.

'But if you're Stephen Lewis, then who—?'

'I'm sorry about this,' said the other man. 'I don't know who this guy is but he's clearly delusional. He accosted my wife at the party in the Palm Grove Hotel yesterday. He came barging in, claiming that *he* was her husband. She was, as you can probably imagine, quite scared. We had to get hotel security to remove him. Perhaps you remember the disturbance when the security guys intervened?'

'He's lying!' cried Stephen. 'That man is *not* Stephen Lewis. I don't know what the hell is going on here or what he wants, but he's clearly up to no good.'

'I ... I *do* remember some sort of scuffle at the far side of the room last night,' said Mandelson. 'Was that when this guy approached you and your wife?'

The other man nodded. 'Yes ... it was quite frightening. We thought he was going to—'

'This is madness,' protested Stephen. 'Richard ... you know me – we've been corresponding for months. I'd have made contact earlier, but I got attacked in an alleyway the day I arrived in Miami.'

'Attacked?' repeated the bemused professor.

'Yes, I suffered a blow to the head and lost my memory ... but it's starting to come back to me now. I can remember—'

The bogus Stephen cut him off. 'Listen mister, I don't know who you are, or what you want, but this is a private meeting' – he took a step towards Stephen, jabbing the air with his finger – 'so why don't you just clear off, right now.'

Stephen stood his ground; he turned to Professor Mandelson. 'I can prove who I am. Just ask me about our research … I know I won't be able to remember everything, but this guy' – he pointed an accusing finger at the other man – 'won't have a clue.'

Mandelson glanced from one man to the other, clearly disoriented.

Stephen decided to press home his advantage. 'Go on – ask me anything,' he persisted. 'I can even tell you the name you're planning to give your new drug. It's—'

'Tridopamite,' interrupted the imposter.

'How … how do you know that?' spluttered Stephen, his head spinning now.

'Because Professor Mandelson told me during our extensive email correspondence in recent months.'

'No, that wasn't him,' cried Stephen, desperate now to gain control of this rapidly unravelling situation. 'It was me. Richard, you must remember … you even told me how you came up with the name. It was because the medication acts on—'

'The dopamine D_3 receptor in the brain,' cut in the other man.

Stephen was stunned. 'Th-that's impossible … how could you possibly know …?'

'Because *I* am the real Stephen Lewis,' said the other man. 'Look,' he said, turning to Professor Mandelson, 'I think this charade has gone on long enough. Do you have any security here? I think this guy needs to be escorted out of here.'

Mandelson just stood in silence, mouth agape, as he witnessed this verbal sparring between the other two men.

'Professor?' prompted the imposter.

This seemed to shake Mandelson out of the stupor which had enveloped him. 'I … uh … yes … we do have security staff on campus, but—'

Stephen made another desperate attempt to convince the professor. This was something the other man just couldn't *possibly* know.

'Richard, wait. You told me about your family … your two boys, Brady and … and …' *Dammit!* Although he *knew* the names of Mandelson's boys, the second name just wouldn't come.

The look on the pretender's face was something akin to pity, as he watched Stephen struggling to recall the name. 'Mason,' he said, calmly, '… Brady and Mason.'

Professor Mandelson shook his head in bewilderment.

'Look,' continued the imposter, 'why don't you ask him for some I.D.?'

'This bastard knows full well that I don't have any,' muttered Stephen, his fists clenched at his sides in frustration. 'When I was attacked, all my things were lost or stolen.' He turned his head to one side and parted his hair to show the shaved patch and the stitches. 'I was in a coma for three days.' He paused for a moment to allow the professor to absorb what he was saying. 'Look … my memory is still pretty screwed up, but I know who I am, and I know who he's *not*.'

The doubt and confusion evident in Professor Mandelson's eyes at least seemed to show that he hadn't dismissed Stephen's story out of hand.

'Wow,' said Mandelson, shaking his head, his eyebrows raised and his cheeks distended as he blew air through pursed lips, 'this really is a totally bizarre situation …' – something of an understatement in Stephen's view – 'I certainly have not been corresponding with *two* Stephen Lewises, yet somehow you *both* seem to know all about my research.' He fell silent, stroking his chin, as if carefully considering his next words. After a few more seconds' silence, he turned towards the other man, his tone apologetic. 'I'm sorry to have to ask, but do *you* have some I.D. you could show me?'

The other man raised his eyebrows, giving a slight shake of his head as he considered this request. 'Well, I don't actually have my passport with me just now, but—'

'You see,' said Stephen, stepping forward, 'he's lying.'

'But,' repeated the imposter, glaring at Stephen as he reached into his inside jacket pocket, 'I can show you my driver's licence … and credit cards.'

As he opened his wallet, Stephen stepped forward so that he could see just what this man was actually going to produce. To his utter dismay, the driver's licence looked completely authentic … apart from the photograph, which was not his, but that of the smug bastard standing in front of him.

'Th-that's impossible …' stammered Stephen. 'He's … I don't know how—'

'And somewhere here I have some credit cards …'

As the man turned over a central flap in his wallet, Stephen felt a wave of nausea flood through him. There was Emma; the photograph in the transparent pocket was exactly the same as the one he used to keep in his own wallet, except for one thing: the man clasping Emma's hand was not him, but his nemesis: the man standing right in front of him.

He felt the blood drain from his face as he struggled to get to grips with what he was looking at. His vision began to go blurry, and a dark veil descended. The last thing he registered was his knees beginning to buckle, unable to support him any longer, and then … nothing.

Chapter 10

As he turned into the alley, he heard what sounded like a woman's voice, pleading and sobbing; he couldn't make out what she was saying. But moments later a man's voice cut in, loud and threatening.

'You think you can just walk away, bitch? Well, I'm gonna teach you a lesson you won't forget in a hurry.'

Stephen quickened his step, straining to see what was going on ahead, but his eyes had not yet adapted to the gloomy light level in the alley. But then he saw it, silhouetted against the brightly-lit street at the far end of the alley: a woman pinned against the wall by a man with his forearm jammed under her chin. With his other hand, he was wrenching her skirt up around her waist and clawing at her underwear. She struggled to try to tear his arm away from her throat, finally succeeding in letting out a piercing scream.

Stephen looked over his shoulder to see if any help was at hand; there was none. He wasn't a particularly brave man, but faced with this situation he acted instinctively.

'Hey, you – what the hell's going on here?' he yelled, breaking into a run.

The man let go of his hapless victim and whirled around to face Stephen, who pulled up a few yards short of the attacker. The woman backed away, awkwardly pulling up her panties with one hand while massaging her throat with the other.

'What the fuck's it got to do with you, asshole?' growled the man.

Up close, the attacker did not look so threatening. He was a small, wiry man, dwarfed by Stephen's muscular, six-foot-three, two-hundred-and-twenty-pound frame. Stephen thought he saw fear and uncertainty in those small, dark eyes.

'Just leave her alone and go home,' said Stephen. 'There's no need for anyone to get hurt.'

The fear in the man's eyes vanished, as his face twisted in an ugly scowl. He reached behind his waist and produced a wicked-looking knife.

'So nobody's gonna get hurt, huh? Well I've got news for you, you interfering fucker.'

He advanced on Stephen, step by step, waving the knife slowly and deliberately from side to side ahead of him. Stephen began to back away, unsure whether to turn and run, or try to defend himself somehow.

Suddenly the man lunged forward, holding the knife aloft before sweeping it diagonally across in front of him in a vicious cleaving action. Stephen tried to defend himself with the only thing he had to hand. He held up his briefcase with both hands, shoving it forward to deflect the strike. He heard a ripping sound as the blade sliced through the leather cladding of the lid, but the case had saved him … for now at least. As Stephen continued backing away, his attacker looked to be tensing for another strike, murderous intent in his eyes.

Suddenly, he caught sight of movement in the dim light behind his attacker. The woman had stepped forward and thrust her hand in the air, pointing urgently towards Stephen. She cried out in a pronounced accent, which could have been South American.

'Look out, there's another—'

He felt a crushing blow and a searing pain to the back of his head, and then … blackness.

***

He could hear voices – muffled and distant. The words seemed to meld into an amorphous continuum with no form or reason. Gradually, though, fragments of comprehensible dialogue began to penetrate his dark, fuzzy world.

Eventually, he was able to distinguish a male voice: American accent, warm tones.

'We should never have let him out so soon … always a possibility … or a complete relapse.'

'But what could you have done?' came a soft female voice. '… hospital, not a prison. You really had no option.'

He realised where he was.

With a considerable effort, he forced his eyelids open. His vision was blurry and indistinct. He blinked and rubbed his eyes and, as his vision cleared a little, he registered the familiar surroundings of the very same hospital room where he had previously been treated. He tried to call out, but his throat felt like sandpaper, and all he could manage was a feeble croak. No-one responded. He remembered the call button alongside the bed and, twisting sideways, he reached out and pressed it.

Seconds later, Kelly, the nurse who had been so kind and generous, came into view, followed a few seconds later by the tall figure of Doctor Holt.

'Stephen? Can you hear me?' said the nurse, pouring some water from a jug on the bedside table into a tumbler and lifting Stephen's head, helping him to drink.

As the cooling liquid coursed down his throat, he finally found his voice. 'What happened? How did I end up back here?'

'An ambulance brought you in,' said Doctor Holt, moving forward to stand over Stephen. 'Do you remember where you were before that?'

The memory came flooding back. He propped himself up on one elbow, taking another long swallow of water before replying.

'Yes. I was at Professor Mandelson's lab, but this other guy who's impersonating me was there. I tried to convince the professor who I really was but ... but I didn't have any papers. And the other guy ... the bastard, he had—'

The words were spilling out on a feverish rush until the doctor placed a gentle, restraining hand on his arm. 'OK, take your time, Stephen. It's good that you have a clear memory of what happened, but—'

'Did I pass out? I remember everything going sort of blurry, and my legs ... they felt weak ... but then, I don't remember anything until I woke up back here.'

'You did, indeed, pass out. As luck would have it, the ambulance crew that picked you up was the same one that brought you here previously. They recognised you and brought you straight back here.'

'But Doctor,' continued Stephen, excitedly, 'I've remembered a whole lot more about what happened to me before ... I know how I got this head injury ...' He instinctively reached for the back of his head, to feel the stitches which had become increasingly itchy of late. He was surprised to feel nothing more than a carpet of stubble surrounding a raised, slightly tender ridge of skin.

'We removed the stitches while you were unconscious,' explained the doctor.

'Oh ... well, anyway, I know what happened. I took a short cut through the alley to try to get to a dinner appointment with Professor Mandelson, and came across this girl being attacked by some young thug. I tried to help her, but there must have been another guy there, because I got whacked over the back of the head. That's how I ended up here in the first place.'

'The fact that so much of your memory of events just before you were assaulted is coming back is excellent news but—'

'And I know who the girl is ... I know her name and where she works. If I can just get her to talk to me, she may be able to shed some light on what's going on.'

The doctor once again placed his hand on Stephen's arm. 'I'm delighted to see that your short-term memory is returning, but ... well, we need to understand much more about the longer-term picture which ... well ... which is in your mind.'

The realisation hit him like a blow to the stomach. 'You don't believe me. You don't believe I *am* Stephen Lewis.'

Kelly, who had said practically nothing so far, intervened. 'Stephen, please ... listen to what the doctor has to say.'

He sank back into his pillow with a weary sigh.

'You have suffered a severe trauma,' said the doctor, 'and it's clear that some of your mental faculties have been affected.'

'But I'm remembering so much more now: my flight here, the girl in the alley, the attack, the conference, Professor Mandelson ... Surely, it's obvious that I'm gradually recovering?'

'Yes, all of this is excellent,' agreed the doctor, 'but this business about another man impersonating you ... it's very difficult to find a rational explanation for such a situation.' The doctor paused, appearing to be choosing his words very carefully. 'Please don't take this the wrong way, but I believe we have to consider the possibility that you are suffering some sort of delusion about your former life.'

Stephen let out a long, slow sigh.

'I know it sounds incredible, Doctor; I can hardly believe it myself, but ... well, if I'm *not* Stephen Lewis, how do I know so much about him?'

'I don't know … maybe you met him sometime. You could have read about his research. Who knows?'

Stephen fell silent as he considered Doctor Holt's words. *Could I? Could I really know all this just from meeting him or reading about him?*

'I … I don't know. It just seems so …well … improbable.'

The doctor nodded, pursing his lips slightly. When he replied his voice was calming, conciliatory. 'Stephen, you have to appreciate that the human brain is an extremely complex organ, about which there is much we still don't understand. The effects of a severe blow to the head, such as you suffered, are very unpredictable.'

'But my wife … I remember our marriage, holidays we went on together. I can even remember having sex with her …' He checked himself, suddenly conscious of Kelly's presence, but when he glanced at her, she seemed unfazed by his remark. 'I … I'm sorry, but it all seems so *real*.'

'As I said,' responded the doctor, 'the brain is an incredibly complex organ. If you have met Stephen Lewis at some time, it is entirely possible that you have met his wife too. From what you have said, she is a very attractive woman. It wouldn't be beyond the bounds of possibility that your brain is creating fantasies about her.'

Could it? Could this really be? He just couldn't believe it possible.

'No,' he insisted, 'I can't accept that. I understand what you are saying, but I just can't believe that such vivid memories are nothing more than fantasies.'

'Then why does she not seem to know you?'

'I don't know. I can only think they are forcing her to take part in something against her will.'

'But why, Stephen? Why would they do that? And who are "they" anyway?'

'I … I don't know,' he admitted.

'And the man you believe is impersonating you – he has a driver's licence, credit cards … even a photograph of himself together with the woman you believe is your wife. How could he have faked all these things?'

Stephen didn't answer – he didn't *have* an answer. He closed his eyes, trying to make some sense of it all. Then he remembered something else …

'But, what about the guy who was following me?'

The doctor shrugged. 'Maybe he wasn't actually following you. Maybe he was just running to catch the train.'

Stephen exhaled heavily and sank back into the pillow once more. 'What's happening to me, Doctor? Am I going mad?'

'"Mad" is a very emotive, and not very precise term, Stephen. My best guess is that the blow to your head has somehow prevented access to most of your long-term memories and, to fill the vacuum, your brain has constructed a whole alternative persona, constructed from snippets about people you have met, with the gaps filled in by your imagination.'

Crazy as it seemed, he had to accept that this explanation was, at least, consistent with all the evidence. 'What the hell am I going to do, Doctor?'

'Look, I am not a specialist in this specific area, so I'm going to arrange for someone who is to see you tomorrow. Doctor Marco Scarucci is one of the very best experts in this field. If anyone can properly diagnose your condition, he can.'

Stephen nodded, grateful for any straw to clutch at in his quest to understand what was happening to him.

'First though,' continued the doctor, 'I want to give you an MRI scan to double check that the fracture to your skull has not impinged upon any brain tissue. It looked OK on the x-rays but ... well, one can't be too careful in matters like this. The nurse will give you a mild sedative to help you relax during the scan, and get some much-needed rest afterwards.'

Stephen nodded, weakly.

As Doctor Holt left the room the nurse offered Stephen two capsules. 'Take these, and then we'll get you straight down to radiology.'

He swallowed the capsules, washing them down with water from the tumbler she offered him. As he passed the tumbler back to her, he looked directly into her eyes. 'Are you married, Kelly?'

She pulled her head back a little, widening her eyes in surprise. 'I ... er, well no I'm not, actually. Why do you—?'

'Boyfriend then?'

'Well, yes. His name is Rick, we've been going out together for over three years.'

'OK, so a pretty serious relationship then?'

'Yes, of course,' she said. 'Actually, we're saving up for the deposit to buy a house together. We want to get married as soon as we can afford it.' She paused, tilting her head to one side, a half-smile dancing around her lips. 'But, why are you asking about *my* life all of a sudden?'

'Imagine,' he said, 'waking up one day to find Rick didn't know you.'

'I can't,' she said, shaking her head.

'And imagine he showed up with another woman who claimed that she was the real Kelly, engaged to marry your Rick.'

'It's … impossible.'

'But if it happened,' he persisted, 'do you really think that it could be true? That he really didn't *know* you? That those three years you spent with him were an illusion? All in your mind?'

She sighed. 'No,' she admitted, 'I couldn't accept that.'

The silence hung heavily in the air for several seconds before Stephen spoke again. 'Do *you* think I'm going mad, Kelly?'

Her eyes were filled with compassion as she laid her hand on his. 'Let's just see what the MRI scan shows and what the specialist comes up with.'

As he lay back and closed his eyes, he no longer knew just *what* to think.

Chapter 11

Carla Fernandez Garrido was torn.

There was no way on earth she could allow herself to become involved in anything which might result in her being questioned by the police. Like millions of other Mexicans, she had entered the USA illegally, and like most of them, she had remained undetected as she slipped seamlessly into North American society. But any contact with the police – even a parking ticket – could result in her cover being blown. If that happened, the very least she could expect was deportation. Worse still, though, if they found out she had become mixed up with drug dealers, she would probably end up in jail. She just couldn't let that happen.

And yet, she owed a huge debt of gratitude to the tall stranger who had come to her aid the previous week. Without his intervention she would surely have been raped … or even worse. She hated herself for having shunned him so brusquely when he had come to the diner, but what else could she do?

She thought back to the shocking events which had ensued in that darkened alley …

***

She clasped a hand to her mouth as the stranger, who had tried to help her, sank to the ground as if poleaxed. His assailant used the bottom of his tee shirt to wipe the iron bar where he had been holding it, before dropping it on the ground; the sound rang out like a bell as it hit the ground.

'Let's get the hell outta here,' he yelled to his partner, who stood hunched over the stranger's prone figure, still brandishing the knife, his eyes wild with bloodlust.

'I should gut the interfering bastard first,' he hissed.

The other man grabbed his knife arm, restraining him. 'C'mon – he's probably already dead anyway. Let's split right now ... before the cops arrive.'

The man with the knife stood motionless over the stranger for several seconds, the other man still clutching his arm. Eventually he shook the restraining hand from his arm and lowered the knife. He gave the lifeless body on the ground a vicious kick in the ribs.

'That's for poking yer fucking nose inta business which don't concern ya,' he growled.

'C'mon ...' urged his partner, 'let's get outta here.'

'What about her?' demanded the first man, raising the knife and pointing it directly at Carla.

Terror rose in her throat once more as she caught the wild gleam in the man's eyes. Her heart was hammering furiously.

'Leave the bitch ... we can deal with her later.'

Finally, he relented, turning to face his partner and returning the knife to its sheath. Carla sank to her knees, still uncertain whether this maniac would suddenly change his mind and attack her again.

But it seemed he now had other priorities. 'Wait,' he said, bending down to go through the fallen man's pockets. He found what looked like a small book or diary, which he flung carelessly aside, and then a wallet, which he flipped open in order to inspect the contents. 'Plenty of cash in here,' he declared, closing the wallet and slipping it into the back pocket of his jeans. He then grabbed the mutilated briefcase. 'There could be more money in here.' He tried to open the case, but it was locked. 'Shit,' he hissed, punching the case in frustration.

'C'mon,' yelled the other man. 'We don't got much time. Leave the case.'

'I ain't leaving it. Look at this leather;' he said, thrusting the case forward, 'this thing musta cost five hundred dollars.'

'Well it ain't worth five hundred dollars now. Just leave it.'

'No. He must be some rich bastard to have a case like this. There's bound to be something valuable inside. Let's just take it with us ... we can force it open later.'

The other man just shook his head and shrugged. 'OK, but c'mon ... we gotta go.'

'Bastard,' growled the man with the knife, giving the lifeless figure on the ground another spiteful kick.

Finally, the two of them ran for it.

Carla dragged herself to her feet and staggered over to the motionless body on the floor. A pool of blood was rapidly spreading behind the man's head. She peeled back one of his eyelids; only the white of the eye was showing. She put her cheek right up to his open mouth to check his breathing: nothing. She pulled back his sleeve and fumbled to locate the pulse in his wrist: nothing.

Her heart was racing as she rushed over to the point where she had been attacked. Her handbag was lying on the ground, its contents scattered far and wide. She dropped to her hands and knees, scrabbling in the dirt as she desperately searched for her cell phone. Her efforts were badly hampered by the poor light in the alley, but finally she found it. Her fingers were trembling so much that it took her three attempts to dial 911. Once the operator had assured her that the police and ambulance were on their way, she hung up, without giving her name.

She hurried back to the fallen stranger, checking for breathing or a pulse once more; still there was nothing. He must have been like that for around three or four minutes now. If he wasn't dead already, he soon would be. She couldn't just stand there and do nothing while waiting for the ambulance to arrive. She had had no medical training but she had to do *something*. She knelt down and tried to roll the body onto its back; she managed to get him about halfway there but then he rolled back onto his side. She tried again, but the result was the same. Christ, he was heavy. She took a deep breath, gritting her teeth and, with a superhuman effort, she finally succeeded in getting him onto his back

Trying to recall what she had seen in countless movies, she placed the heel of her hand in the centre of the man's chest, before placing her other hand on top of the first. She positioned her shoulders above him, and then, using her full body weight – which wasn't much, for she was of slight build – began pumping up and down. After about twenty compressions she stopped to check his breathing again: still nothing. Again trying to replicate what she had seen in the movies, she placed her hand under his chin and tipped his head back; Christ, there was so much *blood* behind his head. Trying to ignore the dark, spreading pool, she pinched his nose, sealed her mouth over his, and blew, firmly and steadily. She could feel, and see, his chest slowly rising; she kept blowing until her own lungs were empty. Pausing for a few seconds to take a deep breath, she once again covered his mouth with hers and repeated the procedure.

The effort was now leaving her breathless and faint; she didn't think she could keep this up much longer and, in any case, she really didn't know whether she was actually doing it right. Still there was no sign of life.

She repositioned her body and resumed the chest pumping; after another twenty compressions, there was still nothing. By now she was exhausted; she couldn't go on any longer.

But then his eyes flickered, and she heard him utter a low groan; her heart leapt in her chest. She checked his pulse again. Yes, it was there now: weak and erratic, but a pulse nevertheless. Encouraged, she once again pinched his nostrils shut and sealed her mouth over his, ready to blow into his lungs again, but this time he seemed to gag and cough. Maybe it would be best to stop now that he was starting to breathe on his own? She pulled back a little, but kept her face within inches of his, ready to resume mouth-to-mouth if necessary. His eyes opened fully and he raised a hand to touch the side of her cheek.

'Emma?' he croaked.

'I'm not Emma. I don't know who Emma is. You've been ...' Her voice tailed off as she realised he was slipping back into unconsciousness.

She straddled his body, positioning herself to start the chest pumping once more, but no sooner had she placed her hands on his chest, she heard the undulating wail of a siren. The emergency services were on their way. She was torn: she wanted to help him, to keep him alive until they arrived, but she couldn't allow herself to be questioned by the police. When a second siren joined the sound of the first, creating a discordant cacophony, her mind was made up. She had to get away ... as soon as possible.

She scrambled to her feet and rushed over to where her handbag was lying on the ground. With the aid of the flashlight built into her phone, she hurriedly gathered up all the contents which were strewn across the filthy pavement and bundled them into her handbag: she could not afford to leave anything which might identify her.

Which way to run? It sounded as though the sirens were approaching from the end of the alley from which the stranger had entered, so she made for the other end, sprinting as fast as her finely-muscled legs would carry her. As she reached the end of the alley, she paused for a moment to glance over her shoulder; the sirens were louder than ever, but no-one was following her. She hoped that she had done enough to save this man who had come to her aid, but there was no time to linger now. As she stepped towards the exit onto the street, she tripped over something, pitching forward and painfully skinning her knee. Cursing, she looked down to see what had tripped her: it was the briefcase.

Without really stopping to think what she was doing or why, she picked it up before stepping out onto the street and heading for the nearby sanctuary of her apartment.

***

Her smile was radiant as she took his hand and turned towards the camera, brushing away a strand of hair from her porcelain-smooth cheek.

'Great,' said the photographer, 'now let's get a shot of the rings.' He fussed around them, arranging and rearranging their positions until satisfied. 'OK, just make sure you keep your hands in exactly that position.'

Stephen looked down at the rings: matching gold bands each with three sparkling stones inset. Emma's slender fingers and elegantly manicured nails contrasted starkly with his own shovel-like paw, but he just knew it was an image he would treasure.

'Right, how about a nice kiss now?' chirped the photographer, fiddling with the settings on his camera.

She turned towards him, her beautiful blue eyes sparkling with happiness. He placed a hand behind her neck and gently drew her towards him. As their lips met and he savoured the taste of her, he was oblivious to the photographer's inane babbling – he was lost in the moment.

When their lips finally parted and he slowly opened his eyes, his heart skipped a beat. Where were those beautiful, azure blue eyes? The eyes which locked onto his were a deep brown colour. Her skin was dark, her hair black. The aquiline nose bore no resemblance to Emma's, which was delicate, and slightly upturned.

'Emma?' he whispered, 'What's happening? Why—?'

He felt an abrupt jolt … and she was gone.

***

The sedative must have been very powerful. In spite of the deafening cacophony of buzzes, clicks, and bangs made by the MRI scanner, Stephen had actually drifted off to sleep.

But now all was silent; it must have been the sudden cessation of the noise made by the machine which had jolted him awake.

As he was being wheeled back to his own room, he thought about the two women who were now haunting his dreams. He resolved that, one way or another, he would have to persuade both of them to talk to him. As he wrestled with how on earth he would manage this, his thoughts became increasingly jumbled and disconnected.

Sleep overtook him again.

Chapter 12

He was drifting in that strange world midway between sleep and wakefulness, where dreams and reality seem to meld seamlessly into one. As his eyelids flickered, he became dimly aware of the presence of a tall figure in a white coat alongside him. Was that part of his dream, or was that the real world? Through blurred vision, he was just able to discern that the doctor was making some sort of adjustment to the drip attached to the tube which snaked down to the cannula in his wrist. Within seconds, he felt a warm, comforting fuzziness suffuse his body; the urge to return to the sanctuary of sleep was almost irresistible, yet something inside him told that all was not well.

'Doctor Holt?' he murmured, 'how long ... I mean, what ...?' Somehow, he could not form a coherent sentence.

'Don't worry, Stephen,' came the reassuring voice, 'this is just something to help you relax.'

Yes, relax ... It was nice to relax. He closed his eyes and began to let the delicious sensation envelop him.

He felt something pressing into the skin just above his left ankle, followed by a gentle tugging sensation. It wasn't enough to significantly disturb his euphoric state; he allowed himself to sink a little deeper into the warm, cosy cocoon which enveloped him. Then something tugged at his left wrist, much harder this time. The pain he felt as something cut right into his flesh was enough to jolt him into full consciousness. By now, the doctor was no longer fussing with the drip; he was busy looping something around Stephen's right ankle. As he looked down, he realised that the doctor was about to secure his ankle with a plastic cable tie.

'What ... what are you doing?' he croaked, every word an effort to force from his lips.

The doctor looked up; it wasn't Doctor Holt. The thin, angular features; the dark, penetrating eyes; the slicked-back hair – there was no mistaking the face of the man who had pursued him in the Metrorail station as he raced for the train. He tried to jerk his foot away, but the response of his muscles to the signal from his brain was leaden; he felt as though he were trying to move through a sea of treacle.

The face of the bogus doctor broke into a wicked grin. 'Finding it a bit difficult to move, eh? Well, I really wouldn't bother trying, because—'

Another voice cut in, urgent and indignant. 'What is going on here?'

Stephen tried to sit up, but found himself pinned by his left ankle and wrist. He rolled over as far as he could to see what was happening. The familiar figure of Doctor Holt stood in front of them, pointing an accusing finger at the other man.

'This is my patient,' asserted Doctor Holt, 'and I demand to know—'

Phut! The doctor's eyes widened and his mouth sprang open as he staggered backward clutching his chest, coming to rest with his back against the wall. When he held up his bloodied hand in front of his face, his expression was one of uncomprehending astonishment. As he lowered his hand and looked up at the man holding the gun, it seemed as though the scene was frozen in time: the doctor standing there, back to the wall, gazing in bewilderment and shock at the man who had just shot him. Finally though, his legs buckled and he slid slowly to the floor.

His assailant stepped forward to stand over the stricken figure sitting propped against the wall.

'P-please ...' murmured Doctor Holt, weakly raising his hand in a defensive gesture.

'You talk too much,' growled the other man.

Stephen looked on in horror as the man raised his gun once more. *Phut!* A small, neat hole appeared in the centre of Doctor Holt's forehead; his head slumped to one side leaving a crimson streak on the wall behind, leading to a hole in the wall where the slug had slammed into it after passing through the doctor's skull.

It was like watching a movie in slow motion; Stephen couldn't process what he was seeing. 'Doctor Holt?' he gasped, but as he looked into those dull, lifeless eyes, he realised that Doctor Holt was dead.

'Now,' said the bogus doctor, apparently completely untroubled by the fact that he had just killed a man, 'I have to clear things up a little here, so why don't you just relax and wait for a few minutes? Then,' he continued, slipping the gun back into the shoulder holster inside his white coat, 'I'm going to wheel you down to the front entrance and into the ambulance which is waiting. Oh, and don't bother trying to call out to anyone – within a few more moments your vocal cords will be completely inoperative.'

'But, why ...? What ...?' He felt his throat seize solid; he couldn't form any more words.

He watched, helpless, as the man took hold of the doctor's feet and began dragging him, slowly and painfully, towards the door to an adjoining room, the blood trail forming a gruesome witness to the route taken.

Suddenly, the shocking reality of what he had just witnessed snapped Stephen out of his drug-induced, trancelike state. Perhaps it was adrenaline, perhaps just sheer force of will but, one way or another, he was now able to start fighting against the effects of the drug.

He had to get out of there – but how? His left wrist and ankle were pinned and there was no way he could release the cable ties with his other hand. His brain went into overdrive.

The first thing he did was to yank the cannula from his wrist: he had to stop whatever that bastard was pumping into his bloodstream. Oblivious to the blood now streaming from his wrist he glanced all around, searching for something, anything, which could help him.

And then he saw it: on top of the cabinet to his right lay a surgical dressing kit. Together with the sterile packs of gauze, bandages, and surgical tape was a small pair of scissors. But it was out of reach. He strained against the bonds restraining him, desperately trying to wrench his hand free, but the plastic strip merely cut deeper into his wrist. The pain was excruciating, but his energetic struggle revealed something: the gurney was moving slightly beneath him as he lurched back and forth in frustration.

The wheels were not locked!

His eyes alighted on an exposed pipe running down the wall to his right. Stretching to the limit of his reach, he managed to touch the pipe with his free hand. With a herculean effort, he managed to stretch a couple of inches further until he was able to curl his fingers around the pipe. Using all the strength he could muster, he pulled hard, and … the gurney moved around a foot closer to the cabinet and those precious scissors.

How much time did he have? Surely the other man would return very soon.

Another hard pull drew him a further couple of feet towards the cabinet. He was almost within touching distance of the scissors when he heard footsteps approaching.

Chapter 13

The bogus doctor stepped through the open door, stopping dead in his tracks when he saw that the gurney had moved several feet from where it had been. As he registered the crumpled pile of bedclothes lying where his prisoner should have been, he whirled around, reaching inside his white coat for his gun.

But Stephen was ready: he jumped forward from his hiding place behind the door, plunging the scissors into the side of the man's neck before he could draw his gun. He cried out in pain, abandoning his grab for the gun and clutching his neck, staggering against the gurney before falling to the floor.

This was Stephen's chance, but he knew he would have to act quickly. The man was incapacitated for the moment, but the scissors were small, and the wound probably quite shallow. He wouldn't be out of action for long. Stephen dashed towards the bedside cabinet, wrenching the door open and grabbing the large plastic bag which contained his clothes and other meagre belongings. He heard a groan and turned to see the man he had stabbed trying to rise to his feet.

In the heat of the struggle, Stephen had dropped the scissors, and now he couldn't see where they had fallen; he scanned the room for some other form of weapon. Finding nothing better, he dropped the plastic bag and picked up the metal bedside chair with both hands, bringing it crashing down on the man's head. The man cried out and fell to the floor once more. Leaving the prone figure behind, Stephen grabbed the plastic bag and rushed for the door.

As he pounded down the corridors, barefoot and wearing only his hospital gown, he was acutely aware of the astonished glances he was attracting from hospital staff and patients alike. But he was concentrating on just one thing: forcing his drug-weakened legs forward as fast as they would go, lest his attacker should be right behind him. As he rounded a corner, he crashed into a trolley piled high with meals and drinks. As the whole thing went flying, so did the hapless porter, who fired a string of obscenities in Stephen's direction. He pressed on regardless.

Finally, he emerged in the hospital lobby, pausing for a second or so to locate the main entrance.

'Excuse me, sir,' called out the receptionist from behind her desk, rising to her feet as she took in Stephen's dishevelled state and obvious distress, 'where are you—?'

But Stephen was already sprinting for the door. As he burst into the warm, humid air outside he stopped for a moment, trying to figure out his next move.

An ambulance stood waiting at the kerb, its rear doors open and a stocky, uniformed figure standing alongside. The man was bald, with dark, close-set eyes, and a bull neck. As they made eye contact, his expression hardened and, with a chilling certainty, Stephen *knew* that this was the man who was meant to take him away.

Shit! Should he try to make a run for it? In bare feet, and still partially under the influence of the debilitating drug which he had been given, he didn't hold out much hope of outrunning his potential kidnapper. Maybe he should retreat back into the hospital and try to find a hiding place there? He turned around to see an elderly lady on crutches being assisted out of the main entrance by a tall, thin man. They were blocking his route back inside.

As he looked past them, through the glass doors, he realised that going back inside wasn't an option anyway: the figure in the white coat, clutching a bloodstained pad to the side of his neck, was inside, making his way, unsteadily, towards the entrance.

'Only a few yards, ma'am,' said the man in the doorway, as he struggled to negotiate the spring-loaded door with the old lady and her crutches. 'The cab's just over there.'

As Stephen's eyes followed the man's pointing finger, he spotted the taxi, its engine idling. There was no driver in the car; Stephen figured he must be the guy helping the old lady. He glanced back at the heavy-set man by the ambulance, who was now reaching inside his jacket and moving towards him.

The decision was made: Stephen rushed towards the waiting taxi, wrenching open the driver's door and flinging his bag of clothes inside, before jumping inside, behind the wheel.

'Hey! What the fuck do you think you're doing?' called out the cab driver, letting go of the old lady's arm and rushing forward.

Stephen didn't respond; he shoved the selector lever into 'Drive' and floored the accelerator. As he sped off, in a cloud of tyre smoke, he could see, in his rear-view mirror, the old lady sprawled on the floor and the cab driver wildly gesticulating. Behind them, the man who had shot Doctor Holt had just staggered out of the main entrance, still holding the blood-soaked pad to his neck. The uniformed ambulance driver rushed to his aid. The last thing that Stephen saw in his mirror, before rounding a corner and leaving the whole scene behind him, was the injured man being helped towards the waiting ambulance: the ambulance which had been meant for *him*.

Stephen had no idea where he was going – he just drove blindly until he had put a few miles between himself and the hospital, and he was sure he was not being pursued. Finally, he pulled up in a quiet side street to let his racing heart settle and try to decide what to do next.

Should he just go straight to the police? That's what any sane and rational person would do, but Stephen was no longer sure of either his sanity or his rationality. And, with no witnesses as to what had happened at the hospital, and the two men who had come to abduct him probably having fled the scene, he was worried that *he* might be considered a suspect in relation to the murder of Doctor Holt.

Above all he wanted, now more than ever, answers.

Just what had happened back in that dark alley? What was the significance of the diary with just two dates highlighted? Why did Emma seem not to know him? Why was someone impersonating him … or were they? Was it *him* who was the impersonator? Why had these people tried to abduct him? What could possibly be so important that these people were prepared to murder the doctor so callously?

The last of these questions had added yet another perplexing dimension to the puzzle. These people obviously had no compunction about committing murder in pursuit of their objectives, but what *were* their objectives? If they had wanted him dead, they could easily have accomplished this in the hospital with a minimum of fuss. Yet they had gone to considerable lengths to try to take him alive. None of it made any sense.

He decided to try, once more, to get Carla, the waitress, to talk to him.

***

Having driven to within half a mile of Eduardo's Restaurant, he parked the stolen taxi in a quiet corner of a largely-empty car park. He climbed into the back of the car and scrambled awkwardly into his clothes, stuffing the hospital gown into the plastic bag. He left the car unlocked and the key in the ignition, reasoning that it would eventually find its way back to the taxi company. And even if someone else stole it, at least it wouldn't be *him* that the police would be after. He set off on foot, depositing the plastic bag containing the hospital gown in the first garbage dumpster that he came across.

It was dark by the time he reached the restaurant, but the brightly-lit interior meant that, through the glass frontage, he could clearly see everything inside. He was dismayed to see that the waitress clearing tables was not Carla; this girl, while also of Latina appearance, was shorter and of heavier build. *Dammit!* Stupidly, he admitted to himself, it had not occurred to him that Carla might not be on duty. His heart sank as he realised that, other than catching her at the restaurant, he had no means of locating her.

What next? He couldn't just hang about waiting for her to show up – it could be hours, or even the following day, before her next shift. The only thing he could think of was to go inside, order something to eat – he was, after all, pretty hungry – and see if he could get the other waitress to help him. This was not without risk, as the big guy who had shooed him away previously was there, behind the counter. If he recognised Stephen or if the other waitress reacted badly to being asked about Carla, there could be an awkward scene or, worse still, the police might be called. There was no other way though – he would have to chance it.

As he sat down, the waitress came right over. 'What can I get you sir?'

'Well, what would you recommend?'

Her brow creased in a puzzled frown as she inclined her head. 'Recommend? I don't know. You want something to eat?'

He nodded. 'I'm really hungry – what's a good choice?'

'It's all good,' she said, laughing. 'Now, am I going to tell you some of it's bad?'

'I guess not,' he replied, smiling.

'Well just choose something from the menu, then.' She took the menu from the stand on the table and placed it in front of him. 'You want something to drink while you're choosing?'

'Thanks,' he said, smiling. 'Tea please.'

'Sure ... say, are you Australian?'

Again? He had to smile, in spite of the desperate situation in which he found himself.

'English.'

'Oh, well ... I love the accent.'

'And yours,' he said, keen to build some sort of rapport with this girl but anxious not to appear to be flirting. 'Where are you from?'

Her eyes narrowed. 'You're not a cop are you?'

'Me? No ... do I look like a cop?'

Her expression relaxed and her smile returned. 'No, I guess not. I'm from Mexico.'

From her initial reaction to his question, Stephen surmised that she probably didn't have the proper immigration papers, but she seemed OK with him now.

'I've never been to Mexico,' said Stephen, 'but I'd love to go sometime. Maybe you could suggest some good places to visit.'

'I'd be glad to, but we're a bit busy right now. Eduardo' – she inclined her head towards the big man in the grubby apron – 'don't like us spending too much time chatting to the customers when it's busy. Anyway, I'll go get your tea while you make your selection from our *a la carte* menu.' She giggled at her own joke.

From the slight cloud which had flitted across her face when she indicated the guy behind the counter, Stephen guessed there wasn't too much love lost between them. He felt he could risk asking her about Carla when she returned.

'OK, what's it to be?' said the waitress, setting down the tea and taking out her notebook.

'Thanks' – he paused as he read her name badge – 'María. I'll go for the cheeseburger.'

'Oh, excellent choice,' she giggled. 'That should chase away the hunger pangs real good.'

OK, now or never. 'Say, do you know Carla who works here?'

'Carla? Sure ... why ... do you know her?'

'Not exactly, but ... well, I'd like to talk to her.'

'Oh, right … like most of the guys who come in here. What's she got that I don't?' The sparkle in her eyes and the smile dancing around her lips made it clear that the remark was made in good humour.

'No,' said Stephen, 'it's not like that. I just … well I need to talk to her. When's she next going to be here?'

'Oh, she's here right now … working out back. She should be out here soon … you want me to send her over?'

Now, that was a difficult question. How would she react?

'Er, no, that's OK, I'll just catch her when she comes out.'

The cheeseburger turned up before Carla did. Stephen had devoured around half of it when Carla finally emerged from the door which led to the kitchen. She showed no signs of anxiety or disquiet as she set about her normal duties; he assumed that the other girl had not mentioned his presence. He kept his head down while he continued eating, but all the time keeping a watchful eye on Carla, who seemed to be working the far side of the diner while the other waitress worked Stephen's side.

Eventually, however, she came right past his table.

'Carla,' he whispered, looking up and catching her eye.

She stopped dead in her tracks, shooting a nervous glance in the direction of the big guy behind the counter, before looking back at Stephen.

'What do you want? You shouldn't be here.'

'Carla, I'm in big trouble. You're the only one who can help me.'

She leaned forward, lowering her voice to a whisper. 'Look, I've got enough troubles of my own. I'm really sorry about what happened, but—'

'But that's just it … I don't *know* what happened: I've lost most of my memory. I know you tried to help me before … and now there are some really bad people after me, and I don't know why.'

'Look,' she said, glancing over again at the man behind the counter, 'all I know is what happened in that alley. I can't help with anything else.'

'Then just tell me about that,' he pleaded. 'Maybe that will help me figure out what's going on.'

Her eyes were now filled with compassion. 'I … I don't know. It's—'

'Carla? You goin' to stand chatting all night or are you goin' to clear those tables?' The big man's tone telegraphed his obvious irritation.

'OK,' she whispered to Stephen, 'I'm off duty in about forty-five minutes. We can talk then. Now I have to go.' She hurried away from Stephen's table.

'How was the burger?' enquired the other waitress when she came to clear the table. As she eyed the empty plate, her face broke into a grin. 'Oh, I guess it must have been OK,' she said. 'You want any dessert?'

'No thanks, I'm pretty full now.'

'The check then?'

'Er ... not yet, I have to wait for Carla to finish her shift.'

'You pulled already?' she said, eyes wide and mouth agape. 'You must have something all the other hopefuls who come in here don't. She's pretty picky you know.' She looked at him, appraisingly, her head tilted to one side. 'Hmm, not bad, I must admit ... but I reckon it's the accent that clinched it.'

'No, said Stephen, laughing, 'I told you it's nothing like that ... we just need to talk.'

'Yeah, right ... talking first is good,' she said, eyes sparkling with mirth.

'No, really I—'

'And here was me thinking that it was *me* you had the hots for.'

'Honestly, I'm just ... oh, maybe I'll have another cup of tea while I wait.'

'You got it.'

Chapter 14

'It's not exactly the height of luxury,' said Carla, as she led Stephen up the stairs to her second floor apartment.

And it wasn't. The front door opened straight into a tiny living room furnished with an old, saggy couch upholstered in faded brown fabric; a wooden rocking chair; and a small, plastic-laminate-topped dining table, with two chairs. The paintwork was faded and patchy, and the dark grey carpet threadbare in places. And yet the place was clean and tidy, with little feminine touches such as a vase of fresh flowers on the table and a row of small soft toys sitting obediently alongside each other on a shelf on the far wall, bookended by a couple of framed photographs – presumably of her family and friends.

'The landlord won't spend a cent on the place,' she continued, 'but if I complain he just says to move on if I don't like it. Says he can get someone else in a heartbeat. And the truth is, he's probably right ... I honestly don't think I could find anywhere else for the price.'

'It's ... homely,' he ventured.

She stifled a laugh as she dropped her handbag onto the couch. 'You're a real bad liar ... Stephen, is it?'

'Yes ... or at least, I think so.'

She cocked her head to one side, drawing her eyebrows together, creating attractive little vertical crinkles in the skin above the bridge of her nose. 'You *think* so?'

'It's a long, and frankly very scary, story,' he sighed – 'one full of holes. But I'm hoping you can maybe help me to fill in some of those holes'

'I'll do my best, but first things first. You hungry?'

'After that monster cheeseburger? You must be kidding.'

'Well, I don't have time to eat while I'm working, so I'm starving. I'm going to fix myself something right now. Make yourself at home while I do that, and then we can talk.'

'Any chance I could take a shower or a bath? I've been in these clothes for quite a while and I'm feeling pretty grubby now.'

'Sure but do you have anything to change into?'

He shook his head.

'Wait a minute.' She disappeared into the bedroom which led off from the living room, reappearing a couple of minutes later with a small pile of clothes, which she laid on the couch. 'Here ... some boxer shorts, socks, and a tee-shirt. I'm afraid I don't have any pants, so you'll have to stick with those you have on.'

Stephen raised his eyebrows. 'You keep spare sets of men's clothes here ... just in case some random guy shows up looking for a shower?'

She laughed. 'They're my old boyfriend's. He left a few things behind when I threw him out.'

'You threw him out? I guess I shouldn't ask why.'

She shrugged. 'It's no big secret – he was screwing one of the other girls who worked at the diner.'

'Oh, I see,' said Stephen, a little taken aback at her forthright response. 'It wasn't ... er, María, the girl who was working there tonight?'

'No, María's my friend ... we look out for each other. The other bitch left after I confronted her. Anyway, that's history ... he's long gone now. Good thing I didn't get rid of all his clothes, though, isn't it?'

'I guess so,' replied Stephen.

'Mike was a big guy like you, so hopefully the clothes'll fit OK.'

'Thank you ... I can't say how grateful I am.'

'OK, well ... bathroom's down there,' she said, indicating a small hallway which led off from the living room.

He gathered up the clothes and made his way to the bathroom. He was gratified to find that, in spite of its almost antique appearance, the shower worked well, with a plentiful supply of hot water delivered in powerful jets. He luxuriated for at least ten minutes in the soothing stream, almost allowing himself to believe it could wash away his troubles.

It couldn't – but by the time he had dried himself off and changed into clean clothes, Stephen was feeling a whole lot better. He returned to the living room, where Carla was just finishing off a toasted sandwich.

'Beer?' she said, standing up and taking her plate over to the kitchen – which was really nothing more than an alcove off the living room with a sink, a cooker, a small fridge, and a couple of wall-mounted cupboards above a short length of laminate-topped work surface.

'I could murder one,' he replied, the casually-uttered words bringing back, with a jolt, the shocking memory of Doctor Holt's violent demise.

Carla, however, seemed untroubled by his remark. 'OK,' she said, opening the fridge and grabbing two cans. She popped the ring pull on her own can, while handing the other to Stephen as she sat down alongside him on the ancient couch. 'First some ground rules …' Stephen looked at her enquiringly. 'I can't get involved with the cops in any way, shape, or form.'

'Because?'

'Because I came here from Mexico illegally, and I don't have the proper papers or anything.'

'And you're worried you might get deported?'

She nodded. 'But it's not just that … I've got mixed up with some very bad people. If they were to get even the slightest idea that I might be grassing on them, they'd really hurt me … or worse.'

Stephen gasped, involuntarily, at this revelation. He took a couple of seconds to find his voice.

'But how? I mean what happened?'

She suddenly clammed up. 'I don't think I should tell you any more … for your sake and mine. Let's just agree that the police are off limits, OK?'

He found it difficult to believe that this woman, who had already shown him considerable kindness, was some sort of hardened criminal. On the contrary, she seemed to display a vulnerability which made him want to help her, distracting him a little from his own desperate situation. This was not the moment to pry though.

'OK,' he agreed.

She nodded, her mouth set in a thin, straight line. 'So what do you want to know?'

***

It was over an hour later. Carla, had recounted the events which had taken place in that darkened alley, filling in the gaps between the fragmented memories that Stephen could recall and explaining how she had called 911, and administered CPR.

'I dreamt about it,' gasped Stephen. 'I saw your face …right in front of mine … I felt your breath filling my lungs … I felt the weight of your body pressing down on me …' He fell silent for a moment before looking directly into her eyes. 'You saved my life.'

She held his gaze for a brief moment before casting her eyes downward. 'I couldn't just leave you there. I … well, I just did what I could until I could hear the ambulance coming.'

'I don't know how I'll ever be able to repay you, but well … thank you for what you did.'

She gave a nervous-looking smile, seemingly embarrassed by his fulsome display of gratitude. 'So what about you? Just what sort of trouble are you in, exactly?'

'Well, some of this is going to sound pretty unbelievable but … well, here goes …'

Stephen told her everything he could remember about his former life and the recent events which had shattered it, including the mysterious dates in the diary, the baffling behaviour of his wife, the shadowy people who were after him, and the horrendous murder of Doctor Holt.

Carla listened in stunned silence. 'That's quite a story,' she said. There was no irony or disbelief in her voice – just shock and puzzlement.

'And still, none of it makes sense,' he sighed. 'But something you just told me might help.'

She tilted her head to one side, drawing her eyebrows together, creating those attractive little vertical creases just above the bridge of her nose. 'And what would that be?'

'The briefcase: I have no recollection whatsoever of what it contained. If I can see what's inside, that might provide some answers.'

Her face fell. 'I'm afraid it's not here.'

'But, I thought you said you picked it up.'

'I did, but it was locked.'

'So we force it open. Where is it?'

'I asked my friend, Sylvia, to look after it for me. Those two guys who tried to ...' – tears welled in her eyes, but she fought them back – 'well, one of them's dead now, but the other knows where I live. If he knew that I had the briefcase ...' Her voice tailed off.

More shocking revelations. Just what the hell *was* Carla mixed up in?

'I was scared,' she continued, 'of what they might do if they found out I had taken the case.'

He placed a comforting arm around her shoulders. 'So can we get it back from your friend?'

'Not tonight,' she said. 'Sylvia works nights – she'll have already left for work by now. Look,' – she sounded a little hesitant – 'do you have somewhere to stay tonight?'

'No, and I've used up most of the cash which the nurse lent me.'

'OK ... I only have one bedroom, but you can crash on my couch for tonight if you like.'

'Are you sure? I mean you've already done so much for me.'

'Well, I figure I kind of owe you,' she said, smiling. 'If you hadn't come to help me, you would never have wound up in the mess you're in right now. And as for me ... well, I just don't know what would have happened.'

'Then I guess we both sort of helped each other.'

She nodded, offering a small smile. 'Get a good night's sleep, and then I'll take you round to Sylvia's tomorrow to get the case.'

'You'd really do that for me?'

'Well, as it happens, I have a day off tomorrow, anyway, and it's such a weird story ... I'm kind of intrigued to find out what's going on.'

'But these are really bad people. I don't want to get you involved in something dangerous.'

She stifled an ironic laugh. 'I'm already involved with bad people ... and something dangerous.'

Again, she had alluded to some awful situation in which she had become entangled but, still, Stephen judged that it wasn't the time to ask questions. Instead, he just responded to her generous offer.

'Well ... if you're sure ...'

She nodded, smiling. 'I'll get you a pillow and a blanket. The couch is right there … just don't try creeping into my room in the middle of the night. I may be skinny, but I've got a mean right hook.'

He raised both hands, palms-outward in a defensive gesture. 'Scouts' honour,' he said, smiling.

Ten minutes later he was fast asleep. In spite of everything swirling around in his mind, exhaustion had finally taken over.

Chapter 15

The next morning, he woke with a start. It was still dark outside but the digital clock, which nestled between the soft toys on the shelf, cast a faint red glow across the room. Rubbing the sleep from his eyes, he checked the time: 4.57 a.m. He groaned and slumped back down. Why on earth had he woken so early?

And then it came to him: he had remembered something important. It was almost as though his brain had been working on the problem in background mode as he slept, and then, once it had found the answer, shouted inside his head, 'Wake up – I have something to tell you!'

He was eager to share what he had remembered with Carla, but bearing in mind the early hour, and her stern warning the previous evening, he thought better of going into her room and waking her. Instead, he lay back in the darkness, trying desperately to build upon this latest recollection. Eventually, as the soft light of dawn began to suffuse the room, his reluctant memory banks gave up another vital snippet of information. By the time Carla emerged from her room, some two hours later, bleary-eyed, in baggy, pink pyjamas, hair all awry, he was bursting to tell her.

'I can't function until I've had my first coffee of the day,' she protested, as Stephen began gabbling away.

'I'm sorry,' he replied, 'it's just that I've remembered something, and—'

'Coffee first,' she insisted. 'You want one?'

'OK,' he sighed, 'I guess it can wait a few more minutes … but do you have any tea?'

She drew her head back, giving an amused frown. 'Afraid not … never touch the stuff.'

He smiled. 'Coffee then … white, no sugar.'

Ten minutes later, they were sitting, side by side, on the couch, each nursing their steaming cups.

'So what is it then?' said Carla. 'What have you remembered?

He set down his cup on the upturned wooden box which served as a coffee table. 'I've remembered what I'm supposed to be doing today.'

'You have?'

'Yes – I'm meant to be meeting with Professor Mandelson again this morning.'

She put her hand to her chin and her forehead puckered in a thoughtful frown. 'Thursday March 9th,' she mused. 'Isn't that one of the dates in the diary?'

'Yes, it is … but I can't see why this particular meeting would be so important when the dates for the other events this week – or even the conference itself – aren't highlighted.'

'And the second date in the diary is months away – July, isn't it?'

He nodded.

'So,' she continued, 'that date obviously can't be anything to do with the conference.'

'I know,' he sighed. 'I've been racking my brains to try to figure out what the connection might be, but' – he hung his head, sighing in frustration – 'it's no use.'

'So are you going to go to your meeting with the professor this morning?'

He gave a wry smile. 'After the last episode? I think any shred of credibility I might have had with Professor Mandelson is well and truly shot to pieces. And, what's more, I'll bet you anything you like that the other guy who's impersonating me will be there.'

She nodded, pursing her lips. 'So what are you going to do?'

He locked eyes with her. 'There's something else – after my meeting with Professor Mandelson, I'm supposed to meet Emma for Lunch at the Delano Hotel. Around one, I think.'

'So what are you going to do?' she repeated.

'I'm worried sick about Emma. I know for sure now that these are really bad people. I've no idea what they are up to, but they must be forcing Emma to go along with their plans – whatever those plans might be. Having seen the way they murdered Doctor Holt without hesitation, I'm terrified what could happen to her.'

Carla nodded, thoughtfully, her face creased in a concerned frown. 'So what … I mean how are you going to—?'

'I need to get her on her own … so that she can speak freely and tell me what the hell's going on. If she's going to be at the Delano today, maybe I can try to get a few minutes with her alone.'

'Hmm … well, what about your briefcase?'

'I don't need to be at the Delano until around twelve, so could we go round to your friend's place this morning?'

She shook her head. 'Not in the morning. Sylvia works in an all-night club; she'll only just have got home; she'll be asleep until this afternoon.'

Stephen felt a twinge of irritation – he *needed* to see what was in that briefcase. However, he had to admit that Carla had already gone out of her way to help him, and he certainly didn't have the right to complain.

She must have picked up some change in his facial expression, for she seemed, somehow, to sense what he was thinking. 'Look, why don't I drive you round to the Delano, where you can try to catch Emma on her own, and then take you round to Sylvia's in the afternoon?'

Any annoyance he had felt evaporated in an instant. This girl really was going above and beyond anything he had a right to expect.

'Look,' he said, 'I'm not entirely sure what I'm mixed up in, but whatever it is, it's not your fight. I really don't want to drag you into it.'

She smiled; it was an attractive smile, softening her somewhat angular features. Stephen could certainly see why she was – according to her friend, María – very popular with the regular male customers at the diner.

'Oh, don't worry,' she said, 'I have no intention of getting involved. All I'm going to do is take you there and hang about while you try to speak to Emma. Anyway,' she added, her expression more serious now, 'considering what you did for me back in that alley, and what it's now cost you, I think it's *me* who has dragged *you* into something you didn't deserve. The least I can do in return is to try to help you now.'

There it was again … just what *was* she mixed up in?

'Carla,' he said, 'you're obviously in some sort of trouble yourself. Do you want to talk about it?'

A shadow flitted across her face. 'I … I don't know.' She stood up, gathering up the cups and taking them over to the sink. When she turned around he could see the tears welling up in the corners of her eyes. 'I'm going to get dressed and fix us some breakfast ... then, maybe ...'

Stephen didn't push her; if she wanted to share her troubles with him, it would be best that she do so in her own time, and her own way.

***

'Can I show you something?' said Carla, once they had cleared up the breakfast things. She walked towards her bedroom, beckoning Stephen to follow.

Curious, he stepped into the room after her. She pulled out, from alongside her closet, an artist's easel. Bending down, she also retrieved a canvas, stretched across a wooden frame, which she placed on the easel.

'What do you think?' she asked, standing to one side so that Stephen could see it properly.

The painting was of an eagle, swooping majestically, talons outstretched. The sweep of the wings and the curve of its neck lent it a strikingly lifelike quality. And the eyes – gleaming with a golden-yellow glow – drew his gaze like a magnet. Stephen was not an art expert, but he could appreciate a striking picture when he saw one; the way that this creature came alive on the canvas quite literally took his breath away.

'You painted that?' said Stephen, swept away by the magnificent image he was looking at.

She nodded. 'Do you like it?' she said, her eyes wide and enquiring.

'It's wonderful. I've never seen anything like it.'

Her smile was radiant. 'I've always loved painting, ever since I was a little girl – especially wildlife.'

'Have you been to art school, or had some other sort of training?'

She gave an ironic laugh. 'My mother could never have afforded anything like that.'

'So you're self-taught?'

'Uh-huh.'

'Well, that's just incredible.'

'Do you *really* like it, or are you just being kind?'

'No, honestly - I think it's fantastic. I'm no expert but, in my opinion, you could paint professionally. You should get a proper art critic to assess your work. Maybe you could actually make painting a full-time career.'

Her eyes took on a faraway look. 'Oh my God – that would be a dream come true, but I can't ever see it happening.'

'Why not? You have the talent.'

'You're very kind to say so, but' – she sighed deeply – 'I just can't see any way out of my current situation, never mind make a whole new life as an artist.'

Stephen sensed she was on the brink of sharing much more information about herself; he gave her the opening to encourage her to do so.

'So what exactly *is* your situation?'

'OK,' she said, sitting down on the bed, 'you've told me your story, so I guess I should tell you mine.'

She patted the bed alongside her, and Stephen sat down too. And then she began ...

'After my mother died, there was nothing for me in Mexico. I have no brothers, sisters, cousins ... no-one. It's hard for a girl on her own to make anything of her life there, so I decided to try to make a fresh start in the USA.'

Stephen judged that it wasn't the right time to ask about the circumstances of her mother's death, or the whereabouts of her father; she would tell him in her own time if she wanted to.

She continued, 'As a single Mexican female with no connections here and no special skills, it would have been impossible for me to enter the States legally, but it's not hard to get in undetected. Hundreds of thousands do it every year.

'Once you're in, of course, there's a chance that they'll find you out and deport you, but if you've got enough money you can get false papers. I know others who have lived here for years after doing that. They've got good lives now and aren't likely to ever be found out.'

'So is that your plan?'

'Yeah, but I need about three thousand dollars to get the false papers. I came here with practically nothing, and the only job I could get was waitressing – which doesn't exactly pay megabucks. By the time I've paid the rent on this dump' – she indicated the patchy paintwork and shabby furnishings around them with a sweep of her hand – 'and covered my basic living expenses, it don't leave much over for saving.'

She paused, a frown creasing her forehead. Stephen had the sense that she was uncertain how much more to share.

'You said earlier that you had become involved with some bad people,' he said.

'Yeah ... worse luck. About a year ago, this guy came into the diner and started sort of flirting with me. He was quite good-looking and kind of funny, so I didn't mind. Anyway, he kept coming back and, one day, he asked me if I wanted to earn a bit of extra money. By now, I kind of trusted him, so I asked him what would be involved. He said that all I had to do was deliver a package to someone, and he'd pay me three hundred dollars. Christ – that was more than a full week's wages at the diner. I knew it must be something shady, of course, but for that sort of money, I didn't really care.

'Anyway, there were no problems. I delivered the package and he paid me just like he said he would. A couple of weeks later, he asked me to deliver another package – again for three hundred dollars. I thought, "At this rate, I'll be able to save up enough for my papers in no time".

'But after a while, I realised what I was delivering: it was drugs. I guess I shouldn't have been surprised ... and in all honesty I wasn't really. I just preferred not to know, particularly when I could see what drugs were doing to some of the kids around here.

'Before long, I realised that the guy who was paying me was part of a vicious gang, responsible for a whole string of murders, as well as God knows how many more deaths due to drug addiction.

'By now, I wanted out. I had saved around half of what I needed, and I didn't want anything more to do with these people. But when I told them, they said I couldn't get out. And that episode in the alley' – she stifled a sob – 'was their way of reminding me that I was their property now.'

Tears had started to well from the corners of her eyes. Her voice tailed off as she reached for a tissue.

'Oh, Christ, Carla,' said Stephen, placing a protective arm around her shoulders, 'I don't know what to say.'

She screwed up the tissue, dropping it on the table and forcing a small smile. 'So I guess you could say we're both in a bit of trouble here.'

Stephen's heart went out to this girl who, in spite of her own desperate situation, was willing to go out of her way to try to help him. Was there anything he could do to help her in return?

It took him only a few seconds to decide. Under normal circumstances he wouldn't even consider doing what he was about to do ... but these were hardly normal circumstances. He slipped his wedding ring off his finger and placed it on the table. 'This is probably worth at least four thousand dollars. Take it.'

Her head went back and her eyes widened. 'Your wedding ring? I ... I can't take that. What about Emma?'

'Look, you need the money and, right now, I don't have any. If you sell this you'll have enough to get your papers, and probably a bit left over. You can then skip to the other end of the country and disappear. I doubt those thugs would bother to try to track you down – they'll just find some other unsuspecting person to do their dirty work for them.'

'But ... your wife ...'

'I know, but ... look, in the end it's just a ring. My priority is to rescue Emma from whatever it is that she ... and I ... have become involved in. Once we're out of danger, we can renew our vows, get new rings ... whatever. So, take it.'

'OK,' she said, taking the ring from the table, 'but I won't sell it unless I absolutely have to. Maybe, once this whole mess is sorted out, I'll find some other way.'

Maybe, thought Stephen but, at that moment, that light at the end of the tunnel seemed very distant indeed.

***

They arrived at the Delano at 11.45 a.m. If Stephen's recollection that lunch was booked for 1 p.m. was correct then they were very early, but Stephen was hoping that perhaps Emma might also arrive early. If so, there might be a chance to get her alone before the other 'Stephen' turned up.

As they walked through the main doors, they were confronted by a huge foyer, predominantly white, which extended for the entire depth of the hotel. Two rows of pillars flanked a wide, central walkway leading to large, open doors at the back of the building. To either side of the central walkway were various items of somewhat unconventional furniture: a huge, button-backed couch; a double bed, on which a couple lounged, sipping champagne; and a chair whose feet actually wore high heels! Many more, equally unusual, pieces lined both sides of the wide central area. It was an eclectic mix with little to suggest a common theme, other than all being rather eccentric. Huge, white voile curtains hung from ceiling to floor at regular intervals along the walkway, swaying gently in the breeze which wafted through the foyer due to the open doors at both ends.

'Wow! Quite some place,' said Stephen. 'Have you been in here before?'

Carla gave him a quizzical look. 'You've seen my apartment. You think this sort of place is in my league?'

He smiled. 'I guess not. Let's find the restaurant.'

As they neared the back of the foyer, they could see that the back doors opened onto a garden and pool area. Through a small gap in the trees ahead, they could see the sparkling blue ocean beyond. And then they saw, to their left, the bar and the entrance to the restaurant.

'Wait there for a minute,' said Stephen, indicating a couch, nestling in an alcove to the right of the foyer. 'I'll go and take a look inside.'

He sidled up to the restaurant entrance and stole a glance inside. There were only three couples seated there and, as expected, no sign of Emma yet.

'Is it just one dining today, sir?' The waiter had seemingly materialised from nowhere in the few seconds Stephen had taken to scan the room.

'No … thank you. I only checked in today and I was just taking a look around.'

'Well, welcome to the Delano, sir. I hope you enjoy your stay with us.'

'Thanks.' He beat a hasty retreat and went over to where Carla was waiting.

'She's hasn't arrived yet. Let's just wait right here – we can see anyone entering or leaving the restaurant, so if she arrives on her own, maybe I can intercept her.'

'OK – sounds like a plan,' said Carla.

'Say, you want a drink?' he said, reaching in his pocket and pulling out fifteen dollars and a few coins.

'If that's all you've got left, I think you'd better hang on to it. In any case, I don't drink these days.'

'Well, *I* could certainly use one – I've got a whole kaleidoscope of butterflies swirling round in my stomach.'

'A kaleidoscope?' she repeated, tilting her head and drawing her eyebrows together in a puzzled frown.

'Well that's what you call a bunch of butterflies isn't it? You know … like a flock, or a shoal or something.'

She shook her head in bewilderment. 'I'm afraid I really wouldn't know.'

Weird, thought Stephen. *Most of my memory is shot to pieces, yet a bloody useless fact like that is still lodged in there somewhere.*

'Anyway, maybe I won't have a drink either,' he said. 'I need to be stone-cold sober when I talk to Emma. And,' he added, gazing at the meagre stash of money in his hand, 'you're probably right – as I'm down to my last fifteen dollars, I should probably save the money for something more important.'

They settled back to wait, the nervous silence between them punctuated only by the exchange of the odd word or two, mostly commenting on the unusual surroundings or the diverse cast of characters drifting to and fro through the foyer. Every so often, a couple or a small group would stop at the entrance to the restaurant, causing Stephen to lean forward and check whether Emma was among them.

At around 12.45 p.m. she arrived. Although she had her back to him, there was no mistaking the slim figure, elegant walk, and luxuriant mass of blonde hair draped down the back of her vibrant blue dress.

'That's her,' said Stephen, making to rise to his feet.

'Wait!' cautioned Carla, placing a restraining hand on his arm. 'There's someone with her.' The other person was hidden from Stephen's view by one of the large pillars in the foyer, but Carla could see him. 'Come over here,' she whispered, pulling him towards her so that he could crane his neck for a better view.

The man standing next to Emma, as they waited to be seated, wore a dark business suit. Stephen couldn't see his face, but assumed it must be his nemesis, the bogus 'Stephen'.

But it wasn't. When the man turned his head, a wave of nausea swept over Stephen. The thin, angular features; the dark piercing eyes; the dark, greasy, slicked-back hair. It was the man who had

pursued him in the subway – the same man who had murdered
Doctor Holt.

Chapter 16

Stephen's heart sank. Now he knew for sure that Emma was in danger – she had just arrived in the company of a murderer. And yet, she showed no signs of distress as this man placed his hand in the small of her back and guided her gently through to the restaurant. Maybe she didn't realise just what these people were capable of.

'Is that the man who is impersonating you?' breathed Carla, leaning towards him to whisper in his ear.

'No – worse I'm afraid. That is the man who murdered Doctor Holt.'

She gasped. 'But I thought she was meant to meet *you* here, so … well, if anyone else was to show up you'd think it would be him … I mean the other you.'

'I don't get it either. I thought she'd be arriving alone to meet me … or *him*. But this … it means Emma really is in serious danger. How the hell am I going to get her away from him so that I can talk to her alone?'

'Let's just wait a bit. Maybe there'll be a chance later.'

'Or maybe I should just go right in there and drag her out … get her away from that monster. What could he do to stop me in a public setting like this?'

'Stephen, no. You'll just cause a horrible scene, and even if you don't get carted off by Hotel Security you'll have alerted those people to the fact that you're watching them. Who knows what would happen then?'

He blew out his cheeks, exhaling in a long, steady stream. 'I guess you're right.'

'Let's just wait and bide our time.'

So they did and, ten minutes later, came the second surprise: the other Stephen arrived. He walked up to the restaurant entrance, spoke briefly to the waiter who greeted him, and pointed his finger towards somewhere inside the restaurant. The waiter nodded, exchanging a few words with him before ushering him inside.

'Is *that* the imposter?' whispered Carla.

He nodded, sighing heavily. 'So now she's trapped in there with the two of them. How on earth am I going to get her on her own now?'

'I don't know,' admitted Carla, 'but there's nothing to be gained by barging in there. Let's just continue to wait – maybe there'll be a chance at some point.'

'Maybe,' he sighed but, in truth, he was feeling increasingly despondent.

'Look, I have to go to the bathroom. You keep watching and waiting while I go and find the ladies' room.'

She was gone for just a few minutes.

'Anything?' she enquired, when she returned, sitting down alongside him once more.

He shook his head, but at that precise moment, the dark-haired guy with whom Emma had arrived emerged from the restaurant entrance. He buttoned his jacket and began striding purposefully down the centre of the foyer. As he disappeared from sight, Stephen rose to his feet and risked a peep around the pillar which was obscuring his view. To his surprise, the man did not break stride, but walked all the way to the main entrance and stepped outside. Stephen continued to watch for a minute or two, but the man did not return.

'He's gone,' murmured Stephen, as he sat back down.

'But why?' mused Carla. 'He can only have been in there for about fifteen minutes – he wouldn't even have had time to have a starter.'

'And he's left Emma with the other guy in there.'

A chilling possibility struck him; as he looked into Carla's eyes, she said, out loud, what he was already thinking.

'Maybe they don't want to allow her to be on her own. Maybe that guy's job was just to guard her until your ... well, the other Stephen arrived.'

'If so, it's clear that they're holding her against her will – forcing her to go along with whatever scheme they're plotting. I *have* to get her out of there. Maybe I *should* call the police.'

'Not yet,' she urged. 'Look, there's still a chance you'll be able to get her alone – a better chance now that the other guy's gone. And even if you don't, we could always follow them in my car when they leave and see where they end up. If you *do* decide to call the cops I need to be long gone before they arrive ... and you need to promise that you won't mention anything about me. OK?'

'OK,' he agreed, with a sigh.

And so they resumed their vigil.

The air was thick with a palpable tension; each minute that passed felt more like an hour. They barely spoke at all – they were just waiting for something, *anything* to happen.

And finally, it did.

Carla grabbed Stephen's arm, gripping it firmly. 'Look!' she whispered.

Emma had just stepped out of the restaurant and was walking across the foyer. Were they leaving already? Stephen waited to see if the man would follow her, but there was no sign of him.

'She's got her handbag, but she's not wearing the wrap which she had around her shoulders,' observed Carla.

It dawned on Stephen what that meant. 'So she's not actually leaving the hotel, then.'

They watched as she disappeared around a corner leading off the main foyer.

'She's heading for the ladies' room,' said Carla. 'This could be your chance – you could catch her when she comes out.'

Stephen was already on his feet. 'OK, you wait here,' he said, setting off after Emma.

As he rounded the corner, he caught sight of her entering the ladies' room. Given the gravity of the situation and the very short time that he probably had available to speak to her, he considered following her in, but quickly rejected the idea. If there were other women in there, they might freak out and alert the hotel authorities, and then the game would be well and truly up. No, better to wait and catch her when she came out. He took up position just around the corner and waited.

After a few minutes, she emerged. As Stephen stepped towards her, her jaw dropped in astonishment. 'What on earth are you doing here?' she gasped.

'Emma ... thank God I've finally got you alone. Are you alright? What the hell is going on?'

'You … you can't be here,' she whispered, shooting a fearful glance over his shoulder as though anxious that they were being watched. 'It isn't safe.'

'But what's happening? Who's that guy pretending to be me? And why?'

'Look, I need to get back in there right away. If I'm gone too long he'll—'

Stephen grabbed her firmly by both shoulders. 'Come with me now – we can get away before he finds out.'

'No … you don't understand. I can't just … leave.'

'Why not? Come on – let's go.' He took her hand and tried to pull her after him, but she stubbornly resisted.

'Is this guy bothering you?' came an unfamiliar male voice from behind him. Stephen looked around to see a tall stranger who had evidently decided to play the knight in shining armour and rescue the damsel in distress. A surge of anger flared within him, but before he could respond, Emma pre-empted him.

'Oh, no – I'm fine … really.' She flashed that winning smile which Stephen knew so well. 'But thank you so much for your attention.'

'We-ell, if you're sure …'

'Yes … we're fine.'

He looked at Emma and Stephen in turn, his expression dubious. 'Well, OK then.' He turned and walked away.

'Look,' said Emma. 'I don't have time to explain just now – I have to get back, but …'

***

Carla waited … and waited. She didn't have a watch on, and there was no clock within sight, so she wasn't sure how long Stephen had been gone. It felt like an age, though. She kept an anxious eye on the entrance to the restaurant. More minutes – which felt like hours – ticked by. No sign of Stephen, no sign of Emma, and no sign of the man she had been dining with. Then, to her horror, she saw the man emerge from the restaurant entrance. He looked up and down the foyer a couple of times before heading off in the direction of the rest rooms.

Unsure of just what she actually intended to do, she jumped to her feet and set off at an angle to the man's direction of travel, on a course to intercept him. As she got closer to him, she opened her handbag and began rummaging inside, appearing to be intent on inspecting its contents while, in fact, keeping the man in her peripheral vision, tracking his path.

She judged the angle of approach perfectly, so that the man didn't see that she was on a collision course with him until it was too late. As she bumped into him, entangling her feet with his, she pitched headlong to the floor, the contents of her handbag flying in all directions.

'Oh … so sorry miss,' he said leaning down to help her to her feet. 'Are you OK?'

'Yes, I think so' she gasped, clambering awkwardly to her feet. 'It was my fault – I wasn't looking where I was going.' She looked up at him and treated him to a glowing smile.

'Are you sure you're not hurt?' he said, his face a picture of kindly concern – it was hard to believe that this man was a murderer's accomplice.

'I … I'm fine, thank you,' she said, probing her knee as though trying to reassure herself.

'Well, let me help you with your things,' he said, bending down to start gathering up the scattered contents of her handbag.

When everything had been recovered and stowed in her handbag, he said, 'Well if you're sure you're OK, I'll just be—'

'Look,' she interrupted, desperate to try to delay him a little longer, 'I'm sure that was my fault entirely – would you like to join me for a drink so I can apologise properly?'

Now she had overplayed her hand. His demeanour changed as abruptly as if someone had thrown an invisible switch. 'Damned hookers,' he snarled. 'You had me fooled for a moment there. Now, I suggest you get out of here right now, before I call—'

'Stephen?' said Emma, as she approached from the direction of the ladies' room. 'Do you know this … lady?'

'She's no lady,' he said. 'Now you,' he growled, turning towards Carla, 'had better—'

But she was already heading towards the main entrance. Before she stepped outside, she stole a glance over her shoulder. The man had evidently lost interest in pursuing any action against her, for he and Emma were heading back towards the restaurant. Seconds later, she saw Stephen coming down the foyer towards her.

Once outside the hotel, the two of them stopped to compare notes.

'Well?' she said.

'Thank God you managed to delay him,' said Stephen. 'That extra minute or two was all I needed.'

'So now you know what's happening?'

'Not exactly, but I will soon.'

'How do you mean?'

'At last, Emma is no longer pretending not to know me. There wasn't time for her to explain properly, and she's clearly frightened, but ...'

'But what?'

'She's going to meet me tomorrow ... alone. Then I'll finally find out what's going on.'

He felt as though a massive weight had been lifted from his shoulders. He was still a very long way away from getting to the bottom of this unfathomable mess, but the fact that Emma was now back on his side made everything seem so much more bearable. By this time the following day he would finally know what was happening.

**

The engine in Carla's ancient Nissan turned over painfully slowly as she cranked the starter; it coughed but wouldn't start. She waited a few seconds and tried again. The wheezy sound grew slower and slower, eliciting nothing more than a few reluctant misfires from the engine. Then, just as it seemed that the battery was about to give up completely, the engine caught, and with a cacophony of rattles, accompanied by a dense cloud of black smoke from the exhaust, settled to an irregular idle.

'I need to get rid of this heap,' she said. 'It's been on borrowed time for a while now. Trouble is, I could never afford to buy another car without using up the money I'm saving for my papers.'

'Do you really need a car to get around Miami?'

'Well, not for just getting to work and so on, but ... oh, I'll explain as we drive. Let's get going before the damned thing conks out again. If we go back to my place and have something to eat, I'll run you round to Sylvia's later to get your briefcase.'

'That's if the car will start again,' he said.

She gave a wry smile. 'Well it's all we've got, so let's hope so.' She engaged 'Drive' and, with a protesting judder, the car pulled away.

'So ... you were about to explain why you needed a car,' said Stephen.

She sighed, giving a slight shake of her head. 'It's because of what I've been doing to earn the money for my papers ... you know, making deliveries for those bastards I've gotten mixed up with. Sometimes I have to make the drops at some pretty remote locations.'

'Ah, I see.'

'When I told them I didn't have a car, they gave me this one. I didn't have to pay anything for it. I guess they considered it an investment.'

'Not a very substantial one though' said Stephen, his observation underlined by a loud backfire from the exhaust.

'You're right there,' she laughed. 'It never was worth much in the first place. Still, it's kept going for best part of a year, so I can't complain. It's really only fit for scrapping now though.'

'But you said you wanted out from this whole business anyway, right?'

'I do, but ... I'm in a real fix. I want out, but they won't let me *get* out. You saw what they tried to do to me in that alley.' A dark shadow crossed her face as she turned for a moment to face him.

Stephen nodded, taking a few moments to digest what she had said. 'Sell the ring, get your false papers, and run.'

'You'd really let me do that?'

'Yes – we already talked about it. You've done so much to help me; it's a small thing for me to do in return.'

She smiled. 'You're a good man, Stephen.'

Was he? Was he a good man? With so much of his former life shrouded in darkness, how could he possibly know? And if he was a good man, how had he become mixed up with this bunch of thugs and murderers? Hopefully, the contents of his briefcase might provide some answers, and then tomorrow, he would finally get to speak to Emma. At last it seemed that he was on the road to untangling this Godawful mess.

They sat in silence for the remainder of the journey to Carla's apartment.

As they reached the top of the stairs, it was immediately apparent that something was wrong: the door to the apartment was open, the frame split, with pale shards of splintered wood protruding from the drab, dark green paint coating.

Chapter 17

Stephen put a finger to his lips and motioned with his other hand for Carla to stay where she was. Very slowly, he pushed the door open and, holding his breath, stepped cautiously inside. The scene which met his eyes was one of utter devastation: the furniture had been knocked over; the floor littered with cushions, books, crockery, and cutlery; every drawer in the apartment upturned, contents scattered far and wide.

He glanced anxiously around, but there was no sign of any intruder in the room. There was, however, still the bedroom …

He looked around for anything which could serve as a weapon; there was a large carving knife lying right at his feet, where the cutlery drawer had been carelessly upturned. As silently as possible, he bent down and picked it up, adjusting his grip for a powerful underarm thrust if necessary. Thus armed, he tiptoed towards the bedroom, whose door was wide open. He had never – as far as he knew, at least – even *held* a knife with the intent of inflicting harm on another human being. Right now, though, fuelled by adrenaline, he was ready to plunge the weapon into any intruder who confronted him.

With his heart in his mouth, he paused at the door for a second or two, before bursting inside, wrenching the door back lest someone lurked behind it.

There was no-one in the bedroom. The whole room, however, was in a similar state to the living room. The mattress had been wrenched from the bed and flung against the wall; the freestanding closet had been pulled away from the wall and overturned; Carla's clothes were strewn everywhere. And then he saw the painting: a jagged rip rent the canvas, running right through the regal face of that magnificent eagle.

'Stephen, are you alright?' came the tremulous voice from behind him.

'Yes ... there's no-one here now, but I'm afraid—'

'Oh, my God,' she gasped as she stepped through the bedroom door. 'It's ... but, why ... I just can't ...'

Her voice tailed off as her gaze alighted on the ruined painting. Her lower lip began to tremble and she sank to her knees, picking up the ripped canvas and gazing at it in disbelief. She looked up at Stephen, her face frozen for a second or two in an expression of utter anguish. And then the floodgates burst: she let out a piercing wail and erupted in a torrent of tears, her shoulders heaving with each tormented sob.

Her tortured cries cut him to the core. He knelt down and pulled her to him; she buried her head in his chest. They clung together like that for several long seconds until her sobs had subsided sufficiently for her to speak.

'Why, Stephen? Why would anyone do this?'

'I assume,' he said, a hard edge to his voice as the anger seethed within him, 'that they were looking for something.'

'But what ...? I don't have anything of value here.'

His jaw took on a grim set. 'Maybe it was the briefcase.'

She wiped her face with the back of her hand, spreading dark streaks of mascara across her cheek. 'Of course! I saw them run off with the case after they attacked you, but they obviously abandoned it at the end of the alley. Maybe they realised that I had picked it up. They know where I live, so I guess they decided to come and turn the place over to find it.'

'There is another possibility,' said Stephen, his stomach churning as he evaluated the chilling prospect.

'What?'

'Maybe it wasn't those people at all. Maybe it was the bastards who are impersonating me and holding Emma against her will.'

'You think so?'

He nodded, his expression dark and intense. 'They could have followed us back here and then waited until we went out, before breaking in and ransacking the place. Maybe there's something in that briefcase which could interfere with their plans ... whatever their damned plans are.'

Her eyes widened. 'Y-yes, I suppose so.'

'Either way, it's not safe to stay here tonight,' he said, taking her hand and helping her to her feet. 'Oh Carla, what the hell have I dragged you into?'

Her sobbing had stopped now, and her face took on a look of fierce determination. 'You didn't drag me into anything; you tried to help me back in that alley. It's not your fault. We have both managed to get tangled up with some really bad people, but we're both in it together now ... and we're going to help each other out of this mess, right?'

There was a steel in this girl that Stephen had not hitherto appreciated. In spite of everything, he was glad to have her at his side.

'Right,' he replied. 'The first thing we need to do is recover that briefcase and see what's inside. Then we need somewhere to stay tonight ... not here.'

She looked at her watch. 'It's gone four now. We can go right round to Sylvia's and get the case. I'm sure she'll let us crash at her place for tonight. I don't think any of these people would have any idea that we've gone there, so we should be safe enough.'

'OK,' he said, 'then tomorrow, I'll catch up with Emma and, hopefully, find out just what the hell is going on.'

Carla's forehead creased in a frown. 'Are you sure it's a good idea to go there to see her alone?'

Stephen was completely wrong-footed by this question. 'Why? What do you mean?'

'It's just that ... well, you've seen the kind of people she's mixed up with, and you've said yourself that you don't know why she's helping them.'

'It's obvious isn't it? They're clearly forcing her somehow.'

'You don't know that for sure.'

'But ... what on earth are you suggesting?'

'I'm not suggesting anything. It's just that ... well, you should be careful.'

'Carla,' he said, placing his hands on her shoulders and looking her directly in the eyes, 'she's my *wife* ... I *know* her.'

'Oh, I know,' said Carla. 'But what if one of them follows her?'

'I'll be careful,' he assured her.

Her concerned expression gave way to a smile. 'Well, OK – but let me drive you round to meet her ... that's if my damned car will actually start, of course.'

'Thank you ... thank you for everything,' he replied. 'But then you have to run ... I've already put you in far too much danger. Get out of Miami and as far away as possible from those thugs. Sell the ring, get your papers, and make a new life for yourself.'

She cupped his face in her hands and kissed him on the cheek. 'And you find your old one.'

***

Sylvia was a Brooklyn girl. Long, dark hair, angular cheekbones and dark green eyes. She wore a closely tailored white shirt teamed with a very short skirt and dark, fishnet stockings. Judging by her attire, her scarlet lipstick, and very heavy eye makeup, Stephen guessed that she was already preparing to leave for her night shift. Her surname, Romano, suggested that she was of Italian origin, though certainly not first-generation Italian, as her distinctive New York twang testified.

'We-ell,' she said, eyeing Stephen up and down, 'this one's a bit more upmarket than your usual type.'

'Please,' said Carla, laughing, 'can you just behave yourself for once?'

'Never have,' she replied, with a shrug, '...don't know why I should start now.'

The two women hugged each other.

'Come on in, guys,' said Sylvia ushering them inside.

The apartment was rather larger than Carla's though barely any more salubrious. Maybe waitressing at an all-night club didn't pay that much better than doing so at the diner where Carla worked.

'I can't thank you enough for this,' said Carla. 'I just wouldn't have felt safe staying at my place tonight.'

'Aw ... it's nut'n. You'd have done the same for me.'

'And thanks from me too,' added Stephen. 'You don't even know me, so it was a big ask.'

'If Carla says you're OK, that's good enough for me. Anyway it sounds like you guys are in some sort of trouble so I'm glad to help.'

'Thanks, babe,' said Carla. 'I owe you.'

'Look, I'd love to stay and chat – find out what the hell's going on with you guys, but I gotta run. Oh, before I go, though, I guess you want that briefcase ... I'll get it.'

She disappeared into her bedroom and reappeared holding the case, the rip sliced into the fine leather surface testament to the vicious assault in the alley. She set it down on the coffee table in front of the couch. Stephen stared at it, trancelike; would the contents finally provide some answers?

'OK,' continued Sylvia, 'there's plenty of food in the kitchen; use whatever you like. No booze, I'm afraid – can't seem to keep it in the place without drinking it.' She laughed. 'Bathroom's over there' – she pointed to the door – 'and the spare bedroom's through here.' She indicated another door. 'Got a nice double bed in there, and I ain't prudish so … well, sleeping arrangements are up to you guys.'

'*Sylvia*, squealed Carla, 'will you just *stop* it?'

'Just sayin' like … the couch is kinda lumpy.'

'Thanks again,' said Stephen, I don't know how I can ever repay you, but … well, thanks.'

'I gotta go now,' she said, grabbing a pair of sky-high stilettos from alongside the door and slipping them into her voluminous handbag. She pulled on a pair of white sneakers, explaining, 'I gotta wear those things at the club, but I'm damned if I'll cripple myself by wearing them on the way there.'

Carla smiled. 'Thanks again, babe.'

'See ya in the morning,' said Sylvia, as she opened the door to leave. 'Then you can tell me all about this weird situation you seem to have gotten yourselves into.'

'Bye,' chimed Stephen and Carla, in unison.

Seconds later, they were alone.

'Seems like a pretty … uh, forthright … sort of girl,' said Stephen.

'Oh, don't mind her direct manner. Sylvia just says what she's thinking and doesn't give a damn how it comes out. She's got a heart of gold, though … can't do enough to help when her friends need her.'

'I can see that,' he replied. 'There aren't many people who would allow a complete stranger to crash at their place, especially one who's become mixed up with a bunch of vicious criminals.'

'Well, like I already said, the people who inhabit the world that Sylvia and I live in aren't exactly saints, either. We're used to dealing with these bastards. Anyway, I don't think any of those animals would have any idea that we're here tonight, so we should be safe enough.'

'Let's see what's in here,' said Stephen, turning to the briefcase.

It was locked. There were two combination locks: 3 digits each.

'Do you know the combination?' said Carla.

'I … I think so,' he whispered. 'It's something to do with a date … or dates.'

He racked his brains. The number was there … almost within his grasp, tantalisingly close, yet somehow refusing to give itself up.

'What about the dates in the diary?' said Carla, leaning forward eagerly as the thought struck her.

'Maybe …' He checked the two dates: Thursday March 9th – today – and Sunday July 23rd.

Picking up on the first date he tried the left hand lock with 093 – no use; then 903 – no use; he tried both combinations on the right hand lock – still no good. He slammed his hand on the lid of the case in frustration.

'Try the other date,' urged Carla.

'July 23rd,' he muttered. 'Let's try 723.'

It didn't work on either lock.

'Maybe it's got something to do with the days of the week as well as the actual dates,' suggested Carla.

'I … I don't know,' he said.

The answer was so close he could almost touch it, yet … no, it just wouldn't come.

'Look,' he said, 'I'm sure the answer's there in what's left of my brain somewhere. I just need to give it a little time and maybe it will come back to me. Do you think Sylvia would mind if I used her shower? Maybe a good soaking and some concentrated thinking might work.'

'Sure … she won't mind. Not sure she has a spare stash of men's clothes like I did, though.'

He laughed. 'Well, I'm not going to rummage through her things to find out.'

'You go and have your shower. I'll take a look around to see if there's anything you can wear. I think she's at least got a towelling bathrobe that might fit so, worst case, we could wash what you're wearing now to use again tomorrow. Sylvia actually has a tumble dryer – pretty upmarket for a place like this, huh?'

He grinned. 'OK, thanks. Look, if I *can't* remember the combination it shouldn't be too difficult to force the case open with a large screwdriver or something.'

'Well, I shouldn't think Sylvia's likely to have a tool kit in the apartment, but I'll take a look around to see if there's anything we could use to force the locks.'

Stephen stepped into the bathroom. When he looked in the mirror he hardly recognised the haggard face staring back at him. He hadn't shaved for days and there were dark circles around his eyes. When would this nightmare end?

To his surprise, he spotted a man's razor and a pack of blades on the glass shelf below the mirror. Maybe Sylvia had a boyfriend who was a regular visitor. Anyway, given the generosity that she had already shown, he didn't think she would begrudge him the use of a fresh razor blade. He couldn't see any shaving foam but, using the bar of soap by the sink and plenty of water, he was able to produce enough of a slippery lather to manage a shave without inflicting too much carnage on his face. As he ran his hand over his now-smooth chin he began to feel better already.

Now for that shower …

***

Carla was searching the kitchen for any sort of implement which might serve to force the briefcase open. So far, the best thing she could find was a corkscrew; she wasn't too confident that would do the job, but she left it out on the kitchen counter anyway.

What about some clean clothes for Stephen? She knew that Sylvia's boyfriend, Kyle, stayed over quite often; maybe he kept some clothes there. Sure enough in the right hand side of Sylvia's closet hung a couple of men's shirts. Kyle wasn't as tall or well-built as Stephen, but maybe one of the shirts might fit well enough. A further search of Sylvia's drawers turned up some boxer shorts and a few pairs of socks. Maybe they wouldn't need to resort to washing and drying the clothes that Stephen was currently wearing. Kyle was such a kind, helpful sort of guy, she didn't think he'd mind.

As she laid the clothes on the bed, she heard the sound of the water in the shower being turned on. Lifting her arm and taking a tentative sniff at her own armpit, she resolved to take a shower too, as soon as Stephen was finished in the bathroom. She wouldn't have any problem finding something to wear; she and Sylvia were of very similar height and build and they were always lending each other clothes anyway.

Her thoughts were interrupted by the gentle chimes of the doorbell.

Chapter 18

Having pressed the button for the doorbell, the man took a step backward, checking that the safety catch on his gun was off and tensing for action. There was a delay of only a few seconds before he heard the sound of the latch being released. Good – they obviously weren't expecting anything untoward. However, the door opened only a few inches, before stopping short, constrained by a security chain. The curious expression on the face of the Latina girl who peered through the gap changed in an instant when she saw him; her eyes widened and her mouth flew open. He had to act fast.

Without hesitation, he put his shoulder to the door, and flung his full weight against it; the flimsy security chain snapped like cotton, and the girl staggered backward, letting out a strangled cry. He burst past her, levelling his weapon in a two-handed grip, crouching as he swept it back and forth, scanning the room. There was no-one else in sight.

His partner was only a split second behind him. Before she could utter another sound, the girl was staring straight down the muzzle of a handgun, her eyes bulging in terror. The man locked eyes with her, placing a finger against his lips, emphasising the unspoken message by moving the gun further forward until the tip of the silencer touched the centre of her forehead.

The three of them stood like that, locked motionless like a freeze-frame in a movie. The only sound which could be heard was the noisy splashing of water from the bathroom, whose door was open a crack, a few tendrils of steam escaping from the gap. For several tense seconds they waited; he kept his gun trained on the bathroom door while his partner kept his weapon pressed against the forehead of the terrified girl. Nothing happened. The noise of the water in the shower had evidently masked the sound of the doorbell and the brief scuffle which had ensued when the Latina girl had cracked open the door.

He nodded to his partner, who shifted position, moving behind the girl and clamping a hand over her mouth, while bringing the gun around the side of her head and pressing it against her temple. She did not resist.

Now that his partner had the girl secured, so that she could not utter a sound, he began moving stealthily towards the bathroom, his handgun extended before him. As he reached the door, he paused again, listening for any sound which might indicate that he had been discovered; there was none. Using the silencer on his gun, very carefully, he edged the door open, inch by inch. The plastic shower curtain was drawn shut and the water continued cascading down in a noisy torrent. *This*, he thought, *should be easy*.

***

Stephen *had* heard the doorbell. He had been standing outside the shower, still fully dressed, fiddling with the impossibly temperamental temperature control in an effort to achieve something between stone cold and scalding hot water.

Who could it be? Perhaps Sylvia had forgotten something and come back for it? But why wouldn't she have used her key? Maybe she had tried to do so but been thwarted by the security chain? But then why hadn't he heard her talking to Carla?

Feeling distinctly uneasy, he cracked the bathroom door open a little, just in time to see the two men burst in. He immediately recognised the one who grabbed Carla as Doctor Holt's murderer. The other one looked like the guy who had been standing by the open ambulance doors when he had fled the hospital just a couple of days earlier.

What to do? It would be crazy to jump out and confront them – both men were armed, and one of them had his gun pressed against Carla's temple. He looked around for anything which would serve as a weapon. The only thing he could find was an ancient-looking set of bathroom scales on the floor. He bent down and picked it up; it was satisfyingly heavy in his hands. He stepped back to a position just alongside the door, where he would be hidden if the door was opened, and waited, his heart pounding.

As the door gradually inched open, he shrank back behind it, gripping the bathroom scales as though his life depended on it – which, in all likelihood, it did. He couldn't see the intruder. Was he advancing on the shower, about to pump several bullets through the flimsy curtain? Was he about to whirl around and wrench the door back, shooting Stephen dead where he stood? When was the right moment to strike? Perspiration streamed down his face in torrents … and it wasn't due to the steam which filled the room. Eventually, he stole a tentative peep around the edge of the door; he was just in time to see the man lay down his gun on the counter surrounding the sink.

Why? Why would he lay down his weapon at this critical moment?

The man reached into his pocket and withdrew a hypodermic syringe, removing a protective sleeve before holding the syringe up and depressing the plunger, ejecting a small fountain of clear liquid. What was in that syringe? Did they want to poison him rather than shoot him? Why?

The man grasped the edge of the shower curtain with his left hand, the syringe poised in his right. With one swift movement, he yanked back the curtain. He was met with a swirling mass of steam, through which all that was visible was a cascade of scalding hot water.

This was the moment. Seizing the brief element of surprise afforded to him, Stephen leapt from his hiding place, raising the bathroom scales high in the air before bringing them down on the back of the man's head with crushing force. The intruder's knees buckled, and he collapsed in a crumpled heap. Stephen raised his improvised weapon once more, ready to strike again, but it wasn't necessary: the man wasn't moving.

'Did ya get him?' came the other man's voice from the living room. American accent, harsh tones.

'Yeah, no problem,' responded Stephen, effecting a gruff tone and the best American accent he could muster. In all honesty, though, he had no idea whether the voice he contrived bore any resemblance to that of his would-be assailant. He just had to hope it was close enough.

He grabbed the gun from the counter and moved silently towards the door. Christ, just how should he play this? He had never handled a gun before in his life … at least as far as he knew. How could he get a clean shot at his opponent without harming Carla in the split second he would have available to him before the man fired back? Maybe if he could appear in an unexpected position …

He dropped to a low crouch, pausing for a moment before shoving the door wide open, hoping to perhaps get a shot at the man in the brief moment before he refocused his gaze downward and registered who was facing him.

It didn't work. Although the man appeared momentarily disoriented by Stephen's tactic, he was using Carla as a human shield. There was no way Stephen could get a shot at him without risking hitting her instead. It took the man only a fraction of a second to register what was happening and train his gun directly on Stephen.

'Lay down the gun,' he growled.

Stephen was paralysed by indecision. He couldn't get a clear shot at the man holding Carla, but if he gave up his weapon now, then they were surely both finished.

The man moved the gun away from Stephen and back to Carla's temple; her eyes bulged in abject terror 'You got five seconds to put the gun down, or I'll kill her … and I'll still drop you before you can get a shot past her dead body.' He fixed Stephen with an icy glare. 'One … two … three …'

Stephen bent down and laid the weapon on the floor.

The man's face twisted in an unpleasant smile. 'Get up.' Stephen did so. 'Now kick the gun over here.'

Stephen's mind was racing as he tried to figure out what to do. Any attempt to tackle the man directly would almost certainly result in Carla's immediate death and probably his own too. But if he did nothing they would both surely die anyway. The man didn't give him long to consider his options.

'Kick it over here – RIGHT NOW – or I swear I'll kill her.'

He had no choice. He kicked the gun forward; it went spinning across the floor, coming to rest against the man's feet.

Suddenly, Carla's eyes widened; at exactly the same moment the man lifted his gaze for a split second. It took Stephen barely a heartbeat to realise they had both seen something behind him. But he wasn't quick enough.

Before he could turn to face the new threat, he felt an arm encircle his neck from behind in an iron grip. Stephen was a powerfully-built man, but he couldn't shake free. He twisted his head as far as he could, just in time to see the hypodermic syringe inches from his neck. He reached back and grabbed the other man's wrist before he could deliver the injection. Mustering all his strength, he tried to force the man's hand away, but the awkward angle at which his arm was held meant that he could not bring full force to bear. It was a stalemate.

The man holding Carla flung her aside, striding forward to assist his partner. In the heat of the moment, it seemed that he had forgotten about the gun which Stephen had kicked across the floor towards him. Carla grabbed the gun from the floor, jumping to her feet and rushing at the man from behind. She hefted the weapon, gripping it by the muzzle and delivering a crushing blow to the back of the man's head. The adrenaline coursing through her body must have endowed her with strength beyond her normal reach, for the man's eyes rolled skyward and his legs buckled as he sank to the floor, his gun falling from his hand.

Stephen was still locked in a battle of gradually failing strength with the other man; the syringe edged closer to his neck. But seconds later Carla was on his assailant's back, her fingernails clawing at his eyes and her legs clasped around his waist in a scissor grip. The man screamed in pain as Carla's nails raked across his eyes and down his cheek.

Her intervention provided Stephen with the brief respite he needed; he wrenched himself free and twisted around, now able to get both his hands on the man's wrist. It was no longer an even contest. With his opponent half-blinded and battling to fight off Carla's frenzied attack, Stephen was able to turn the syringe around, forcing it closer and closer to the other man's neck until, finally, he was able to plunge it into his flesh, fully depressing the plunger as he did so.

Almost immediately, the man's strength began ebbing away, and within fifteen seconds his body had gone completely limp as he slumped to the floor.

'Is he dead?' gasped Carla.

Stephen probed the man's neck, feeling for the Carotid Artery; the pulse was strong and regular.

'No,' he panted, gasping to recover his breath. 'God knows what was in that syringe but it clearly wasn't a lethal drug.'

The other man – the one who Carla had hit over the head emitted a weak groan.

'We have to get out of here – right now,' said Stephen, taking Carla's hand. He bent down to retrieve the fallen man's gun from the floor and grabbed the briefcase from where it lay on the coffee table. 'Where are your car keys?'

'In my handbag … by the front door.'

The man gave another moan; this time he moved his foot slightly.

'OK – let's go,' ordered Stephen.

They rushed through the open door, Carla pausing just long enough to grab her handbag.

The sight which met them at the bottom of the stairs caused Carla to freeze in her tracks. Her hand flew to her mouth as she stifled a silent scream.

Chapter 19

Stephen's stomach churned as he stared in disbelief at Sylvia's lifeless eyes, blood streaming from the hole in the centre of her forehead, coating her face and fanning out in an ugly dark stain down the front of her shirt. He was paralysed with shock.

Carla took a step forward, stretching her hand towards her friend's crumpled body. 'Sylvia ... oh, Sylvia ... no.'

Stephen snapped out of the stupor which had enveloped him and took Carla's outstretched hand, gently pulling her towards him, but she refused to respond or turn her head; her gaze was locked on the horrific sight in front of her.

'Carla,' said Stephen, gently but firmly, 'we have to go.'

Finally, she turned to face him, her features frozen in an expression of shock and confusion. 'We ... we can't just leave her there like that. We have to help her.'

Stephen let go of her hand and kneeled down, laying the gun on the floor as he probed Sylvia's neck, feeling for a pulse, all the while knowing that it was hopeless.

After some seconds, he turned to face Carla. 'We can't help her Carla – she's dead.'

'No,' wailed Carla. 'She can't be.'

'Carla,' said Stephen, picking up the gun and rising to his feet, 'we have to get out of here – right now.'

She looked at him, blankly. 'She's my best friend.'

It tore at Stephen's heart to see the abject grief which had consumed her. He wanted to hold her, console her, give her time to absorb what had happened. But there simply wasn't time: they needed to get away – and fast.

The decision was abruptly made for him. A loud groan emanated from upstairs, followed by erratic scraping and banging sounds. At least one of their assailants was still a threat.

There was no time left for sensitivity and consideration – Stephen grabbed Carla by the hand and physically pulled her away from the lifeless body of her friend.

'Give me your car keys,' he yelled as they stepped out onto the street.

In spite of everything which had just happened, Carla had kept a firm grasp on her handbag – maybe she had realised its importance, or maybe it was just force of habit. In a daze, she reached inside and found the keys, holding them up in front of her. Stephen grabbed them from her hand and, stuffing the gun into his waistband, took her wrist in his hand, sprinting across the road to where Carla's car was parked, dragging Carla behind him. He unlocked the car and shoved her into the passenger seat before rushing around and jumping into the driver's seat. With fumbling fingers, he inserted the key into the ignition and twisted it.

The car wouldn't start.

He let the starter motor churn for maybe ten seconds, but the engine wouldn't catch. 'Come on, damn you... come on ...' he hissed, through gritted teeth. He tried again – after a few seconds the engine coughed and spluttered, but it still wouldn't catch. The speed at which the starter motor was turning the engine began to slow as the tired battery began to give up.

Suddenly, the air was rent by a sharp, high-pitched sound – something between a shriek and a crash. He felt a rush of hot air graze the back of his neck. He jerked his head to the left just in time to see the side window of the car disintegrate into a myriad of tiny fragments and fall out of the frame. In the doorway of Sylvia's apartment block he could see a figure grasping a gun in a double-handed grip, pointed right at them. The man was swaying unsteadily on his feet, which were planted wide apart as he tried to stabilise his stance. Stephen was still trying to process what was happening when he saw the muzzle flash as the man loosed a second shot. The bullet glanced off the windshield at a shallow angle without penetrating it.

Stephen yanked the gun from his waistband; he had never fired a gun before in his life but, with the car refusing to start and their pursuer closing on them, it seemed the only chance. As he took the weapon in both hands and braced his forearms on the sill of the shattered window, his panic seemed to subside and a strange feeling of confidence filled him. Taking aim, he held his breath for a moment and squeezed the trigger. *Pfut!* The silenced weapon made very little sound as it kicked in his hands. The gun spun from the hand of the figure in the doorway as he staggered backward, clutching his upper arm.

In the few brief moments since the first shot had been fired, Stephen had not had the chance to steal even a fleeting glance at Carla. Now he seized the opportunity to spin round and check on her; thankfully she still sat bolt upright, and there was no sign of any blood. She was staring straight ahead, as though in a trance, seemingly oblivious of the mayhem erupting around her.

'Carla – are you OK?' he yelled, grabbing her shoulder and shaking her.

She turned her head towards him, blinking as she shook off the dazed stupor that had consumed her. 'Y-yes, I think so. What ... why ...?'

There was no time to talk: Stephen glanced back towards the apartment doorway to see the man staggering to his feet, still clutching his injured arm, but once again holding the gun. *Shit!*

What should he do? Should he fire again to try to take the bastard down? His first shot had been remarkably accurate considering the range and his own total inexperience with firearms, but that must have been down to luck – he doubted that he would stand much chance in a gunfight with someone who was surely a hardened killer. Should they get out of the car and make a run for it? He feared, though, that they would be sitting ducks outside of the car. He decided to have one last try at starting the car.

As he twisted the key in the ignition, the engine turned over painfully slowly, but then coughed twice before bursting into life. *Thank God!* He shoved the selector lever into 'Drive' and floored the accelerator. With a brief chirrup from the tyres, the little car surged forward. Stealing a brief glance over his shoulder, Stephen saw another muzzle flash, followed a moment later by the sight of the back window of the car crazing over before breaking up and falling, in a cascade of tiny pieces, onto the rear seat. Thankfully, neither he nor Carla had been hit.

They sped away, running a red light and executing several hazardous overtaking manoeuvres before Stephen was satisfied they were safe; only then did he slow to a sensible pace.

'You OK?' he breathed, turning to Carla.

She turned towards him, nodding weakly, her face a mask of shock and grief. 'Sylvia … they killed her. Why? She wasn't supposed to be involved in any of this.'

Stephen had no answer.

'It's my fault,' she continued, 'I should never have asked her to let us stay at her place.' A tear welled from the corner of her eye and trickled down her cheek.

'No,' insisted Stephen, 'if it's anyone's fault it's mine.'

She didn't respond, either to accept or refute what he had said, but instead asked, 'Who are they Stephen? What do they want?'

'I just don't know,' he muttered, shaking his head in rage and frustration. 'For whatever reason, they just seem to—'

'LOOK!' she yelled, clutching his arm. 'BEHIND!' She had twisted in her seat and was looking through the shattered remains of the back window.

Stephen glanced up at the rear-view mirror to see a silver SUV speeding towards them.

Chapter 20

Stephen floored the accelerator pedal, willing the tired old Nissan to find a little more pace, but it was no use – the other car was relentlessly closing the gap between them.

And then their plight became even worse, for straight ahead was a red light. There were already several cars waiting, and there was no way through or around them. Behind, the silver SUV was now only about a hundred yards back, and closing rapidly. Stephen's brain was racing as he tried to decide what to do. There was only one possible option.

'Hang on!' he yelled, as he stood on the brakes and wrenched the steering wheel hard over to the left. The tortured tyres screamed in protest, emitting a cloud of acrid-smelling smoke as the car slewed round in an untidy U-turn.

The manoeuvre seemed to catch their pursuer by surprise, for he had no time to react as they sped back towards him on the opposite side of the road. As they drew alongside him, the man fired a hurried shot though his open side window. But he had had no time to aim properly, and the shot was wild; Stephen heard it slam into the bodywork somewhere behind them. As they sped past, he caught a glimpse of their attacker: blood streamed down his left arm; his face was twisted with rage.

Stephen floored the accelerator again. As they raced away, he glanced again in the rear-view mirror to see the SUV also performing a wild U-turn, snaking erratically from side to side as the driver fought to regain control. Seconds later, it was speeding towards them once more.

The next light was, mercifully, on green but, as Stephen flew through the junction, he was dismayed to see that the silver car was rapidly gaining on them. He cursed as their pursuer also made it across the junction before the lights changed to red. He urged

Carla's car forward but it was already giving all it had to give; there was no way they could outrun the other vehicle.

What could he do? Try another U-turn? His pursuer would probably be ready for such a move this time. Try and shoot back at the other car? Practically impossible while still driving. Give the gun to Carla? She looked way too traumatised to shoot back, even if she knew how to handle the gun. The prospects looked bleak.

The next light turned to red just before they reached it. There were no other cars in front of them this time, so Stephen just kept the accelerator pinned to the floor and surged toward the junction. The blare of a horn proclaimed the outrage of the driver coming from his right as Stephen swerved to avoid hitting him. But, against the odds, they made it across, and as Stephen looked in his mirror, the stream of traffic now flowing rapidly across in both directions would surely make it impossible for their pursuer to follow.

But he was a determined bastard – Stephen was astonished to see the silver SUV cutting through the stream of traffic, fishtailing wildly as the driver tried to avoid other vehicles. Finally, another car clipped his rear corner causing the car to spin, and then, a second or two later a massive truck ploughed into the car, carrying the twisted wreck forward for perhaps thirty yards before coming to a halt.

His heart pounding, Stephen slowed the car to a normal pace: he didn't want to attract any unnecessary attention from the police, although the battered state of the car would probably do so anyway, before long.

'I think we're safe – for now at least,' he gasped.

Carla turned her head sideways, still looking dazed and confused. 'Is he … gone?'

Stephen nodded. 'The car's trashed, and he's either dead or injured.'

'You sure?'

'I'm sure … he won't be following us any longer.'

'Thank God,' she breathed, her chin sinking to her chest.

'But we still need to find somewhere to stay tonight.'

'But where?' said Carla. 'We can't risk going back to my place … or Sylvia's.' Her voice caught in her throat as she uttered her friend's name.

Stephen thought for a moment. 'How much money do you have on you?'

'I don't know exactly … probably about fifty or sixty dollars, I guess.'

'And I still have a few dollars left. OK … I know a place.'

**

The proprietor at El Refugio evidently remembered Stephen.

'Well, hello again,' he said, licking his lips salaciously as his gaze flickered from Stephen towards Carla. 'I see you have a friend with you tonight.' The sly intonation in his voice as he said the word 'friend' was obvious. 'So would you be wanting a room for the whole night or would you prefer to pay by the hour?'

Stephen felt a surge of anger erupt within him, but chose to suppress it. 'For the night,' he said, laying fifty dollars on the counter.

'You want twin beds or a double?' he said, eying Carla's slim, shapely body up and down. 'You see it's an extra ten for a double.'

Stephen was just about to remonstrate with the seedy slob of a man when Carla beat him to it. To his surprise, she stepped forward and leaned across the counter, looking up at the man, her face just inches from his stubbly chin.

'Listen to me you fuckwit. This is not what you're implying, and it would be none of your damned business even if it was. We just want a room for the night, and I don't give a shit what sort of bed – or beds – it's got. We've just had a *really* bad day, and I'm not in the mood for any more your smartass comments. Now, one more fucking wrong word out of that foul mouth of yours and I'll come around that counter and knee you right in the balls. Got it?'

Were it not for their desperate situation, Stephen might have laughed out loud at the expression on the man's face. His jaw had dropped and his eyes were like saucers. He appeared to be dumbstruck.

'Well? You heard the lady,' said Stephen.

It took the man a couple of seconds to gather his wits enough to respond. When he did, all of the innuendo had evaporated; he became meek as a lamb. 'Er … yeah, sure. Twin beds then?' he said, nervously.

Stephen nodded. 'Just give us the key.'

When they got into their room, the two of them sat down facing each other, one on each of the twin beds.

'I'm so sorry you got dragged into all this,' said Stephen. 'And especially for what has happened to Sylvia. All she was guilty of was trying to help us – she didn't deserve to ...' His voice tailed off – whatever words he could find just seemed woefully inadequate.

But Carla was no longer tearful – her expression now portrayed anger and grim determination. 'It's not your fault. You saved me from being raped, or possibly even killed. You'd never have been attacked and lost your memory if you hadn't come to help me. It was my choice to try to repay you in some way. It seems we have both become mixed up with some truly evil bastards.'

'I guess we have,' murmured Stephen, hanging his head and shaking it from side to side.

'So what now?' asked Carla. 'Should we go to the police?'

Stephen shook his head. 'If we go to the police now – after everything that has happened, they're bound to keep us in for questioning while they try to untangle what the hell's going on. I'm worried sick about Emma, and I can't afford to miss the opportunity to get to her tomorrow. In any case, if you were the police, would you believe a crazy story like mine?'

She managed a half smile. 'I guess not.'

'I'd more than likely be considered a suspect for the murder of Doctor Holt,' said Stephen '... maybe Sylvia, too.'

'And as for me ... well, I'm not even supposed to be in the country at all,' added Carla.

'You need to get away,' he reaffirmed. 'Sell the ring, get your papers, and get as far away from here as possible. I can't ever thank you enough for everything you've done for me, but there's no reason for you to stay tangled up in my mess any longer.'

She leaned forward and placed her tiny hand on top of his. 'At least, I'll drive you over to meet with Emma and hang around until she shows up.'

'You don't need to do that.'

She smiled. 'I want to.'

He squeezed her hand gently. 'OK – but then get the hell away from Miami as fast as possible. And ditch the car as soon as you can ... with the windows all shot out like that it'll be a magnet for the cops.'

She nodded.

They sat like that, in silence, looking into each other's eyes for several seconds before her expression changed and she turned her head sideways. 'What about your briefcase?'

In spite of the hectic events of the last few hours Stephen had hung on to the case, which now lay alongside him on the bed. He picked it up and set it down on his knees, gazing at the two combination locks. Were some of the answers he was seeking inside that case?

'Maybe,' said Carla panning her gaze from side to side, 'there's something in the room we can use to force it open.'

As Stephen continued staring at the locks, a dawning realisation settled. 'There's no need,' he said, looking up at Carla.

'Why?'

'I've remembered the combination.'

'You have? But how ...?'

'Remember I told you that I thought it was something to do with significant dates?'

'Yes, but you already tried numbers based on the dates in the diary.'

He shook his head. 'Not those dates.'

'What then?'

'The first combination is based on my birthday ... 3rd of November.'

He turned the wheels to show '311'. Tentatively, he slid the square button to the left; the latch obediently flipped open.

'Yes!' exclaimed Carla, clapping her hands together. 'What about the other lock?'

'My wedding anniversary ... 26th of August.'

He set the wheels on '268'and slid the button to the right. '*Click*'. The latch sprung open.

He looked up at Carla, a slow smile spreading across his face.

'Open it!' cried Carla, moving across to sit next to Stephen on the bed as he raised the lid.

The case was mostly full of papers, but protruding from a pocket in the lid was a UK passport. Stephen took it from the pocket and, with trembling fingers, opened it. There, staring back at him, was his own photograph. When he read, out loud, the name below it, an overwhelming wave of relief swept through him. 'Stephen Mark Lewis'.

Carla grabbed his arm. 'You see? You weren't going crazy … it's *you*.'

He stared and stared at the page, almost afraid to believe it was true. So the other Stephen Lewis *was* the imposter. But why? What did anyone have to gain by impersonating him and abducting his wife? And what was important enough to justify the indiscriminate murders of Doctor Holt and Sylvia? The confirmation of his identity might have reassured him of his own sanity but it raised even more questions than it answered.

'See what else is in there,' urged Carla.

The contents were mostly medical research documents, and there was a brochure about the conference at the Palm Grove Hotel, but as Stephen carefully removed the papers, laying them out carefully on the bed, what he found underneath them made his breath catch in his throat.

Chapter 21

They both gazed, open-mouthed, at the several thick wads of banknotes in the briefcase.

Carla was first to find her voice. 'But why would you have been carrying so much cash?'

'I ... I don't know,' he admitted.

'What about your wallet?' she prompted. 'You said you didn't have it on you when you were taken into hospital.'

'That's true,' he said. 'Maybe it's here somewhere.' He pulled absolutely everything out of the briefcase, but there was no sign of the missing wallet. His shoulders slumped. 'I guess those bastards who attacked me must have taken it.'

'Hey, why so miserable?' You've got your passport for I.D. now, and with all this cash, you really don't need your wallet.'

He looked into her eyes. 'It's just that ... well, the only photo of Emma and me together, that I stood any chance of retrieving, was in that wallet.'

'Oh,' she whispered, 'I understand.'

They sat in silence for several seconds before Carla continued. 'Look, you're going to see her very soon now. You won't need that photo – you're going to be together again ... and get your life back on track.'

He sighed. 'I guess you're right.'

'Anyway' she said, lightening her tone, 'come on, let's count this money – since you were down to your last fifteen dollars it hasn't come a moment too soon.'

He smiled, shaking himself free of the emotion which had engulfed him.

They organised the banknotes into neat piles according to denomination and counted them carefully. Carla announced the result. 'Twelve thousand, three hundred and seventy bucks.' She gave a low whistle. 'Now you can afford to buy your own wedding ring back,' she said, a small smile creasing her pretty face.

She reached into her handbag and withdrew the ring, passing it to Stephen. He smiled, counting out six thousand dollars and offering it to Carla.

She pushed his hand away. 'I don't need that much. Three thousand is enough to get my false papers.'

'Take it,' he insisted. 'You'll need transport, living expenses … enough to get settled and make a new life somewhere.'

She leaned forward and kissed him on the cheek. 'Thank you – I'll never forget you, you know.'

He hugged her to him. 'Nor me.'

***

Emma had arranged to meet Stephen at Loews Hotel in the South Beach area. Carla parked her battered car in a dark corner of the parking garage across the street and they approached the hotel on foot.

The impressive building, like many in Miami Beach, was built in the Art Deco style, its most notable feature a circular turret running all the way up one corner, topped with a terraced spire. As Stephen and Carla approached the main entrance, flanked by manicured lawns and sparkling fountains, they looked at each other and, as if Carla had read Stephen's mind, she vocalised just what he was thinking.

Looking Stephen up and down, she said, 'We're not exactly dressed for an upmarket joint like this, are we?'

It was true that their clothes, which they had had no chance to change since the chaotic events of the previous day, were looking somewhat the worse for wear. It was strange, thought Stephen, how such an insignificant thing – in the overall scheme of things – was bothering both of them.

'I suppose not,' he said, doing his best to smooth down the creases in the front of his shirt with the palm of his hand. 'I guess we just need to look confident and front it out. After all, a lot of rich folk deliberately dress scruffy.'

She laughed – for the first time since the tragic events of the previous day. 'OK … let's go for it.'

They strode up to the main entrance and stepped inside. Bar Collins – the place where he was supposed to meet Emma – was centrally located within the hotel, and easy to find. They paused before entering the bar as Carla checked her watch: 12.04 p.m.

'We're about twenty-five minutes early,' she said. 'Do you want to wait a while before we go in?'

Stephen shook his head. 'No … and, actually, I could use a drink to steady my nerves.'

'Me too,' she agreed.

'I thought you said you don't drink?'

'I don't, usually, but today, I'll make an exception. I need something to settle my nerves.'

The lounge – already quite busy – was furnished in a modern, minimalist style. The bar itself was a central island, with tables arranged all around it. They took a slow stroll to check out all corners of the lounge; there was no sign of Emma yet. They went up to the bar and ordered drinks; Stephen had a double bourbon and Carla a bottled beer.

They took their drinks over to a table near the entrance to the bar and sat down. Carla downed about half of her beer in just a couple of deep swallows.

'Wow!' said Stephen. 'For a non-drinker, you're making a pretty good job of demolishing that beer.'

She barely even smiled. 'I told you, I'm feeling nervous as hell.'

'Me too,' he said, taking a sip of his own drink, pausing for a moment to swirl the fiery liquid around his mouth, before letting it course down his throat.

'So this is it then,' said Carla. 'This is when you find out what's happening, and you get your wife back.'

He locked eyes with Carla. 'Yes it is … and I hope to Christ that it's the beginning of the end of this damned nightmare.'

She nodded, placing her hand on his as he set his drink down.

'I should go,' she said.

'Go? But—'

She cut him off. 'It's best if I'm not here when Emma arrives. You may not have that much time to talk, and my presence here would just be an unnecessary … complication.'

Stephen cast his eyes downward, gazing at Carla's hand still resting on his. After a couple of seconds he looked up. 'I guess you're right.'

'I'm glad you've finally got your life back ... now I need to get on with mine.' She sniffed and wiped her eyes – now glistening with a film of tears – with a napkin she took from the table. 'Look,' she said, 'I won't actually leave until I know that Emma's arrived. I'll just go and sit at a table over at the far side of the bar where I can still see you, but once Emma has sat down with you, I'll slip away.'

Stephen, too, felt the powerful emotion of the moment, fighting back the tears which threatened to erupt. He clasped her hand between both of his and gently squeezed. 'Thank you, Carla ... for everything. Maybe sometime, when we have both got our lives back on track we could ...'

'I don't think so,' she sniffed. 'Good luck and ... goodbye.'

With that, she pulled her hand away, picked up her beer, and hurried over to the far side of the bar.

The next fifteen minutes felt like an eternity. Stephen finished his drink and ordered another. He looked up at the clock: 12.26 p.m. She should be here any moment. But what if her captors had found out about her plan? They could have stopped her coming ... or worse. With every second that passed, he became more and more convinced that something was wrong. He drained his glass and checked the clock again: 12.37 p.m. She was late now. What should he do? He looked across to the other side of the bar. Carla was still there, and for a moment their eyes met; her anxiety was plain to see. He was about to get up and go over to her when he heard a familiar voice.

'Stephen, thank God I've found you at last.'

But it wasn't Emma's voice – in fact, it wasn't even a woman's voice at all.

'Henry? What are you doing here?' gasped Stephen.

Chapter 22

Stephen was astonished to see his Oxford colleague and good friend, Doctor Henry Parker, looking down at him, his face a picture of concern. Henry was a round-faced, kindly-looking man with abundant swathes of dense, grey hair either side of his shining bald pate. He and Stephen had been friends for years.

'How did you find me?' said Stephen, standing up to shake his friend's hand.

'I picked up your phone messages, but when I tried to return the calls there was no answer. Eventually I managed to get in touch with Emma, who told me that you were both in big trouble. Naturally, I got the first flight out here that I could.'

'But how did you know you could find me here?'

'I spoke to Emma on the phone. She told me she had arranged to meet you here.'

Stephen looked all around. 'So where is she?'

'Apparently she couldn't make it – she says she has people watching her every move.'

'Damn!' hissed Stephen, slamming his hand down on the table, evoking curious glances from some of those on the adjoining tables.

'Don't worry,' said Henry, 'she says she should be able to get away later this afternoon. I've given her details of the hotel where I'm staying. If you come with me, we can wait for her there.'

'But did she explain what's happening to her?'

'No ... I got the impression that she was being watched and didn't have time to talk.'

'Oh God, Henry ... this situation is such a bloody mess. There's someone claiming to be me, my wife's been kidnapped, and I have no fucking idea what it's all about. People have been *murdered* for Christ's sake.'

'My God … it sounds utterly horrific. Come on, let's get out of here. Maybe when Emma arrives at my hotel room we can make some sense of what's happening.'

***

Carla was mystified. She had no idea who the man talking to Stephen actually was, but she didn't have a good feeling about it.

And now she had another problem to contend with: an overweight, middle-aged man with slicked-back hair and a grey business suit had invited himself to sit at her table.

'Now what's a good-looking girl like you doing all on your own like this – you looking for some company?' In spite of the early hour, his breath smelled strongly of alcohol and his speech was slightly slurred.

'Actually,' she said, 'I'm waiting for someone.'

He was now blocking her view of what was happening at Stephen's table; she shuffled sideways a little so as to be able to see past him.

'Someone like me?' he drooled, leaning forward so as to block her view again.

She shifted position again for a better view. 'No,' she bristled, 'no-one at all like you.'

'Aw, c'mon honey … I've always had a bit of a thing for Latina girls.' He reached across the table and laid his hand on her arm.

As she craned her neck to see past him, she realised that Stephen was following the man who had met with him through the exit door. She needed to get rid of this creep right now. With her free hand she knocked the remains of her beer over, carefully directing it so that most of it landed in the man's lap.

'What the fuck?' he yelled, jumping to his feet and frantically pawing at his saturated crotch area.

'Oh, my God … I'm *so* sorry,' said Carla. 'Here' – she passed him a few paper napkins from the pile in the centre of the table – 'maybe these will help.'

'Clumsy bitch,' he hissed. 'I'm going to the men's room to try to sort this out.'

'Oh, I'll wait here for you then.' She flashed him her sweetest smile.

As soon as he was gone she hurried towards the door. Stepping out into the lobby, she could see no sign of Stephen or the stranger he had been talking to. She sprinted across the lobby towards the main entrance, attracting curious glances from staff and guests alike. As she burst through the doors, she was momentarily blinded by the intense sunshine. Blinking furiously, and shading her eyes with her hand, she scanned the street. Nothing. Maybe they hadn't actually left the hotel at all. She was about to step back inside when she spotted them – right across the other side of the street, heading for the parking garage where she had left her own car. Breathing a sigh of relief, she set off after them.

Keeping a discreet distance, she followed them as they approached a large, black van. As the stranger opened the passenger door for Stephen to step inside, the back door of the van opened and another man stepped out. To her horror, she realised it was one of the men who had attacked them in Sylvia's apartment – the one they had subdued with the syringe. Now he was, once again, holding a hypodermic syringe. He crept up behind Stephen, clamped a hand over his mouth, and plunged the syringe into his neck. Stephen struggled for a few seconds but it was obvious that his strength was fading fast; it wasn't long before the briefcase slipped from his hand and fell to the ground. Seconds later, his knees crumpled and he collapsed.

The bald guy stepped forward and prodded Stephen's limp form with his toe, apparently ensuring he was completely unconscious … or dead. Once satisfied that Stephen could not fight back, he nodded to his accomplice.

With some difficulty, the two men picked up Stephen's limp body and shoved it into the back of the van. The bald guy then climbed into the driver's seat while the other man picked up the briefcase and climbed into the back of the van alongside Stephen's body.

It had all happened so fast; Carla hadn't had time to process what was happening or decide what on earth she should do. And now it was too late.

***

Everything was black; his head was pounding furiously. He felt strong hands dragging him … and then a moment's weightlessness, followed by an agonising blow to his hip. His cheek was pressed against a hard, rough surface and his hand was trapped beneath his body. When he tried to moisten his lips, his tongue became coated with dry, earthy, foul-tasting grains of something.

'Get up!' commanded a harsh voice.

He wasn't sure that he actually could, but the vicious blow to his kidney that followed certainly concentrated his attention.

'Get up!' repeated the voice.

With some difficulty, he forced his eyes open and lifted his head. He realised he was lying on the ground behind the black van which Henry had been driving.

'Get up, you sonofabitch!' goaded his tormentor, this time with an additional edge of malice to his voice.

Then, a much softer, friendlier voice intervened. 'I suggest you do as he says if you want to avoid further pain.'

'Henry?' he croaked.

'Come on Stephen – you can get up now,' coaxed the familiar voice of Doctor Henry Parker.

With a considerable effort he staggered to his feet. Everything hurt – his head, his hip, his lower back – everything.

The first thing he registered was the muzzle of a gun, pointing right at his face. Wielding it, one-handed, was the man Stephen had struggled with in Sylvia's apartment. In his other hand the man held Stephen's briefcase. Looking around, Stephen could see scaffolding, piles of bricks, a stack of steel girders, and bags of cement. A building site ... they had brought him to a building site. But they were up high – it was a multi-storey car park which was under construction, and they were on one of the higher levels. But today, the entire site was deserted.

'I'm sorry it has come to this,' came the voice of Henry Parker, from behind him.

He whirled around. 'Henry ... why? What's going on?'

'We really tried, you know,' Henry replied, 'but it just didn't work out.'

'What do you mean? Why are you helping these bastards?'

'We thought there was a chance, but I'm afraid you're just too far gone.'

'Too far gone? What do you mean?'

'You have to be removed from the picture and let Stephen Lewis do what he came here to do.'

'That other guy? You know that he's not the real Stephen Lewis.'

'Of course he isn't,' said Henry, a pitying tone in his voice, 'but then neither are you.' He paused for a moment, sighing deeply. 'Stephen Lewis doesn't exist.'

Chapter 23

Henry's words hit him like a pile driver. 'Wh-what do you mean ... "doesn't exist"? You've known me for years. We've worked together for years. It's that other guy who's the imposter.'

Henry shook his head, his expression pained. 'You really do believe it, don't you?'

'Believe what? Henry, you're not making sense.'

'My name's not Henry, and we don't work together at Oxford.'

This was crazy. 'What are you talking about? You're my oldest friend.'

'And your name is not Stephen Lewis.'

Stephen pressed the palms of his hands against his temples, as though that would somehow coax some sense out of what he was hearing. It didn't help.

'Look, I know my head's been totally screwed up, but now I've found my passport. I *know* who I am now.'

'No ... you really don't.'

'Well if my name's not Stephen Lewis, what is it?' he challenged.

'It really doesn't matter now.'

'Of course it matters,' he yelled. 'I need to know who I am ... *what* I am.'

'Ah, *what* you are ... yes, I can help you with that. You are a professional assassin'.

Now Stephen doubted that his ears were even sending the correct signals to his brain. 'An *assassin*? Don't be ridiculous.'

'How do you think you were able to pick up an unfamiliar handgun – even one hampered by the fitment of a silencer – and hit my associate with your first shot, from a range of around a hundred yards?'

'Your *associate*? Henry, what the hell are you talking about?'

'I told you, I am not Henry Parker … not a research scientist … and not your friend.'

'But, I googled you. It's all there on the internet – your profile, your field of research – everything.'

He shrugged. 'These things are not difficult to fake, if you have the right resources. And the organisation I work for has considerable resources.'

'Organisation? What organisation?' said Stephen, uncomprehending.

'We run a network of professional assassins, available for hire by anyone who can afford our fees – which are *very* expensive, by the way. We employ only the very best … and that's what you are … or were. You really were one of the best.'

'No,' insisted Stephen. 'I don't know why you're telling me this, but I know it's not true. When I managed to talk to Emma yesterday she confirmed it – she said she was being held against her will. Are they forcing *you* to help them as well?'

'Her name is not Emma, and she's not your wife.'

'Not my wife? Don't be absurd.'

'She's a professional assassin too. She's your partner on your current mission … or was, until you stupidly tried to help that Latina bitch and almost got yourself killed in the process.'

By now, Stephen's head was fit to explode. 'No … as my memory has started to come back I've remembered our wedding day, the photographs, the rings … everything.'

'We coached you both for well over a year for this mission, until you were both word perfect on your supposed lives together. We took the photographs, provided the rings, the I.D.s … everything. You were the perfect couple for the job: you, with your previous medical training to win the confidence of Professor Mandelson and her, with her looks and charm, to persuade him to let down his guard.'

'B-but I can remember so much about my time with her … even …' His words tailed off as a fleeting vision of their lovemaking flashed through his mind. 'I *know* that Emma is my wife.'

'I have to admit it *is* remarkable,' said Henry. 'It seems that you learned your script so well that, after the blow to your head, you have come to completely believe your own legend. Your brain seems to have filled in all the gaps between the bits you remembered to

150

create a whole alternative life. Remarkable,' he repeated, shaking his head.

'That's … impossible,' breathed Stephen.

'I'd have thought so, too … and yet here we are. Why, you've even accepted *me*, your handler, as your fictitious colleague at Oxford.'

No, this was all too much. 'Why are you lying to me about all this? It doesn't make any sense.'

Henry ignored the question. 'We tried very hard to get you back; we thought perhaps that, with careful coaching, you could be brought back to reality. After all, we have invested huge amounts of time and money in training you and preparing you for this particular mission. But, unfortunately, it seems that you have gone well beyond the point where that would be possible. I'm sure it would make a fascinating case study for certain scientists, but unfortunately that won't be possible now.'

'What is this "mission" you are talking about?'

'Oh, you and your partner were to steal Professor Mandelson's research and then kill him, as well as his sponsor – that do-gooder, Bob Gench – and everyone else who was involved with his research.'

'I don't believe you,' cried Stephen. 'Emma could never do such a thing … and neither could I. Why are you lying to me?'

Henry shrugged. 'Believe me or not … it really doesn't matter anymore.'

'In any case,' continued Stephen, ignoring Henry's last remark, 'why would anyone want to kill an eminent scientist and a world-renowned philanthropist?'

'Because they are about to release to the world a revolutionary cure for cocaine addiction.'

Stephen was utterly uncomprehending. 'But … but that can only be good.'

'Not for our client.'

'Your client?'

'A very large and influential Colombian drug cartel. Cocaine is a multi-billion dollar business. Imagine the impact on that business if a fast and effective cure for addiction was readily available – it would be devastating. Conversely, imagine the leverage the cartel would have if they controlled access to such a cure. It's not difficult to see why they are willing to pay a very great deal to get their hands on the research and make sure that Mandelson and Gench do not recreate it.'

The first seeds of doubt began to germinate into insidious tendrils, snaking through Stephen's brain. Could any of this actually be true? There was, after all, a chilling logic in what Henry had told him. Even if some of it *were* true, there was no way he could accept the parts which he and Emma were alleged to have played in such a diabolical plot.

'I could never have agreed to take part in such a scheme,' gasped Stephen, 'and neither could Emma. It's ... evil.'

Henry shrugged. 'Perhaps,' he said, 'but we make a point of not making value judgements about our clients' motives or morality. As long as they can pay our fee, then we adhere to the old adage, "The customer is always right".' He smiled as he delivered this casual assessment of the situation.

Stephen's head was spinning as he tried to sift fact from fiction. There was still so much that didn't make sense. Like why they would lie about his own involvement in such a monstrous conspiracy and ... yes ... the biggest question of all ...

'Who is this other guy posing as Stephen Lewis?' he demanded. 'What's his part in all this?'

'Well,' replied Henry, 'this mission is *very* important to us. It has been well over a year in the planning, and we couldn't afford the possibility that one or other of the assassination team might be unable to complete the project, for whatever reason. So we prepared a reserve operative for each of you, ready to stand in if there were any problems.' He paused, pursing his lips and frowning. 'And I'm afraid *you* have now become a very big problem.'

Stephen still didn't believe what he and Emma were accused of, but one thing, at least, now seemed certain: incredible as it first seemed, Henry was involved in this thing right up to his neck. How, or why, he couldn't fathom, but now he had a more immediate problem. He realised, with a chilling certainty, what Henry's last sentence had meant ... and he could see no possible means of escape.

'Oh, by the way,' continued Henry, 'we are most indebted to you for providing us with the missing briefcase. That was a worrying loose end which could have caused us all sorts of problems if the police had found it.'

'What are you going to do with me?' said Stephen, knowing full well the answer to the question, but desperately playing for time.

'We'll make it look like the result of a clash between rival gangs; the cops are dealing with this kind of thing every day. There'll be no I.D. on you, and you'll have a recently-fired gun alongside you. With a stash of cocaine in your pocket, you'll be just another unidentified John Doe – another sad bastard killed in the course of Miami's ongoing gang warfare.'

Stephen desperately ran through his options. Make a run for it? The nearest cover was about twenty yards away – plenty of time for the guy with the gun to drop him as he ran. Try to rush the guy with the gun? No, he was too far away – he would be dead before he had covered half the distance. Try to rush Henry? He was a bit closer; maybe, just maybe, he could reach him in time and turn him to use as a human shield. It was a very long shot, but what other chance did he have?

'I'm truly sorry it's turned out this way,' continued Henry. You were one of our very best operatives but … well, needs must.' He turned and nodded to the guy with the gun. It was now or never.

The man began to raise his gun, his mouth curling in an unpleasant smile. Time seemed to slow to an unnatural crawl as Stephen planned his move. He measured the distance in his mind. Maybe ten feet – two or three quick strides should do it, but even so he didn't rate his chances. But with no other option, he tensed for action.

Chapter 24

Just as the man levelled his gun, Stephen detected a sudden change in his expression: his eyes – which had been locked onto Stephen's – flickered to the side. The cruel smile evaporated as he dropped to a crouch and swung the gun away from Stephen, and towards something behind him. And then he heard a squeal of tyres. He spun around to see Carla's battered car accelerating towards them.

The man fired three shots in quick succession, three holes appearing in the windshield of the car. The spider's web of radial cracks radiating from each bullet hole rendered the glass more or less opaque, but as he saw the tight grouping of the bullet holes right around where Carla's head would be, Stephen's heart sank.

The car, however, raced relentlessly forward.

The man managed to loose one more shot, which glanced off the roof of the car, leaving a deep gouge just above the windshield, before the car ploughed into him. He was lifted clean off his feet and slammed against the side of the van. His eyes bulged in terror in that split second before his body was crushed and copious gouts of blood sprang from his mouth.

After the noise and fury of the last few seconds, it was suddenly eerily quiet: no movement, no sound, no sign of life. Stephen was rendered inanimate – rooted to the spot as he tried to process what had happened. But then he caught sight of movement off to the side – Henry had gathered his wits and was reaching inside his jacket pocket. By the time Stephen registered what was happening, Henry was already withdrawing a gun from his pocket.

There was no time to think – Stephen launched himself forward, covering the ground between them in two huge strides, before grabbing Henry's wrist, forcing the gun up and away. A shot rang out, but it went harmlessly skyward. That round, kindly face was now twisted into an expression of pure fury. The man fought back with surprising vigour, but for all his ferocity, his strength was no match for Stephen's. As they struggled, he was forced back, step by step but, even so, Stephen could not wrest the gun from his stubborn grip.

Suddenly, Henry's eyes widened, and the gun spun from his grasp. He toppled backwards, breaking through the flimsy red-and-white-striped plastic ribbon which marked the edge of the concrete floor slab and warned of the forty-foot drop beyond. Stephen tried to grab hold of him, but he had passed the point of no return. As he disappeared from view he let out an anguished scream, cut short a second or so later by a sickening thud. His heart thumping, Stephen stepped forward and looked over the edge. The man's body was spread-eagled like a stranded starfish, impaled on the upturned prongs of the bucket of an excavator. The expression frozen on his lifeless face seemed to be one of surprise rather than fear or pain. Stephen gazed, mesmerised, at the gruesome spectacle laid out below him.

But what about Carla? He turned away and began moving towards her wrecked car. With each step, his sense of trepidation grew. He could not see her sitting at the wheel. As he drew nearer, he registered two bullet holes in the driver's headrest. He felt the air sucked from his lungs in a suffocating rush as he crept forward the last few yards and looked through the remains of the shattered driver's door window. She was lying sideways, motionless, her head on the passenger seat, one arm trapped beneath her and the other draped in the floor well.

'Carla!' he cried. There was no response from the prone body.

He wrenched at the door handle, but it wouldn't budge – the crumpled bodywork would not allow the latch to release. 'Shit!' he hissed, thumping his fist on the roof of the car in frustration. He rushed around to the other side of the car, which seemed to have sustained a little less damage. As he looked through the window frame, which still hung on to a few fragments of shattered glass, a leaden boulder descended in his gut. It had not been visible from the other side of the car, but now, the slowly spreading pool of blood on the seat beneath Carla's head was plain to see.

He grabbed the door handle and pulled hard; with a screech of torn metal, the door grudgingly submitted and opened. He reached inside and gently lifted Carla's head. The side of her face was smeared with so much blood that it was impossible to determine its source.

'Carla ... Carla ... can you hear me?'

No response. Was she still alive?

With trembling fingers he gently probed her blood-streaked neck, feeling for a pulse.

There it was – strong and regular. His heart leapt. All of a sudden the medical training which Henry had referred to came flooding back – not that he knew when or where he had received such training. He needed to see where she had been hit if he was to know if she could be saved. His gaze settled on the glove box, which had sprung open in the crash. Inside was a pack of tissues. He grabbed a handful and began cleaning the blood away from her face, searching for the wound.

And then he found it – on her temple. But it wasn't a bullet wound – instead, a jagged gash which, although bleeding freely, didn't appear to be all that deep. She must have hit her head on something when the car crashed. The wave of relief which swept through him was almost overwhelming

As he continued cleaning around the wound, her eyelids flickered.

'Carla ... are you OK?'

Her eyes opened and, with a groan, she propped herself up on one elbow. 'Wh-what happened?' she murmured. 'I ... was driving straight at him, and then ... I don't remember.'

'It's OK,' he whispered. 'He's dead.'

'Did I get him then?' she gasped.

'You did. You crushed him against the van.'

'But what about the other guy?'

'I struggled with him and he went over the edge. He's dead too.' Stephen helped her to sit up and gave her some seconds to settle her breathing before continuing. 'It's a miracle that you weren't hit. That guy's aim was right on target.'

'When I saw him taking aim, I knew I wouldn't be able to get him before he fired, so I just let go of the wheel and threw myself across the seats. I heard the shots and saw them crash through the windshield but I guess he was aiming at where I was a moment earlier. I must have hit him before he had a chance to readjust his aim.'

'Thank God,' breathed Stephen.

'What about you?' she said. 'Are you OK?'

'Yes … but we need to get out of here fast. If anyone saw or heard the commotion, the police are sure to be here soon.' He grabbed a fresh wad of tissues. 'Here … keep these pressed against that head wound. It's still bleeding quite a bit, but it doesn't look too deep. Can you stand up?'

'I think so.'

She wriggled across to the passenger side and placed her feet on the ground. Stephen took her arm and helped her to her feet.

'OK?' he asked.

'Yes, I think so but … wait.'

'What?'

'My handbag … all that money.'

Stephen stuck his head inside the car. Her handbag was on the floor in the passenger-side foot well.

'Here,' he said, handing her the bag. 'And I need to get my briefcase.'

He scanned the chaotic scene but, at first, could not locate the briefcase.

'The guy with the gun had it,' said Carla. 'I think he dropped it when he saw me coming at him.'

Stephen stepped over to where their erstwhile assailant's body was draped over the bonnet of Carla's car, his face frozen in a grotesque death grimace, blood still streaming from his nose and mouth. There was the briefcase, on the ground, partly underneath the car.

The case was now very much the worse for wear: the once-luxurious leather cladding was scuffed and torn, and the underlying frame badly twisted. It had burst open, spilling some of its contents on the ground. Stephen hurriedly gathered everything up and stuffed it all back in the case, closing it up as best he could.

'OK … let's get out of here,' he said.

***

The cab driver had looked a little reluctant to give them a ride – hardly surprising, given their dishevelled state and the amount of blood on Carla's clothing. When Stephen produced a hundred-dollar bill, however, he quickly relented. They needed somewhere to stop, gather their thoughts, and take stock. For want of anywhere better, they headed back, once more, towards the motel, El Refugio.

'Stop the car,' said Stephen.

'But it's another couple of miles yet,' replied the driver.

'Stop ... over there ... by that QVC store,' insisted Stephen.

The driver shrugged and pulled over.

'OK,' said Stephen, producing another fifty-dollar bill – which the driver snatched without hesitation – 'wait here. I won't be long.' He turned to Carla. 'We need some new clothes – what size are you?'

'Er ... well, 6 on a bad day, 4 on a good day.' She even managed a small smile.

'OK – back soon,' he said, stepping out of the car.

Ten minutes later, he was back, clutching a bag full of fresh clothes.

The proprietor in 'El Refugio' took a pace backward when he saw them walk through the door. 'Hey, you guys again? You look ... er, well ... like you've had a bit of a rough time.'

'We have,' said Stephen, without elaborating. 'We need a room.'

'I, er ... well, I don't know,' he said, eyeing Carla's bloodstained shirt. 'You sure you don't need a doctor or something?'

Carla stepped right up to the counter – the man visibly recoiled. 'Listen ... we just need a room. Now, you got one or not?'

'I ... I just need to check,' he said, making a great show as he stared intently at his computer screen and tapped away at his keyboard.

'Will this help?' said Stephen, laying a hundred-dollar bill on the counter.

The man looked up, smiling nervously as he laid his hand on the banknote and started sliding it towards himself. Stephen clamped his own hand over the other man's before he could pocket the money, fixing him with an icy stare.

'Er ... w-well, as it happens,' stammered the fat man, 'I do have two rooms left.' Stephen released his hand. 'Now ... about the sleeping arrangements ...?'

'That's it,' hissed Carla, jabbing the air with her forefinger, 'I've just about had enough of this shithead. One more word out of his mouth and I'll—'

Stephen laid a restraining hand on her arm. 'We'll take whatever you have,' he said, in the calmest voice he could muster.

When they arrived in their room Stephen said, 'OK, let's take a look at that head wound of yours.' He tipped the contents of the QVC bag onto the bed, selecting a bottle of antiseptic spray, a pack of wound-closure strips, and a pack of Band-Aids. 'Come through to the bathroom.'

She sat on the edge of the bath as Stephen tenderly cleaned the wound with the antiseptic liquid. 'What exactly happened back there?' she said, looking into his eyes.

'It's not as bad as it looked,' he said, dodging the question. 'There was a lot of blood but it's not too deep.'

She placed her hand on his wrist. 'Stephen … what happened?'

'Well, you know what happened – you rammed the guy with the gun and—'

'No,' she said, 'I mean what happened about … *you*? You've been sort of … *different* since then. I know it's not just the shock of the whole thing – you've learned something new about yourself, haven't you?'

He dipped his head, shaking it from side to side before, again, making eye contact with her. 'Before you turned up, Henry told me the most incredible and disturbing story.'

She inclined her head. 'Henry? The guy who met you in the bar? So you knew him … but why—'

He raised his hand to restrain further questions. 'Let me finish dressing this wound, and then … then, I'll tell you everything.'

***

After they had cleaned themselves up and changed into the new jeans and tee-shirts he had bought, he sat down and told her everything he now knew.

She stared at him in utter disbelief. 'So you think this plan to kill the professor and steal his research is true?'

'At first I didn't believe it, but it's true that the research Professor Mandelson is due to release to the world is truly revolutionary. It will lead to a cheap and widely available drug which can completely reverse cocaine addiction with just two or three treatments. What he said about the potential effect on the illegal cocaine trade makes perfect sense.'

'But this guy was a colleague at Oxford wasn't he? Why would he be mixed up in such a horrible scheme?'

'I don't know,' admitted Stephen, 'but I do know that he was ready to shoot me back there. I can't imagine how he got involved, but somehow they seem to have turned him.'

'So you really believe the professor and Bob Gench are in danger?'

'I'm afraid I do.' He paused for a second or two, hanging his head before sharing the thought that was torturing him. 'Carla, if Henry was somehow coerced into taking part in this hideous plan, can I really be so sure that I wasn't involved too?'

She placed her hand under his chin, raising his head until his gaze met hers. 'That's not you,' she said '... not the man I have come to know.' She took both of his hands in hers. 'That is *not* who you are.'

'But you don't really know me, Carla. I don't really even know myself.'

'I know enough to know that you're a good man, Stephen.'

He pulled away from her and stood up, pacing the room as he continued. 'When I woke up in hospital after the attack I couldn't remember anything. My head was so screwed up – *is* so screwed up; how can I be sure that the memories which have come back to me are real? Even now there are huge chunks of my life which remain a mystery.'

'Oh, Stephen ... what can I do to help you?'

He didn't respond to her question. 'It's so strange – like trying to recall a dream. You know that feeling? You know it's there, but somehow it stays tantalisingly just out of reach.'

'Let's take another look through all that stuff in the briefcase,' said Carla '... maybe there will something that gives us more clues.'

He nodded, sitting down on the bed as she opened the battered case. But his heart wasn't in it; they had already scoured the contents of the briefcase, and he couldn't believe that those papers had any more truth to yield. Carla, however, began picking through them with a fierce intensity.

'Look!' she cried.

'Huh?' He was miles away, still trying to probe the deepest recesses of his mind for answers.

'Look here!' She grabbed his shoulder and shook him until he eventually focused on what she was showing him.

With all the contents of the case removed, it could be seen that the bottom of the case was coming away. One corner was twisted and raised; there seemed to be a gap below. Carla inserted a couple of fingers into the gap and pulled hard. The entire bottom lining of the case came away. What they found beneath the false bottom of the case reduced them both to a shocked silence.

Chapter 25

How on earth had they failed to realise, before this moment, that the internal depth of the case bore little relationship to the substantial external dimension? Now though, the purpose of the hidden compartment became clear.

There were numerous stacks of banknotes arranged side by side, each bound with a paper sleeve bearing the handwritten inscription '$10,000'. They looked at each other, open-mouthed, as Stephen picked up one of the stacks and examined it. 'Used, hundred-dollar notes,' he observed.

'How many?' breathed Carla.

He counted the stacks of banknotes. 'Fifteen bundles ... so if these labels are right we're looking at—'

'A hundred and fifty thousand dollars,' interrupted Carla.

They sat, staring at each other in disbelieving silence for several long seconds before, eventually, Stephen articulated the troubling thought which he sensed Carla, too, shared. 'Why on earth would Stephen Lewis, Research Scientist, need to be hiding a hundred and fifty thousand dollars in a secret compartment in the bottom of his case?'

She looked into his eyes for a moment, as though searching for the truth there, but quickly looked away before taking the remaining stacks of cash from the case. What lay below was even more disturbing: at least a dozen passports, of various nationalities.

It was with a feeling of growing unease that Stephen picked up the first UK passport he could see. When he opened it, his worst fears were confirmed: there, staring back at him, was his own face. But it was different: the hair was shorter and darker, and the face sported a neatly-trimmed moustache. The name in the passport was Kevin Blake.

'It's you, isn't it?' breathed Carla.

He nodded, setting the passport aside and taking another from the case – this one also UK. As he turned to the title page, his breath caught in his throat. It was Emma, but her tumbling blonde tresses had been replaced by chestnut brown hair, styled in a bob. The name was Diana Blake.

The sensation he felt was like a physical blow to his stomach. So it was all true.

As he worked through all the other passports he found an Australian and a Canadian passport each bearing his photograph – with two more different names. And then there were another nine passports in a variety of nationalities which contained no photograph at all, the plastic film which normally covers the photograph not yet sealed in place: passports customisable, with minimal effort, to suit any purpose.

The despair which he felt hollowed him out from the inside. It felt like a ghastly nightmare, but one from which he knew he could not wake up.

He turned to Carla, his voice flat and lifeless. 'It's all true. I'm not Stephen Lewis … I don't know *who* I am.'

She laid her hand on his. 'I … I don't know what to say.'

'What kind of monster am I, Carla?'

Tears began to well up in her eyes. 'You're not a monster. I don't know what you have done in the past or what you were planning to do before you lost your memory. I only know you as you are now – and that is a good man.'

He shook his head. 'A good man? Carla, I was going to *murder* people – just for money. I was going to rob the world of a revolutionary new addiction cure – in the process propping up a hideous drugs trade destroying countless people's lives. It's just …' He could no longer find the words.

'Stop it,' said Carla, grabbing his shoulders and shaking him. 'What's done is done – you can't change it. Don't let what you *were* define you; it's what you do *now* that matters.'

Chapter 26

At the Palm Grove Hotel, guests were arriving for the pre-conference reception.

'Doctor and Mrs Lewis,' said the other Stephen Lewis, extending his hand to show their invitations.

The man on the door examined the invitations, ran his finger down the guest list and, evidently satisfied, ushered them over to a side table where his colleague was carrying out bag checks.

Emma laid her Gucci evening bag on the table: a compact, elegant bag, encrusted with sparkling crystals and set off by a slim, chain-link shoulder strap. There was really only space for the bare essentials in such a small handbag, and when the security guy opened it, he gave it only the most cursory of inspections.

'Stephen'– real name Ethan Peterson – was carrying a larger, black, over-shoulder bag, which he dutifully laid on the table for inspection. When the security guy undid the zip, his brow creased in puzzlement, for the bag was empty.

'I have to take some papers back at the end of the presentations,' said Ethan, by way of explanation.

The man shrugged and zipped up the bag, handing it back. He indicated, with a sideways nod of his head that they should proceed.

As they stepped through the door, they were greeted by Bob Gench, the billionaire tech entrepreneur and philanthropist who was sponsoring the conference. Emma recognised him immediately, having studied countless photographs.

'Doctor and Mrs Stephen Lewis,' said Ethan.

'Ah, Doctor Lewis,' said Gench, shaking Ethan's hand. 'Professor Mandelson has told me all about you.'

'And me about you,' replied Ethan. 'Without your unwavering support, this whole thing just wouldn't have been possible.'

Gench waved away the compliment without responding directly. 'Well, pleased to meet you at last ... and, of course you, Mrs Lewis.'

'Please ... call me Emma,' said Natasha, proffering her hand to Gench,

'Of course.' He said, gently shaking her hand. 'Let me take your wrap, Emma.'

'Emma' – real name Natasha King – was dressed to kill. Her plan relied on her ability to charm Professor Mandelson into letting down his guard, so she had put a great deal of thought into her clothes and makeup for the evening. She needed to look as alluring as possible, without being too obvious.

'Thank you,' she said, turning her back towards their host to allow him to take her wrap.

As Bob Gench slipped the faux fur garment from her shoulders, she could almost feel his eyes traversing the expanse of her lightly-tanned back, laid bare by the deeply plunging cut of her deep red cocktail dress, which clung to every curve of her slender figure. As she turned to face him, flashing him a dazzling smile, she was gratified to see his eyes flicker momentarily to the glimpse of cleavage on display before he recovered his composure and quickly focused on her face. Noting, also, the envious glances from two women who were standing nearby, she figured she had got the look just about right.

'I'll hang it just over there,' he said, indicating the coat rack alongside the door. He took her wrap, and hung it from one of the coat hooks.

Ethan waited until he turned back towards them. 'Can I leave my bag there, too?'

'Of course,' said Bob Gench.

Ethan moved over to the rack, unslinging his over-shoulder bag and hanging it on the same hook as Natasha's wrap.

'Now, Professor Mandelson has not yet arrived,' said Bob Gench, 'but please grab yourselves a drink and take the opportunity to mingle with the other guests.'

Natasha flashed him another winning smile before they moved through into the body of the room. Funny to think the poor bastard would be dead in a couple of hours' time.

They each took a glass of champagne, but it was mainly for appearances sake, rather than to actually drink – they needed to stay sober for the task ahead. There were about forty or fifty people in the room; the men mostly wore tuxedos and the women elegant evening dresses. Natasha knew that she looked more glamorous than just about every other woman in the room, but she took no particular personal satisfaction from that fact. She was a professional and, for this particular mission, she needed to be the *femme fatale,* a look which she could pull off with ease, given her natural beauty, but she could equally well make herself look cheap and slutty, or even plain, when the mission demanded it.

They didn't bother to mingle with other guests, but rather stayed, as unobtrusively as possible, close to the entrance, just chatting to each other. When the moment was opportune, Ethan moved unhurriedly over to the coat rack and rearranged their things on the coat hook so that the wrap lay over the top of the bag rendering it invisible to a casual glance.

Then they waited … and waited. They changed position from time to time, to avoid looking too obvious, but they never strayed far from the entrance to the room.

When Professor Mandelson finally arrived, he looked a little flustered – red in the face and perspiring heavily. Natasha's gaze homed in, laser-like, on the laptop bag slung over his shoulder.

'So sorry I'm late,' he said, as Bob Gench shook his hand, '… the traffic was terrible.'

'No problem,' said Gench. 'We've allowed plenty of time for guests to mingle and chat before the presentations. They won't start until about eight.'

Natasha knew that the purpose of the reception was not only to allow invited guests to get to know each other, but also to provide a platform for Professor Mandelson to give a preview of the announcement he was to make at the conference proper on Monday.

Ethan Peterson – or rather his alter ego, Stephen Lewis – had been invited to join Professor Mandelson at the top table but had successfully managed to wriggle out of this, by claiming his part in the research had been minimal. But Mandelson, Gench, and a couple of others involved in the project would be seated together at the top table for the presentations; this was when Natasha and Ethan would strike. Before this part of the plan could be enacted, however, they had something else important to accomplish.

Judging their timing to perfection, they wandered past just as Bob Gench was ushering Professor Mandelson through into the main body of the room.

'Stephen,' called out the professor, 'hello.'

Ethan turned at the sound of his voice, feigning surprise. 'Richard, great to see you.'

But Professor Mandelson's eyes were already on Natasha, who smiled back at him.

'And this must be Emma,' he said, extending his hand.

'Delighted to meet you, Professor,' she said, tipping her head, coyly.

'And you too,' he replied. 'Stephen has told me all about the incident at the party the other day. You must have been terrified when this other guy turned up, claiming to be your husband.'

'Well,' she said, 'not exactly terrified, just kind of *unsettled* – it was so weird. After all, why on earth would anyone want to impersonate Stephen?' She gazed up at her supposed husband, her expression quizzical.

'Certainly beats me,' said Ethan. 'I guess the guy must have been unbalanced.'

'Although,' said Professor Mandelson, hesitating as though unsure whether to continue, 'having now met your charming wife, I can see why he might want to be you.' He coloured up slightly, no doubt realising, as the words came out of his mouth, how utterly cringe-worthy they sounded.

What a shmuck, thought Natasha, as she smiled and put a dainty hand to her mouth, pretending to stifle a giggle. 'Oh really, Professor … you're too kind.' This was almost *too* easy.

Her response seemed to quell his embarrassment; his expression relaxed.

'Can I get you a drink?' said Ethan, turning to the professor.

'Yes … I could certainly use one … might help to settle my nerves. I hate standing up in front of people and giving presentations. I've done dozens – no, probably hundreds – of the damned things in my time, but I'm still nervous as hell each time. And this is a really big one.'

'I'm the same,' said Ethan, 'but you have nothing to fear this time. Everyone will be blown away by what you are about to tell them.'

Mandelson smiled, biting his lip.

'Let me get you that drink,' said Ethan '… champagne OK?'

The professor nodded.

As Ethan went to get the drink, Natasha lost no time in building upon the impression she had obviously already made on Professor Mandelson, fluttering her eyelashes as she gazed at him. 'Stephen tells me that your research is absolutely ground-breaking.'

'I … er, well I only hope it will help degrade, and ultimately eliminate, the evil cocaine trade which is destroying so many young lives.'

She nodded, still gazing into his eyes as she continued to pile on the flattery. 'Stephen says you are one of the most brilliant researchers he has ever known.'

'Oh,' he said, the blood rushing to his cheeks, 'that's a bit of an exaggeration … I'm just doing my job.'

Ethan returned with the Professor's champagne. He shifted his laptop bag, awkwardly, as he went to accept the drink.

The perfect moment, thought Natasha. 'Oh, here – let me take that for you,' she said, setting her own glass down on a nearby table so that she had both hands free. 'You look awfully uncomfortable with it.'

'I … er … I think I'd rather keep it with me – it contains some very important information.'

'Oh, Professor—'

'Please … call me Richard.'

She smiled, raising a hand to toss a lock of wavy, blonde hair away from her face. 'Thank you – I will.'

'You see my presentation is on my laptop and all my research findings, too … plus a lot of other important information.' The professor had laid a protective arm over his bag.

'Oh gosh!' she breathed, wide-eyed. 'Then you certainly mustn't let it out of your sight. It does look awfully heavy and awkward to have over your shoulder all evening, though.' She paused for a moment, as though deep in thought. 'Look,' she said, indicating the coat rack near the door, 'my wrap is hanging up just there. Why don't you let me hang your bag right next to it? You'll be able to keep an eye on it all the time until you need it for your presentation.'

'We-ell … I suppose that might be OK.'

'And the only people Security will let in are invited guests. No-one can sneak in from outside.'

'Well, that's true I suppose.'

'Here, let me take it,' she said, smiling and tilting her head as she held out her hands.

Her persuasive smile did the trick.

'Well, OK then.' He slid the bag from his shoulder and handed it to her.

This was the critical part. She had only a few moments, and if the professor should spot what she was doing, the whole plan would be blown.

Chapter 27

Stephen and Carla rushed up to the reception desk of the Palm Grove Hotel. The immaculately-groomed woman behind the desk greeted them with a smile, but could hardly disguise her disdain at their cheap, ill-fitting clothing. Carla's jeans were clearly a size too large, puckering untidily below the waistband where she had cinched them in with her belt. There were even a few spots of blood on the belt, which the receptionist may, or may not, have spotted. Stephen had the opposite problem: his tee-shirt was way too small, his muscular arms threatening to burst the sleeves.

'Checking in, sir?' enquired the woman, quickly regaining her professional demeanour and suppressing the look of disapproval which had momentarily revealed itself on her face.

Stephen wasted no time on pleasantries. 'We need to speak to the Head of Hotel Security – right now.'

She pulled her head back, her face creasing in a puzzled frown. 'Excuse me?'

'The Head of Security – we need to see him, right NOW.'

'I'm sorry sir, we have a very important function taking place this evening, and all our security staff are fully occupied with that. Now if you'd like to give me some details of—'

'Oh, screw this!' muttered Stephen. He grabbed Carla's hand and began striding towards the entrance to the pre-conference reception.

The man on the door saw them approaching and clearly anticipated trouble. He looked over his shoulder and called out something. A moment later, his colleague was alongside him. They were both big men – about the same build as Stephen.

As Stephen and Carla approached, one of the men held up his hand in a 'halt' gesture. 'I'm sorry, sir. We have a private function taking place in here this evening.'

'I know that,' said Stephen, attempting to push past the man.

His colleague intervened, grabbing Stephen's arm, wrenching it up behind his back.

'Let him go,' pleaded Carla. 'There's going to be a mass murder in there if we don't stop it.'

The first man's eyes widened in surprise. 'What are you talking about ... a *murder*?'

'It's true,' hissed Stephen. 'Let me go.'

The two men looked at each other in what appeared to be utter confusion. 'What do we do?' said the one restraining Stephen.

'I'll get Mr. Schultz,' replied his partner, reaching for the discreet intercom attached to his lapel.

Stephen knew full well that they were never going to let him barge straight into the private function, but he had achieved his objective of circumnavigating the woman on the front desk. Derek Schultz was Head of Security, the man Stephen had previously encountered when last in the hotel. That was only a few days ago, but it felt like a lifetime.

He only hoped that they were in time to avert the disaster which was about to unfold.

***

'So now,' said Derek Schultz, 'you are saying you are *not* Doctor Stephen Lewis.'

They were back in the same security office where Stephen had previously been questioned. He had spent the last twenty minutes trying, without success, to convince Schultz to call off the function and evacuate the entire hotel.

'I told you,' said Stephen, 'I now know that's not my real name.'

'And your real name is?'

'I don't know,' he said.

'You don't know?' said Schultz, his voice laden with scepticism.

'No I don't,' admitted Stephen, '... but look, we're wasting time here. If you don't evacuate the hotel right now, many people will die.'

'Because *you* were going to kill them, but now the other man – who you say is also not Doctor Stephen Lewis – is going to do it instead?'

'Yes,' said Stephen. 'I know it sounds far-fetched but—'

'And your wife – who is now not your wife – is helping him?'

Stephen slammed his hand down on the table in frustration. The security guard who had been standing motionless in the corner of the room took a step forward.

'It's OK,' said Schultz, raising his hand to indicate that no intervention was necessary.

He turned back to Stephen. 'Look … you have had a very nasty experience. You said yourself that you have been completely mixed up since that blow to the head. I think you need to return to the hospital and—'

Carla could contain herself no longer. 'He's telling the truth. We have spent the last few days running from these people; we have seen them kill without hesitation. You need to evacuate the hotel and call the police.'

Stephen thought he could detect the first flicker of uncertainty in Schultz's eyes. He needed to open up that chink of doubt.

'Look, I know what the plan was. It's odds-on that it hasn't changed just because I've been replaced.' He locked eyes with Schultz. 'There's a bomb – it will take out everyone on the top table and probably many others too.'

Chapter 28

As Natasha turned to walk toward the coat rack, holding Professor Mandelson's bag, Ethan put into action the distraction strategy which he had prepared in advance. 'Have you seen the seating plan for Monday's conference?' he asked the professor.

'Well, no … I haven't actually.'

'Oh, well come and have a look,' said Ethan. 'They've posted it on the flip-chart stand just over there.' He pointed to the stand in question, taking Mandelson's gaze away from Natasha.

Although she hoped that Ethan would be successful in keeping the professor's attention away from her, she held the bag in front of her as she walked, so that her own body would shield it from Professor Mandelson's view should he turn around. She unzipped the top of the case as she walked.

As she reached the coat rack she stole a glance over her shoulder. Mandelson had his back towards her as Ethan pointed out some feature of the seating plan. *So far so good*. She hung the strap of the bag on the coat hook next to where her wrap was hanging. She pulled her wrap to one side to reveal the other bag, whose zip was already open in readiness for her next move.

The urge to turn and take another look behind her was almost irresistible, but she suppressed it. Now, more than ever, was the moment she had to rely on the professionalism of her partner. Ethan would be watching her every move; she had to trust that he would keep Mandelson's attention away from her until she had completed her task.

Taking a deep breath, she pulled Professor Mandelson's laptop out of the case, slipping it into the other bag and pulling the zip closed before turning around. Ethan made eye contact; she gave a small nod. Ethan turned away from the chart and guided Professor Mandelson back to where they had previously been standing.

As she made her way back towards the two men, Natasha added her own touch to the distraction strategy. Effecting a slightly exaggerated sway to her walk as she approached them was quite sufficient to keep the professor's gaze fixed on her hips rather than his precious laptop case. *God, men are so easy to manipulate.* When Mandelson glanced up and made eye contact with her, she assuaged the guilt in his eyes by flashing her most dazzling smile.

'There, Professor – oh, sorry, I mean Richard – your bag is right over there' – she pointed to where it was hanging – 'where you can keep an eye on it.'

'Thank you,' he said.

She waited another five minutes or so, chatting easily with the two men, before making her next move. 'Now, if you boys will excuse me for a little while, I just need to pay a visit to the ladies' room.'

'Oh, yes … of course,' said the professor.

'I think I'll just grab my wrap. The air conditioning out in the lobby is a little too fierce for a dress like this.' She emphasised the point by turning slightly to one side and running a hand over her bare shoulder. The professor's Adam's apple performed a little dance in his throat.

Now, though, she needed to tone down the charm – the last thing she needed was for the professor's gaze to be fixed on her backside as she approached the coat rack. As she walked away, she adopted a rather less provocative gait.

This was the point where, once again, she had to rely on her partner's distraction skills. As she reached the coat rack, she risked a glance back towards the two men. She needn't have worried: Ethan had, once again, skilfully managed to adjust their positions so that Professor Mandelson had his back to her, while Ethan could see exactly what she was doing. She took both the wrap and the bag from the rack and draped the wrap over the bag as she headed for the door. As expected, the security guys didn't bother to check what was being taken *out* of the room – they were only interested in what was being taken *in*.

She didn't go to the ladies' room; she headed back to the suite where she and Ethan had been staying.

She slid the laptop from the bag and set it down on the desk, flipping up the lid of the machine and powering it up. After a few seconds, Mandelson's name and photograph appeared on the screen. Just below, was a box requiring a password.

This was an absolutely critical moment. If the information provided by her accomplice in Professor Mandelson's employ was incorrect, the entire mission would fail. She took a deep breath to try to steady her nerves.

Chapter 29

Lara Hurst was a lab assistant at the University of Miami's Marsden Medical School. Her résumé was outstanding – it had to be in order for her to land a job working with the renowned Professor Richard Mandelson.

Actually, though, much of what was contained in her résumé was fictitious, including her name. She was, however, sufficiently competent to satisfy the demands of Professor Mandelson, who was usually too absorbed in his work to notice if anything she said or did might be inconsistent with her supposed background. She had worked for the professor for almost a full year, and now had his complete trust.

Her task was to find out exactly where Mandelson stored all his research data and what security measures he used to protect it. She soon found that he committed very little to paper, preferring to store everything on his laptop computer. He guarded the machine closely, invariably closing any files he had been working on when he stepped away from his desk, even for just a few minutes, and always taking it home with him at night. On the very few occasions when she *had* been able to get to the laptop without the professor seeing her, she had found all the relevant files to be password protected. It was infuriatingly frustrating.

At first, she was puzzled by the professor's frequent requests for her to purchase new diaries. For someone who seemed so averse to putting things down on paper he seemed strangely reliant on these things. And why on earth did he need six new diaries during the course of a single year? All her instincts told her that this strange behaviour held some significance beyond the mere quirk of a somewhat eccentric academic.

He often had his diary alongside him when he was working at his computer, and *always* picked it up and slipped it into his jacket pocket before leaving his desk. The strange thing was that every time he got a new diary he would tear out some of the pages from the old one and shred them. The rest of the diary would then be carelessly tossed into the waste bin.

The first time she checked the remains of a discarded diary she was surprised to see that most of the pages were still in place, but that absolutely nothing was written on any of them. Whatever was important must have been on the few pages which had been shredded.

On one occasion, the professor had neglected to pick up his diary when leaving his desk to visit the men's room. She seized the opportunity to examine it while he was gone. One of the dates on the open pages was ringed in ink: January 23rd. She flipped quickly through the rest of the diary and eventually found another date, also highlighted: August 7th. She could not see any significance in either of these dates, but jotted them down in the notebook she always kept with her, before leaving the diary open on the desk, exactly as she had found it.

When, two weeks later, Professor Mandelson discarded the diary in favour of a new one, the pages which had been removed included the ones containing those same two dates which had been highlighted.

When, after another two months, the professor discarded the next diary, she retrieved it from the bin and checked it. Again, there were just a few pages missing, but the dates they contained were different. So the dates were clearly not significant in an absolute sense; they were significant only for a couple of months and then replaced with new ones.

Finally, she worked it out. The professor, for all his brilliance, had an absolutely appalling memory. She had seen ample evidence of this as he went about his daily work: he would frequently ask her where he had left this item or that around the lab. The fact that she was invariably able quickly to locate the missing item only served to increase his dependence on, and confidence in, his trusted lab assistant. Given the professor's dreadful memory, he would probably forget the passwords he used to protect his files if he didn't write them down, but writing them down would make them vulnerable. Instead he had chosen a sort of simple code: he would select dates at random in a diary and use these as passwords, referring back to the diary if he forgot the passwords, which he frequently did. For extra security he would change the dates every two months and destroy the old ones.

Now the only thing she needed to discover was in what format the date had to be entered. Was it 'month/date/day'? 'date/month/day'? Maybe the year was included too? There were many possible permutations.

In spite of much urging by her paymasters, she never did manage to discover this critical piece of information. She never got the opportunity to watch how the professor entered his passwords; nor did she get a chance to access his laptop and experiment with entering the dates in various different formats. The only thing she knew, with near certainty, was that the dates highlighted in the diary at any given time held the key to accessing the files.

The best she could do, as the date of the conference drew near, was to try to find out what the latest dates were. When she bought the professor's new diary, just three weeks before the conference, she also purchased several additional, identical diaries. As the professor was working at his computer, with his diary alongside him on the desk, she sent a text message from her mobile phone. He was far too engrossed in his work to notice. Her accomplice was waiting for that message.

Moments later, the phone in the adjacent room rang.

'I'll get it,' she said. The professor nodded, absent-mindedly, as he waved her away.

She went through to the next room and picked up the phone, waiting a few seconds before moving back into the main lab.

'Professor Mandelson? It's a Doctor Mackenzie from Harvard … he says it's urgent.'

Mandelson's eyebrows drew together in a puzzled frown. He obviously didn't recognize the name – hardly surprising as Lara had just made it up. He tutted and shook his head but, infuriatingly, remembered to close the file he was working on before getting up and moving next door to take the call. He did, however, leave the diary open on the desk.

She had to act fast – it wasn't going to take the professor long to figure out this was a hoax call. She took her diary from her lab coat pocket and quickly turned to the same page as that open in the diary on the table. She ringed the date: Thursday March 9th. Thumbing rapidly through the rest of the professor's diary, she found a second date ringed: Sunday July 23rd. She marked this in her own diary, too. She couldn't find any other dates highlighted in the professor's diary, so she hurriedly turned back the pages to Thursday March 9th, leaving the diary open on the desk, exactly as she had found it.

'Anything important?' enquired Lara, as Professor Mandelson re-entered the room, muttering under his breath.

'No ... just some crank pretending to be a Harvard researcher. How do these idiots manage to get hold of my direct phone number?'

'I'm sure I don't know,' said Lara, shaking her head.

Chapter 30

Natasha opened the diary and located the two ringed dates. She tore both pages out of the diary and laid them side by side on the table alongside the laptop.

Although Lara had been unable to discover the exact format in which the dates had to be entered as passwords, she had at least determined that there were two, and only two, passwords. Furthermore, she had advised that the page at which the diary had been open, at the time she copied the latest dates, probably contained the deeper level password, as the professor had definitely had an individual file open at the time he had been interrupted. Logically then, if there was a top level password protecting the entire computer, it should be the other date: Sunday July 23rd. Her heart was pounding as she made her first attempt to access the professor's computer.

She typed in 'SunJul23'.

Incorrect password - please try again

She tried 'SundayJuly23'.

Incorrect password - please try again

Third try: 'Sun23Jul'

Incorrect password - please try again

There were only a finite number of possible formats, but time was short, and she wouldn't be able to try them all. She tried 'Sunday23Jul'.

Incorrect password - please try again

Fifth try: 'Sun0723'

The screen flickered for a moment and then displayed a long list of folders. She smiled – it really hadn't been too difficult after all.

She scanned the list of folders; most of the titles meant nothing to her, many of them containing esoteric medical terms which she had never heard of but, as she continued working through the list, eventually her eyes alighted on one entitled 'Tridopamite'. That was the one they wanted – Lara had already reported that was to be the name of the new drug.

Clicking on the folder in question, she was confronted by a message –

Folder is password protected
Please enter password

She turned to the other date highlighted in the diary: Thursday March 9th. Now that she knew the format to use, this should be easy. She typed in 'Thu0309'.

A list of one hundred and twenty-seven files appeared. She plugged in a USB flash drive, highlighted all of them, and clicked on 'Copy'.

Copying 127 files – time remaining 1 min 45 seconds.

As she waited for the copy process to complete, she checked the time: 7.10 p.m. The presentations were due to start at eight: so far, things were nicely on schedule.

When the copy process was successfully completed, she sent a text message to Lara, who had made an excuse to stay late at the lab that evening.

'I have the files – delete backups now.'

In spite of Professor Mandelson's fiercely protective attitude towards his files, the IT department at the University had insisted they must be backed up on the main system there, encrypted with security measures which were rather more sophisticated than the professor's passwords. Lara, whose IT skills were considerable, had tried repeatedly, but failed, to find a way to access the contents of these files on the main system. She *had*, however, found a way to delete them when the time was right. That time was now.

Natasha waited, heart racing, for a response to her text message. Just two minutes later, it came.

'Done.'

Now it was time to press ahead with the next phase of the plan.

***

'Impossible,' said Schultz. 'There cannot be a bomb. The entire room was swept for explosives and weapons this very morning, and I've had guards on all the doors since then. No-one could possibly have got into the room and planted a bomb during that time.'

'It's not in the function room,' said Stephen. His memory was flooding back now.

'What do you mean?' demanded Schultz.

'Do you have a set of floor plans for the hotel?'

'Well, yes ... of course.'

'Get them.'

'They are on the computer system.'

'Can you bring them up on that machine?' said Stephen, indicating a large-screen computer on a desk in the corner of the room.

'Yes, but why?'

'Please, just bear with me ... we don't have much time.'

Schultz shook his head in puzzlement, but relented, following Stephen over to the machine.

'Call up the ground floor layout,' said Stephen. Schultz sat down in front of the desk and, after about twenty seconds of moving and clicking the mouse, he brought up the floor plan.

'Now ...' mused Stephen, studying the plan for a few moments before extending a forefinger towards the screen, 'is that the function room where the reception is being held?'

'Yes.'

'So,' said Stephen, pointing at a specific location within the function room, 'the top table where Professor Mandelson, Bob

Gench and the other VIPs will be for the presentations would be about … there.'

'Well, yes, I suppose so, but what is the—?'

Stephen didn't let him finish. 'OK, now can you bring up the plan for the floor above?'

Schultz sighed, raising his eyebrows but, a few moments later, the plan of the floor above was there, in a separate window on the screen.

'Can you superimpose the two?' said Stephen, urging the security chief on.

'I … er … yes, I think so.'

Schultz clicked and tapped away for a few moments until he had succeeded in overlaying one plan upon the other. 'So what exactly are you driving at?'

Stephen pointed at the guest room directly above the location of the top table in the function room. 'Which room is that – the one right there?'

Schultz squinted at the screen for a few moments before looking up and pushing his spectacles up the bridge of his nose a little. 'It's the Miami Suite … why?'

'Now check where the man claiming to be Stephen Lewis is staying.'

Schultz moved over to the other computer in the room and called up a guest list. After a few seconds he turned and looked up at Stephen; for the first time Stephen thought he could detect fear in the eyes which peered through the thick lenses of those round glasses. 'How did you know?'

'Because that's where I was supposed to plant the bomb … and where my replacement will now have done so.'

'What?' gasped Schultz.

'The bomb is in the Miami Suite. It's hidden underneath the bathtub. It's a special type of bomb, designed to direct the main force of the blast downwards. If it detonates, it will bring the ceiling down on everyone at the top table, and probably many others seated nearby.'

'That's … no, surely—'

'It could even bring down that entire side of the hotel,' added Stephen, anxious to capitalise on the security chief's obvious uncertainty.

A myriad beads of perspiration sprung forth on Schultz's forehead and all over his bald pate. His eyes darted this way and that as he grappled with the fear and indecision which had evidently gripped him.

'You have to act NOW,' insisted Stephen.

Stephen's urgent tone seemed finally to galvanise Schultz into action. 'Robert,' he snapped at the security guard who had been silently overseeing the whole exchange, 'get up to the Miami Suite right now, and check whether there is any truth in what this man is telling us.'

'Yes, sir,' he replied and, in a moment, he was gone.

***

She decided to set the bomb to explode at 8.40 p.m. That would ensure that the main targets were in place, directly below the bomb, and allow enough time for the two of them to slip away before it detonated. A few taps and swipes on the screen of her smartphone, and it was done. Now all she needed was to—

The doorbell rang.

Shit! Who the fuck could this be? She really did not need any complications at this critical stage of the mission.

'I'm really sorry to disturb you, ma'am – Hotel Security.'

She had already recovered her composure and immediately turned on the wide-eyed charm. 'Oh, goodness ... well what can I do for you ... Robert?' She figured that using his first name – read from his name badge – would help relax the situation.

'I'm afraid that I need to carry out a quick check on your room, if that's OK.'

'Right now?' she said. 'Only I'm just getting ready for the reception downstairs and I haven't quite finished doing my makeup.'

His eyes performed an involuntary scan up and down her whole body. It was quite evident that he considered her makeup – and, indeed, everything else – looked just fine.

'I'm really sorry – orders, you see,' he said.

Any attempt to refuse him entry would surely look suspicious; she smiled and stepped to one side.

'Then you'd better come in.'

'I need to check the bathroom, ma'am.'

Her heart skipped a beat, but her outward demeanour didn't falter. This development might, however, require some rapid modification to the plan.

When he moved through to the bathroom, he immediately made for the bathtub, bending down to examine the panel at its side. It was secured in place with eight screws. 'Hmm – I'm going to need to go get a screwdriver ma'am. I need to get this panel off.'

'Oh, well actually, my husband always travels with a small toolkit. He's such a Do-It-Yourself nut that he just can't bear to be without it, even when we're travelling. Let me see,' she said, bending down alongside the security guard, leaning in closely so that he could smell her perfume. 'You just need something to undo those screws?'

'Sure,' he said, 'just a regular cross-head screwdriver.'

'Oh, I'm sure he has one of those … let me go and see.'

As she stood up, she allowed her breast to brush, ever so lightly, against his arm. He gave a nervous smile.

She went back into the bedroom and opened the door to the closet, punching in the four-digit code to the safe which was inside. It took her but a few seconds to withdraw the Glock 9mm pistol and screw the silencer in place. The screwdriver which the security guard had requested lay on a shelf above the safe; she picked it up.

Moving back into the bathroom she held the gun at her side, concealing it with her body while she extended her other hand, offering the screwdriver.

'Will this do?' she said.

'Perfect,' replied the guard, smiling as he took the tool from her. He turned back towards the bath panel and set about loosening the first screw.

Sorry Robert, she mouthed, silently, as she raised the pistol and levelled it at the back of his head.

Chapter 31

The delay caused by the unexpected intervention of the security guard was a complication she could well have done without. Every second that she, and Mandelson's laptop, were out of the function room increased the probability of their plan being discovered. She just had to hope that Ethan would be able to hold the professor's attention long enough for her to return to the room and replace the laptop in its case without being noticed.

As she stepped into the lobby, she stopped for a moment to take her phone from her handbag and send a text message. She waited for around 15 seconds and then sent it again. She knew that Ethan would have his phone on silent in his pocket, but would be easily able to detect the vibration as the two messages were received. This was the signal to alert him that she was about to come back in.

The bag-check guy seemed more interested in examining Natasha's cleavage than the contents of the handbag, which received only the most cursory of inspections. 'Hey, didn't you already come in a while ago?' he said, doing his best, but failing, to disguise where he was looking.

'Well, yes I did. I'm surprised you noticed.' She leaned forward to afford him a slightly better view.

'Oh, ma'am,' he said, '... I always notice a classy lady like you.'

She tilted her head and gave a coy smile. 'Well that's so kind of you to say so.'

Having gone through the motions of inspecting her evening bag, he turned his attention to the bag containing the laptop. He clearly wasn't the sharpest tool in the box, but he wasn't completely clueless. As he unzipped the bag and withdrew the machine, his face creased in a puzzled frown; she could almost hear the cogs whirring.

'Um ...' he began, laying a hand on the laptop 'You didn't have this with you earlier, did you?'

'No … it's my husband's. He needs it for his presentation this evening, but he didn't want to be carrying it around all evening so he left it in our room. I just went back to get it for him.' She was counting on the likelihood that the men on the door would have no clue as to who was giving presentations and who was not.

'Oh … got you,' he affirmed.

He flipped up the lid of the laptop and pressed the power button.

Shit! She hadn't expected him to actually power the machine up. When he saw Mandelson's photograph on the welcome screen, the game would be well and truly up, for he looked nothing like the man she had come in with earlier – the man she called her husband. She began frantically weighing up her options. Frankly, none of them looked good.

She had already noted that both men on the door sported the tell-tale bulge, under their jackets, of a handgun in a shoulder holster, and the only weapon she had on her was a small stiletto, concealed in a slim compartment which ran along the bottom of her evening bag, masquerading as part of the hinge between the two halves of the bag. Any confrontation with two armed heavies was never going to end well. Maybe she should just abort the mission and run. Surely they wouldn't shoot an unarmed woman running away from them? But the retribution from her paymasters for the failure of the mission would be severe – probably worse than being shot dead there and then. Right now, though, making a run for it seemed the only credible option.

While the guard's attention was, for a few moments, on the laptop rather than her body, she discreetly lifted her right foot behind her, reaching down to slip off her high-heeled shoe. He didn't seem to notice – she swiftly repeated the manoeuvre with the other shoe. She tensed, ready to run.

The screen lit up, and the professor's smiling face appeared. This was the moment …

***

'Can't you see you're wasting time?' pleaded Stephen. 'You need to get everyone out of the hotel.'

'Seriously?' hissed Schultz. 'This reception has taken weeks to organise. It is being attended by many of the most brilliant minds in the medical scientific community – not to mention the wealthiest philanthropist in the entire country. Do you honestly think I am going to call the whole thing off and evacuate the hotel, on the say-so of a man who doesn't even know his own name?'

'Please,' pleaded Stephen, 'you have to believe me … I know it all sounds incredible, but it's true. Over the last couple of days we've seen innocent bystanders *murdered* by these people, just because they happened to get in the way.'

Schultz put his head back and gazed at the ceiling, his cheeks distended as he blew air through pursed lips. 'If I do this, and it turns out to be a false alarm, the reputation of the hotel will be ruined … and my career will be finished.'

'But what if you *don't* do it … and it's *not* a false alarm?' said Stephen, desperately trying to goad the man into action. 'Can you imagine how that would look?'

Perspiration was streaming down the security chief's face now. He loosened his tie and undid his top shirt button. 'I'm sorry but … a few days ago you didn't even know who you were, and now … you expect me to believe that you're a paid assassin? But that you've suddenly had a change of heart? That your wife – who now isn't your wife – is also an assassin? Put yourself in my position, Doctor … whatever your name is. You have had a severe head injury – I don't believe even you know what is fact and what is fantasy, so how do you expect me to?'

Stephen hung his head. How could he convince this man that he was telling the truth?

Carla intervened. She stepped right up to Schultz, looking him squarely in the eye. 'Look, Mr Schultz, I know that Stephen has suffered memory loss and confusion, but *I* haven't. Everything he's telling you now is true. These people have chased us, attacked us, and tried to kill us. And it's not just us – as Stephen has told you, we have seen innocent people murdered by these bastards. If you don't act now, many more will die.'

Schultz took a step backward, evidently intimidated by Carla's invasion of his personal space and the fierce determination in her eyes. 'H-how do I know you're not just saying what he wants you to say?'

'For Christ's sake,' she screamed, 'why the fuck would I do that? My *best friend* just got murdered – for no reason other than that she was in the wrong place at the wrong time.' She clenched her fists in frustration. 'Unless you do something right now … *you* will be responsible for many more deaths.'

Schultz pressed his fingers against his temples, shaking his head as he grappled with the overload of information which was assailing him. Was he about to relent?

After a few seconds, he stood up straight and panned his gaze from Stephen to Carla in turn. 'We will wait for Robert to report back.' His voice held a chilling air of finality.

Chapter 32

Natasha needn't have worried: the security guard evidently did not recognise the image on the screen as the keynote speaker – nor did he question that it was anyone other than her husband. He closed the laptop down and slipped it back into its case.

'Thank you ma'am – sorry to have troubled you, but we have to check everything really carefully, you see.'

'Oh yes, of course,' she cooed, gazing at him, smiling invitingly, even as her own racing heartbeat began to slow a little.

She was expecting him to comment on the fact that she was suddenly around four inches shorter, and was desperately trying to fabricate a plausible reason to have stepped out of her shoes at that particular moment. However, he didn't seem even to notice. Perhaps the fact that she measured five feet nine inches, even in her bare feet, helped. She breathed a sigh of relief as she slipped her feet back into her shoes, slung the laptop bag over her shoulder, and made for the entrance to the room.

It was critical, now, that Professor Mandelson did not see her enter the room. Although she had sent her partner the signal to distract him while she entered, she was concerned that the delay at the entrance while the laptop was checked might have upset the timing. She entered the room tentatively, her eyes searching for the two men.

All was well: Ethan had managed to continue to keep Mandelson in a position such that his back was towards the door. As he looked over the professor's shoulder and made eye contact with Natasha, he gave an almost-imperceptible nod. She moved swiftly towards the coat rack, stealing another glance towards where the two men were chatting, before slipping the laptop back into Professor Mandelson's bag. She hung Ethan's – now empty – bag on the rack and covered it with her wrap.

It had been a tricky few moments, but Natasha had dealt with it with typical professionalism. By the time she approached Professor Mandelson and Ethan, she was fully back in control and oozing charm once more.

'How do you girls manage to spend so long in the ladies' room?' said Ethan, his tone light and jovial.

'Oh, I got chatting with a charming lady from Seattle named Jolene. She's ...' – Natasha glanced around the room, her eyes apparently searching for the fictitious Jolene – 'oh, I can't actually see her just now.'

'Anyway,' continued Ethan, turning to Professor Mandelson, 'it'll soon be time for the speeches and presentations, so you should probably go and get ready now.'

'Yes ... I should,' he replied. 'Well, delighted to meet you Emma. Perhaps we can chat a little more after the reception.'

'I'd love that,' she purred, tilting her head a little and flashing a radiant smile. *Actually,* she thought, as she watched the unsuspecting professor head off to collect his laptop, *there won't be any 'after the reception' for you.*

'So,' said Ethan, 'everything OK? I was a bit worried when you took so long.'

'Yes – all OK now, but I had a couple of issues to deal with.'

'Issues?'

'I had a damned security guard come snooping around, wanting to look under the bathtub.'

Ethan's forehead creased in a frown. 'He must have known something.'

'Don't worry – I took care of him.'

Ethan didn't bother to ask her to elaborate. It had been an inconvenient glitch, but it had been dealt with.

'You seemed to take quite a while to come back in, even after you sent me the signal.'

'I just had a little delay while the moron on the door checked the laptop.'

'He checked it? I hope he didn't—'

'Relax – when have I ever failed to distract a man's attention when the situation demanded it?' She tilted her head and gave a wicked smile.

Her finely-tuned antennae picked up the momentary flare of desire in his eyes: even a professional like Ethan wasn't entirely immune to her charms. This was hardly germane to the task in hand, but reassuring to know nevertheless. It reinforced her conviction that, whatever kind of corner she was in, provided her adversaries were male, she could, most likely, use her well-honed feminine wiles to escape.

'Well,' he continued, 'it's just as well that you didn't take much longer – I had just about exhausted my medical expertise, and if we'd had to chat much longer, there was every chance that Mandelson would have rumbled me. Truth be told, your first "husband" knew rather more about this stuff than I do.'

'I know – he did actually train to be a doctor before realising he could earn a hell of a lot more in this line of work.' She placed a forefinger on her chin, her expression quizzical. 'Kind of ironic really – swapping a career saving lives for one being paid to take them.'

'I guess … anyway, did you get the files OK?'

'Yes. I have the memory stick here in my handbag, and the bomb is set to detonate at eight forty.'

Ethan checked his watch: 7.25 p.m. 'OK, let's just linger until everyone is asked to sit down for the presentations and slip away then. That should give us plenty of time to—'

Natasha let out a scream, her mouth flying open and her hands spread wide, as she looked down in horror at the deep red stain spreading down the front of her dress.

Chapter 33

'Don't you think your colleague should have been back by now?' said Stephen.

'Please be quiet.' replied Schultz. 'Robert will need a little time to check out your story, which—'

'We don't have the luxury of time,' interrupted Stephen. 'That bomb could go off at any moment.'

'Enough!' snapped Schultz. 'If you think I am going to call off the most important event this hotel has hosted in years – on the basis of a frankly preposterous story which you have spun – then you are very much mistaken.'

'He's telling the truth,' insisted Carla. 'I know that calling off the reception is a big deal, but being responsible for the deaths of many innocent people – including one of the country's pre-eminent scientists and its most well-loved philanthropist – is surely an even bigger one.'

'Shut up!' yelled Schultz. 'We will wait for Robert's return.' He pulled off his jacket revealing, to Stephen's alarm, a handgun in a shoulder holster. Large, damp patches stained his shirt, emanating from his underarm area. He ripped off his tie and flung it on the table.

Carla tried one more time. 'But can't you see that—'

'No! I will not hear any more of this nonsense. We will wait.'

Carla threw Stephen a look of desperation. He shook his head – it was obvious that Schultz was severely rattled but, equally, it was clear that he wouldn't be persuaded by their increasingly desperate pleas. They would have to find an alternative strategy.

They settled back into a tense and uneasy silence. Minutes passed – Stephen had no idea how many. All he knew was that they had to find some way to break this edgy stalemate. He trawled the depths of his brain, searching for a solution, but none was forthcoming.

In his peripheral vision, he detected a subtle change in Carla's demeanour. She was clearly trying to attract his attention – giving small jerks of her head and casting her eyes towards something behind him. Anxious not to alert the security chief's attention, he yawned, using the diversion to turn his head, ever so slowly, to try to ascertain what Carla was trying to show him.

At first, he couldn't figure out what it was. He turned towards her once more, narrowing his eyes in a puzzled frown and giving a slight shake of his head. She glanced at Schultz, obviously concerned that he might pick up on their non-verbal communication. She needn't have worried: he was gazing at his feet, his face grimly set, as he drummed his fingertips on the table. She switched her attention back to Stephen, widening her eyes as she nodded, once again, towards the wall behind him.

Checking, once more, that Schultz was still distracted, he followed her gaze. This time he saw it.

Maybe, just maybe, this would give them a chance.

***

The man who had bumped into Natasha, spilling red wine down the front of her dress, had evidently been taking full advantage of the free drinks on offer.

'Oh my God!' he said, swaying a little unsteadily. 'Whassappened? Did I do that?'

Natasha glared at him in disgust.

A female voice intervened; the accent sounded New York. 'Oh Christ, Charles, look what you've done to this lady's beautiful dress.'

Natasha looked up; she had noticed the woman earlier; with her angular cheekbones, finely shaped nose, and emerald green eyes, she was one of the very few women in the room who came close to rivalling Natasha's own beauty. The way her long, dark, glossy hair lay against her brilliant white evening gown made her look even more striking. She had obviously not consumed as much alcohol as her other half.

'I'm so sorry,' she continued, turning to face Natasha. 'My husband is such an idiot when he's had a few drinks.'

His hand flew to his mouth. 'Oh, yes ... really shorry. Er ... can I do anything to—'

His wife shot him a look which could have silenced a seasoned politician in full flow. 'The best thing you could do to help is go up to our room and sober up.'

'But I can't just—'

'Go on, get out of here while I try to help this poor lady.'

He slunk off.

'I'm so sorry,' she said again. 'Here, come with me to the ladies' room and let's try to sponge that stain off. It's a good thing your dress is red, and not white like mine.'

Natasha exchanged an anxious glance with Ethan who signalled, with his eyes, that she should get rid of this woman so that they could stay on mission without distraction.

'I don't think we really have time to—'

'Oh, come on,' said the woman, glancing at her watch. 'The presentations aren't due to start for another half an hour, and they'll probably start late anyway.' She emphasised the point by gently taking Natasha's arm.

She considered her options. The incident had already attracted the attention of several other nearby guests and, if she continued to resist this interfering bitch's entreaties, it was likely that the exchange would attract even more attention. And attention from other guests was the last thing they needed. It was true that they still had at least half an hour before the presentations were due to start, and quite a bit longer still before the bomb would detonate. Maybe it would be best to go with this woman to the ladies' room and just try to get rid of her as soon as possible. If the worst came to the worst, she had the stiletto concealed in her evening bag. The weapon was small, but Natasha knew exactly where to insert it to bring about near-instantaneous death.

'OK,' she said, smiling, 'let's go.'

When they reached the ladies' room, there was no-one else in there.

'Now then,' said the woman, 'I think just plain, cold water will be best.' She grabbed a fluffy, white hand towel from the stack on the shelf above the washbasins and soaked it under the cold tap. 'What's your name, by the way?'

'Emma.'

'Oh, nice name – I'm Sophie. Say, I love your accent – you English?'

'Yes.'

'Oh, really? Which part?'

'London,' she said, figuring that would avoid more pointless, timewasting chat trying to explain where some less-well-known town or city was located.

'I've always wanted to visit London,' said Sophie. 'My husband's been there, and he says there's so much to see: Big Ben, Buckingham Palace, the—'

'Yes … look, I'd love to chat, but we really should get back in there as soon as possible.'

'Oh, right … yes, of course. Now then, can you hold your arms up out of the way?' Natasha laid her bag down on the counter and spread her hands as the other woman began dabbing at the stain on her dress. 'You here for the conference in your own right, or as a "plus one"?'

'My husband's a research scientist,' was her cryptic reply.

'Mine's an embarrassment,' she laughed, dabbing away with a lot less urgency than Natasha would have liked, 'but then you know that' – Natasha gave a weak smile – 'but he's really not like that when he's sober. Actually,' she continued, 'I'm the medical researcher in our family. He's an accountant.'

For fuck's sake, thought Natasha, *I don't need your damned life history here. Just get on with it will you?* 'Great,' she said. 'Look, can we try and hurry up a bit – I really should be getting back soon.'

'Oh, sure,' she said. 'I think we've probably got it as good as we're going to now, anyway.' She held up the wet towel, much of which had now turned a deep pink colour. 'See how much we've managed to get out.'

Natasha looked down at her dress; to her eyes, now that it was soaked with water, it looked even worse than before. 'Yes,' she said, 'that looks much better. Now can we just—?'

'Let's blot up the water with some dry towels,' said the woman, grabbing a fresh one from the pile, and pressing it against the wet patch on Natasha's dress.

'Thank you – I'm sure that'll be fine now.'

'You got kids?' persisted the woman, as she continued dabbing away.

'No – no time for kids in our busy lives,' replied Natasha, her tone casual.

'Oh, too bad,' said the other woman as she continued fussing and dabbing.

OK, I don't have time for this crap, thought Natasha. She glanced towards the door; still no-one else had come in. If she was going to do it, she needed to do it now.

She turned to see where she had placed her handbag; it was within easy reach. It would be only be a matter of seconds to get the stiletto, drag this troublesome bitch into one of the cubicles and finish her off. She wouldn't want the body discovered too soon, though. She'd have to lock the cubicle from the inside and somehow get out while leaving the door locked. As was common for public toilets in the USA, there was a very large gap between the bottom of the cubicle door and the floor. Given her slender figure, she judged that she would probably be able to slither underneath. If that didn't work, she'd have to scramble over the top of the door. But given the level of fitness and strength which she always worked hard to maintain, that should not be a problem. If she pulled her dress up right around her waist – to free her legs from the constraint of the slim-fitting garment – scaling the door should not present too much difficulty.

What *was* a problem, though, was that it would be impossible to do the deed without splattering her already-ruined dress with copious amounts of blood. Her best bet, she reasoned, would be to rush back to her room, using one of the clean towels to conceal the blood, and change into a clean dress, before re-entering the reception to catch up with Ethan before they would both slip away.

Natasha shifted her stance slightly, positioning herself ready to lunge for the stiletto.

'There,' said the woman, 'I think that'll do it.' She stood back, looking Natasha up and down. 'By the time that's dried off a bit more it shouldn't notice too badly.'

Is that it? thought Natasha, allowing herself to relax a little. *If only you knew just how close you came.* 'Thanks,' she said. 'Now I really need to get back to my husband.'

The other woman's eyes continued to pass up and down Natasha's body. 'Great figure, by the way. You work out? Diet? I always struggle with my weight.'

This, Natasha thought, was hard to believe, as the other woman's figure was easily a match for her own. But now, the meddling bitch had signed her own death warrant; there was simply no time for any more of this shit.

197

'Oh, well, a bit of both, actually,' said Natasha, her tone casual. She tensed, ready to strike.

Chapter 34

The sign below the red button mounted on the wall read 'Emergency Evacuation Signal'. Alongside it was a microphone mounted in a cradle. If he could just get past Schultz, maybe he could raise the alarm himself. Before he could do that, though, there was the small matter of the handgun holstered just below the security chief's left arm.

How much time did he have left? Unfortunately, this was one aspect of the assassination plan, of which he, himself, had previously been an integral part, which just would not come to him, no matter how much he tried to trawl the fragmented memories which had returned to him. Had there even been a set timetable, or had this part been left flexible, according to the circumstances on the night? He just didn't know. The only conclusion he could reach was that he should act just as fast as humanly possible.

He needed to create a distraction of some sort …

***

'Well, I'd love to chat some more,' said the woman, 'but I think I'd better go and check on my husband before the presentations start.'

She flung the soiled towels into the waste bin and, to Natasha's surprise, leaned forward and kissed her on both cheeks. Considering that she had just been on the very brink of killing this woman, Natasha was completely disoriented by this unexpected gesture.

'Yes,' she said, struggling to keep her voice calm and level, while the adrenaline was still pumping hard and her heart racing, 'good idea.'

The woman gave a little wiggle of her fingers which passed as a wave. 'Well, maybe we can chat some more after the presentations are finished.'

No fucking chance, thought Natasha. 'Oh, that would be lovely,' she said, forcing a smile.

When the woman left, Natasha let out a huge exhalation of breath, leaning forward with both hands on the counter facing the mirror. As her heartbeat began to settle, she stared at her own image, willing herself to look calm and composed. Was she ready to re-enter the reception? Not really: her cheeks were a little flushed and the dress looked hardly any better than before that wretched woman had attacked it with wet towels

She checked her watch: 7.50 p.m. There simply wasn't time to go and change now, so she settled for just giving the dress another few dabs with a dry towel; that would have to do.

Just as she made ready to leave the room and re-enter the reception, the door opened and a rather large, silver-haired woman, probably in her late sixties, came in. As she made eye contact with Natasha she smiled but, as she glanced down and registered the state of the dress, the smile changed to a frown.

'Oh, are you alright my dear? Whatever happened to your beautiful dress?'

'Oh, just a little accident with some red wine. It'll be fine when it dries out a bit.'

'I'd offer you one of my evening gowns, but … well, it's been many years since I had a figure like yours.' She emphasised the point by running a hand over her generous stomach, giving a little giggle.

By this time, every scrap of inane conversation was costing precious seconds. She had to go now.

'No really,' said Natasha, grabbing her evening bag from where it lay on the counter, 'I'll be fine. Now, if you'll excuse me, I really must be going.' She virtually barged past the woman in her haste to get to the door.

'Well really …' she heard an indignant voice say, as the door swung shut behind her.

She paused for a few seconds as she entered the lobby, taking a deep breath before exhaling, slowly and steadily, as she endeavoured to compose herself for the final stages of the mission. She forced herself not to rush as she traversed the lobby. Instead she adopted her customary elegant and unhurried walk, searching left and right with her eyes to see whether the people around her appeared to be paying any attention to the state of her dress. She attracted a tentative smile from a tall, middle-aged man – but she was used to that kind of male attention all the time. Reassuringly, no-one seemed to be staring at the dress. Maybe it didn't really look as bad as she had thought, especially as it was now starting to dry out.

As she approached the bag-check area, the security guy smiled. 'Sorry to trouble you ma'am, but I have to take a look in your bag again …rules you see.'

'Of course, she said,' flipping the bag open. 'As you can see it's—'

Her words froze in her mouth as a dead weight sank in the pit of her stomach.

It wasn't her handbag.

***

As Stephen locked eyes with Carla, she somehow understood, without any exchange of words, exactly what he was thinking. She gave an almost-imperceptible nod of acknowledgement. After weighing up her options for a minute or two, she made her play.

'It's so hot in here,' she said, wiping her forehead with the back of her hand, 'I'm really feeling quite faint.' She looked at Schultz. 'Can't you turn the temperature down a few degrees?'

'Yeah, well we're all feeling hot, and there's nothing I can do about it: the air-con in this particular room is broken.' His tone was hardly sympathetic. 'The maintenance guys were all too busy making sure everything was ready for this damned reception to spend ten minutes fixing the air-con in one of the most important parts of the hotel.'

'Well, can I at least get a drink of water?' she pleaded.

'Cooler's over there,' he grunted, indicating the transparent, cylindrical dispenser situated in the corner of the room.

She rose to her feet and made her way over to the cooler. She wasn't sure whether her attempt to feign an unsteady walk was cutting through with Schultz. Certainly, he wasn't displaying any sign of interest in her condition. She guessed he was preoccupied with the far more pressing issues at hand.

She took a paper cup from the stack alongside the cooler and filled it from the small tap at the bottom of the machine. As she took a few sips from the cooling water she made a pretence of steadying herself with her other hand against the water reservoir. 'I really don't feel that well. I'm not sure that I can—'

'Shut up and sit back down,' hissed the security chief. 'You're going to stay right there until Robert gets back.'

She nodded, wiping her hand across her forehead once again, before moving, unsteadily, back across the room. As she drew alongside Schultz, she faltered, allowing her eyes to roll upwards in their sockets – a skill she had mastered as a little girl when she used to compete with her school friends to see who could do the most convincing fainting impression to get out of a boring Math lesson. She allowed her knees to buckle and began to pitch forward, the cup slipping from her grasp and spilling its contents everywhere.

In spite of Schultz's apparent disinterest in Carla's condition he could not help himself when he saw her about to collapse. He rushed forward and thrust his hands beneath her armpits, preventing her from crashing down to a painful impact with the hard, marble floor. Struggling with her dead weight, he staggered the few paces necessary to set her back down on the chair where she had previously been sitting. As he stood back, panting for breath, his eyes became saucers and his jaw dropped. He was staring straight down the muzzle of a gun, held in Carla's trembling hands.

His hand flew instinctively to his shoulder holster, but it was empty. His shoulders slumped in defeat.

***

The evening bag looked identical to her own but, as soon as Natasha opened it, she knew it had been switched. Inside, was a typical collection of items which would suffice for an evening event such as this: lipstick; mascara; a tiny, folding hairbrush; and a small pack of tissues. Crucially, it did not contain her mobile phone or the vital memory stick. As she ran her fingers along the hinge at the bottom of the bag, she also confirmed that the secret compartment for the concealed stiletto was not there.

'Are you OK, ma'am?' said the security guy. 'You look a bit … well, shaken.'

'I'm fine,' she said, recovering her composure, '… I just have a bit of a headache.'

Her mind was racing now. Who was that woman? Had the whole incident with the spilt wine been staged in order to engineer a situation where she could switch the bags? How did she know that the memory stick would be in that bag, and why did she want it anyway? There were a million more unanswered questions swirling in her brain. Right now, though, the most important thing was to decide what to do next; the whole plan had been shot to pieces by this unexpected development, and there was no plan B.

'Would you like me to call the hotel's nurse?' said the security guard, his face a picture of concern.

'No,' she replied, closing the bag – into which the security guard had barely glanced – 'I'll be fine, thank you.'

'Really ma'am it's no trouble. I wouldn't want you to—'

But she was already hurrying through to the function room.

Once inside the room she immediately spotted Ethan, and made her way over to him, forcing herself not to rush, or do anything to draw undue attention to herself.

'At last,' he said. 'What the fuck have you been doing all this time? We need to get out of here as soon as—'

'Shut up and listen! We have a big problem ...'

Chapter 35

The Colombian drug cartels were not the only ones who had an interest in ensuring Professor Mandelson's discovery never saw the light of day. Mexico, too, had a thriving drug-trafficking industry, and the cartels there also stood to lose a great deal if a miracle cure for cocaine addiction ever became widely available. The largest of the Mexican cartels had, via its network of spies, learned of the plan by its Colombian rivals to steal Professor Mandelson's research and then kill him, his billionaire sponsor, and several others associated with the project. If they were to succeed in getting control of the new addiction cure, they would be able to dominate the whole Central and South American illegal drugs trade. The Mexicans could not afford to let that happen; *they* needed to be the ones to get that research data.

They were, however, running from behind. The Colombians had conceived a painstaking and elaborate plan, which they had initiated well over a year earlier. They had hired a crack English assassination team to inveigle its way into the professor's confidence before stealing his research and killing all those involved in its creation. There was no way, starting from scratch, that they could beat the Colombians to the punch. But they could perhaps piggyback on their plan ...

***

Madison Taylor and Brett Freeman had grown up together in the Bronx. From the way that they always hung out together, most people assumed they were boyfriend and girlfriend. The truth, however, was that they were just two bright, ambitious kids, born in the wrong part of town, who shared a common desire to actually make something of themselves.

It was a pretty rough neighbourhood, with few opportunities for kids like them to get on. As they reached their mid-teens, increasingly, they saw their friends turn to crime as the only way to make any serious money and, equally importantly, win some respect from their peers.

Brett and Madison started down the same path, initially with muggings. They usually targeted men – Madison was a strikingly-attractive girl and had no trouble attracting the attention of male passers-by. She would lure them into a doorway or the entrance to an alley, where Brett would be waiting. To begin with, Brett would threaten his victims with a kitchen knife. However, after about a dozen successful muggings – during which time he'd never had to make good on his threat to actually use the knife – he'd made enough money to buy a Smith and Wesson 9mm pistol on the black market. From that point onward, he didn't bother with the knife, preferring instead to see the look on his victims' faces as they stared down the muzzle of the gun.

All continued to go well, until one day they encountered the guy who decided to fight back. When he tried to wrench the gun from Brett's hand, he got a bullet through his eye for his trouble. For that murder, Brett and Madison earned a cheap digital watch, a credit card that they couldn't use, an ancient pay-as-you-go cell phone, and fifty-four dollars in cash. The thing was, though, neither of them felt a great deal of remorse for their victim – just disappointment that the proceeds of the mugging had been so meagre. Once they realised just how easy it was to kill, however, they sought not to step back from this path, but merely to find a way to make it more profitable.

Their first contract killing earned them two thousand dollars – more than they would usually make from a dozen muggings. From that point onward, they never looked back. As the years went by, they won more and more lucrative contracts, gradually honing their craft until they became one of the most sought-after hit teams in the entire USA. If you wanted a politician, a top businessman, or a crime boss disposed of, Madison Taylor and Brett Freeman were the assassination team that you approached first. The fact that, to date, they had never, ever, failed to fulfil the objective of a contract only served to enhance their reputation.

And now they had landed their most lucrative contract ever: it was worth twenty million dollars. It didn't matter that the bomb which would kill Professor Mandelson, Bob Gench, and many more wasn't actually going to be planted by them; as long as they procured the research data and made sure that its creators and sponsors ended up dead, then their Mexican paymasters would be happy.

For this contract, they had been sharing a room in the Palm Grove Hotel for almost two weeks as they prepared their plan. The room had twin beds: in spite of their long association, Madison's striking beauty, and Brett's rugged good looks, they weren't actually sleeping together. Their relationship was purely professional. In fact, neither of them had had any long-term sexual or romantic relationships in their entire lives; in their line of work, secrecy was important, and they couldn't afford to let anyone else into their lives for fear of compromising that secrecy. So, their physical needs were catered for only by occasional one-night stands with complete strangers and if, by chance, one of their fleeting acquaintances should learn anything which they shouldn't, then that was easily dealt with. It had only happened once so far, when a guy who Madison had picked up for the night turned out to be an off-duty cop who became a little too curious. His death was an unpaid job, of course, but they considered it to be a worthwhile investment to protect the future of their enterprise.

And now, that bumper payoff was almost within touching distance.

***

'So,' said Madison, as they entered their hotel room, 'Blondie ain't quite so smart as she thought she was. Fell for the spilt-wine routine just like a first-time amateur.'

'Yeah, well let's make sure we've got that memory stick before we start gloating too much.'

He went to take the handbag from her, but she shrugged him away. 'Not so fast – she may not be so very smart, but she could have rigged the bag. Let me check it first.'

They had been watching the English hit team closely for over a week; Madison had already seen the blonde woman carrying her distinctive Gucci evening bag at the party the previous Tuesday. She had no trouble, the following day, finding an identical bag in the upmarket Bal Harbour shopping mall for the purposes of the planned bag switch.

She inspected the other evening bag carefully, checking, both visually and by feel, for any clue that it had been rigged. When she ran her fingers along the hinge line at the bottom of the bag, something didn't feel right: there was a small protrusion around one third of the way along. As she turned the bag upside down to check it, she realised it was a latch of some kind. What was it? If the bag was booby trapped, she would have expected the trap to be triggered by opening it in the normal way – not by something on the hinge at the bottom. No, this surely had to be something different. Very carefully, she slid the latch back, which released a portion of the hinge from the rest. Taking great care, she slid it to one side.

'What is it?' said Brett, his voice tense.

'Hmm, it seems that Blondie came prepared for trouble,' said Madison. She withdrew the stiletto from its hidden compartment and held it aloft.

'Ha!' said Brett. 'That little thing's barely more than a toy.'

'Not if you know how to use it,' she retorted, twirling the weapon between her fingertips, watching the blade glint in the light cast by the table lamp on the desk, 'and I'm willing to bet that she does.'

'Anyway,' said her partner, 'come on – we're wasting time here.'

After a few more moments spent carefully inspecting the bag, she was satisfied that there was no booby trap. She released the clasp, carefully opened the bag, and tipped its contents onto the bed: a cell phone, a small hairbrush, a hotel key card, and various cosmetics.

A worried frown began to grow on Brett's face. 'Where's the fucking memory stick?' he muttered.

'Just wait,' she said, trying to sound far more confident than she actually felt, 'it'll be in here somewhere.'

Her heart was racing as she continued to pick through the various items on the bed. Perhaps the English bitch had given the memory stick to her partner or hidden it somewhere, before the bags had been switched. There was, however, one last chance: as the bag was identical to her own – apart from the hidden compartment containing the stiletto – she knew that there should be a small zipped pocket inside. She probed the lining with her fingers and felt that there was a small, hard, rectangular object inside the pocket; her heart jumped. Unzipping the pocket and retrieving the object inside brought a wave of relief.

'You see?' she said, as she showed him the memory stick, 'I told you it'd be there.'

'Good,' said Brett, puffing out his cheeks as he exhaled a sigh of relief. 'Now we've got what we came for, we need to get the hell out of here.'

'Not until we make sure this is the right one: it could be a decoy.'

He nodded, flipping up the lid of the laptop on the desk, before taking the flash drive from Madison and inserting it in one of the USB sockets. As he pressed the power button and waited for the machine to wake up, the two of them exchanged an anxious glance. This really *had* to be the genuine article, or they were in deep trouble.

Ten minutes later, however, they had trawled through the list of file headings, and they were both satisfied that they did indeed have Professor Mandelson's research data.

'OK,' said Madison, shooting Brett a satisfied smile, 'now let's get the hell out of here.'

'Sure,' said Brett. 'We need to be well clear of the hotel by the time that bomb blows.'

***

Back in the function room, Natasha had told Ethan about the bag switch.

'Fuck!' he muttered, 'So what do we do now?'

'We have to get that memory stick back … and until we do, we can't let that bomb go off.'

He nodded. 'OK, send the signal to halt the countdown.'

She spread her hands helplessly. 'I can't.'

'What? Why not?'

'Because my phone is in my handbag – I don't have it.'

'Shit!' he hissed. 'And my phone doesn't have the app to connect to the bomb.'

'We'll have to turn it off manually. You know how to do that, right?'

'Well, yes … but we'll have to get the side cover of the bathtub off to access the control panel.'

'Then let's not waste any time. My key card was in my bag; have you got the other one?'

He thrust his hand into his jacket pocket, feeling for the card. 'Yes.'

'Then let's get back to the room right now. You can take care of the bomb while I grab the Glock and go after that bitch. I'll make her wish she never tried to cross me.'

'OK, how will I know when you've got the memory stick back?'

'I'll get my phone back – or take hers – and call you.'

He nodded. 'We can still do this,' he said, locking eyes with her.

Chapter 36

When they returned to their hotel room, Natasha wasted no time in retrieving the Glock from the safe and setting off after the woman in the white dress. Now, Ethan needed to cancel the countdown of the bomb; he stepped through into the bathroom.

Although he was a seasoned killer, the sight which met his eyes nevertheless took him aback for a moment. The pool of blood emanating from the head of the hapless security guard had now spread to cover about a quarter of the entire area of the bathroom floor. Nevertheless, he quickly recovered his composure and focused on the task in hand. It would be impossible, however, to get past the body and remove the bath panel without getting covered in blood. Things had now gone much too far now, though, to worry about getting a bit dirty.

Ethan shrugged off his jacket and laid it on the padded stool in the corner of the room. He returned to the bathtub and bent down, placing one knee on the floor – doing his best to avoid the blood – while bracing his other foot against the side of the bathtub. He hooked both arms over the security guard's dead body and tried to roll it over and away from the bathtub. But the body was heavy; it wouldn't budge.

Taking a deep breath, he tried again, pulling harder this time; it still didn't roll over, but it did slide an inch or two towards him. It was the blood: it formed a layer of lubricant between the body and the floor. With this realisation, he shifted position so as to pull directly towards the main part of the pool of blood. It was as if someone had untied an invisible tether; now the body slid towards him with relative ease, accompanied by a liquid squelching sound, overlaid with a metallic screech as the guard's handcuffs, secured to his belt, scraped against the floor tiles After a couple more determined pulls, the body was far enough from the bathtub to allow unfettered access to the panel at its side.

He checked his watch 8.07 p.m. He had thirty-three minutes before the bomb was due to detonate. He eyed the eight cross-head screws which secured the panel – it shouldn't take more than five or six minutes to remove those, and then it was simply a case of removing the panel and hitting the manual override button to cancel the countdown. He still had plenty of time.

He took several long, slow breaths to compose himself and then made his way to the closet in the bedroom. As he opened the door and surveyed its contents, his heart skipped a beat; the screwdriver wasn't there.

OK, he told himself, *stay calm – it can't be far away.*

He checked every shelf in the closet, but it wasn't there. *Natasha must have moved it.* He checked the drawers in both bedside cabinets and the desk drawer. No luck.

Where the fuck can it be? He couldn't even call Natasha to find out; her mobile phone had been taken, along with the memory stick and everything else in her bag.

How could he have known that the metallic scraping sound he had heard while moving the body was not due solely to the handcuffs, but also the screwdriver, which was trapped between the dead body and the floor?

What now? He was losing precious time and needed to do something right now.

Stay calm. You know you only fastened the screws loosely, just in case they needed to be removed again. Maybe there's some other implement around here which would get them out.

He checked the minibar and found a corkscrew. Rushing back into the bathroom, he tried to hook the point of the implement into one of the corners of a screw head and persuade it to turn. It was useless; he flung the corkscrew down in frustration.

Glancing desperately around the room, his eyes alighted on a small pair of nail scissors on the counter, alongside one of the washbasins. He jumped up and grabbed the scissors. As he examined them, he realised that if he set the blades almost, but not completely closed he could fashion a tool with two sharp points set just a few millimetres apart. If he could get those pointed tips to engage with opposing corners of the cross shaped recess in the screw head, maybe – just maybe – he could get sufficient purchase to turn the screw.

With trembling fingers, he tried it on the first of the screws. Sure enough, he was able to exert some turning force, but although the screws had not been fully tightened, this first one, at least, was refusing to budge. As he tentatively applied more and more force, the blades of the scissors began to flex and move apart from each other. He feared the makeshift tool might break at the pivot point of the blades.

Holding his breath, he applied just a little more force and … the screw turned a little. Suddenly it was easy; once the initial resistance had been overcome, the screw turned freely. A couple more turns raised the screw head sufficiently for Ethan to grip it with his fingers and spin it all the way out. One down – seven to go. He checked his watch: 8.14 p.m. It was going to be tight, but now that he had mastered the technique he figured he could get the rest of the screws out in time to cancel the countdown.

The second screw took him about two minutes to remove and the third less than a minute. He began to breathe a little more easily. The fourth, however, proved to be more problematic: it was tighter than the others. After struggling for several minutes to loosen it, he applied just that little bit too much force. The blades of the scissors separated and fell to the floor, with a tinkling chime of metal against ceramic tiles.

Ethan gazed in dismay at the two parts of the now-useless tool. He checked his watch: 8.21 p.m. With just nineteen minutes left, he needed to make a decision: if he was going to make a run for it, he needed to go now. If he lingered much longer he would be absolutely committed to defusing the bomb.

He made that commitment. He had never yet failed in any assignment he had taken on, and he had an unshakeable faith that, when the chips were down, he could pull through.

The panel was made of white, moulded plastic. It didn't look all that substantial. With three of the screws removed, he was able to hook his fingers behind a corner of the panel. Bracing both feet against the side of the bathtub he pulled hard, and was rewarded with a loud cracking sound as the panel fractured. With the release of tension, he fell backwards, his backside skidding across the pool of blood.

He scrambled to his feet and rushed back to inspect the results of his efforts: a jagged section, representing about one third of the total panel had broken away. Unfortunately, it was at the opposite end of the bathtub to where the bomb was situated. He grasped the sharp edge of the remaining portion of the panel and pulled with all his might. This time, however, it refused to yield; the five intact screws held it firmly in position. He thumped the top of the bathtub with a balled fist, letting out a roar of frustration.

But wait – although he couldn't actually *see* the bomb properly through the hole he had made, he might be able to get his hand inside and hit the override switch. He lay down on his side, now completely oblivious to the amount of blood which smothered his clothes. Reaching though the jagged hole, he grasped at thin air as he sought, in vain, to find the bomb. Pushing himself further forward, he felt the sharp edge of the broken bath panel pressing painfully against the side of his neck. He forced himself even further forward, the broken plastic edge now cutting into his skin. He gritted his teeth against the pain as the warm trickle of blood slid down his neck.

Stretching to the absolute limit of his reach, he finally found it: the control panel of the bomb.

At that precise moment, the air was rent by the harsh, two-tone wail of a siren. The sudden shock made him lose his bearings and his fingers lost contact with the control panel. After around ten seconds, the sound of the siren was overlaid with the amplified and distorted tones of a voice announcement; the accent was English.

'Attention – this is an emergency evacuation announcement. Would all guests and members of staff make their way immediately to the nearest exit and vacate the hotel. This is not a drill. I repeat – this is not a drill. You must evacuate the hotel immediately.'

'Shit!' he hissed, out loud, 'What the fuck do I do now?'

It took him but a matter of seconds to decide that now, more than ever, he *had* to defuse the bomb. If it detonated after the targets had evacuated the room, it would completely fail in its objective. Furthermore, even if Natasha succeeded in retrieving the memory stick, Mandelson and Gench would now have to be eliminated by other means. If the bomb went off while hundreds of people were evacuating the hotel, probably in a state of panic, their chances of locating and eliminating their targets would be minimal at best.

He groped desperately under the bathtub, adrenaline endowing him with the strength to push through the pain caused by the sharp plastic edge cutting into his flesh. Finally, he located the control panel once more. With trembling fingers, he felt along the row of toggle switches. The manual kill switch was third from the left; he felt his way along the row of switches until he located it. Taking a deep breath, he flipped the switch. He was rewarded by an electronic beep, indicating that the command had been successfully received.

Letting out a long, loud exhalation of breath, he extricated himself from the bathtub and staggered to his feet, sitting down on the lid of the toilet while he took a few moments to steady his ragged breathing.

OK, what next? He stood up and regarded his reflection in the mirrored door of the cabinet located above the washbasin. His white shirt was badly bloodstained, and more blood was flowing freely from the wound inflicted by the jagged edge of the bath panel. However, the mission was still alive – albeit severely compromised. If he was to avoid drawing undue attention to himself as he re-joined Natasha and tried to retrieve the situation, he would need to clean himself up.

He opened the mirrored door of the cabinet and was gratified to find a small first-aid kit inside. He cleaned the wound with some gauze and antiseptic spray, before sealing it with two wound-closure strips and finally applying a large Band-Aid. Now all he needed was a change of clothes and he would look presentable enough to take up the hunt for these bastards who had outwitted them.

Fortunately, he and Natasha had not packed away all their clothes. They had planned to slip away from the reception as swiftly and unobtrusively as possible; having to retrieve suitcases and tow them through the main lobby would have been an unnecessary impediment to that plan. Thanks to that decision, he knew there were two clean, white shirts and a spare suit hanging in the closet.

Ripping off his ruined shirt, he dampened a towel and wiped away the remaining streaks of blood from his shoulder and chest, before hurrying over to the closet to grab a clean shirt.

Returning to the bathroom he put on the shirt, fastened his tie and donned the spare suit. Inspecting the results of his efforts in the mirror, he decided he was ready to re-join the fray.

Suddenly, an unexpected sound intruded. *Beep … Beep, Beep … Beep … Beep, Beep … Beep … Beep, Beep …Beep …*

That was the signal that the bomb would detonate in precisely two minutes' time. A hollow dread eviscerated him from inside *I must have flipped the wrong fucking switch!*

Chapter 37

Natasha was fuelled by an all-consuming rage. She and Ethan were now on the brink of losing out on a huge payoff – far more than either of them had ever before earned for a single contract, and probably enough to retire on. What hurt even more, though, was the fact that she had been outsmarted by the woman in the white dress. Naturally she wanted to retrieve the memory stick and rescue the mission, but she wanted, even more, to watch that bitch die. Now it was intensely personal.

But how should she go about finding her? There was no possibility to check inside the main function room: she would never be able to get past the bag-check area with the gun she was now carrying. In any case, it was very unlikely that this woman, and her male accomplice, would have re-entered the function room once they had procured the vital research data. She tried to put herself in the other woman's Louboutins. *What would I have done?*

If this woman was a professional – and Natasha was convinced that she was – then she probably wouldn't just assume that she had the correct memory stick; she would most likely want to check its contents. The chances were that she and her partner would have gone back to their hotel room – assuming that they were, indeed, staying in the hotel – and plugged the flash drive into a computer to make sure that they had the right one. In that case, they would probably not yet have left the hotel. Now, when they *did* leave, which exit would they use? If they were to use an emergency exit, they would probably trigger an alarm somewhere. No, she reasoned, it was more likely they would leave by the main entrance. If Natasha positioned herself so as to be able to observe everyone entering or leaving by the main entrance she stood a reasonable chance of spotting them. If she followed them outside, she could choose the best time and place to kill them both and retrieve the flash drive without attracting the attention of passers-by. It was the best plan she could come up with, under the circumstances.

Concealing the Glock beneath her wrap, she made her way across the hotel lobby, searching for a suitable place to watch and wait. There were two large, circular pillars which flanked the main entrance and, either side of these, some secluded seating areas. She chose the one which gave the clearest view of both the main entrance and the elevators at the far side of the lobby. She sat down to wait, the Glock nestled in her lap, under her wrap, and a newspaper alongside her, with which she could conceal her face if necessary.

She had been sitting for barely a minute when the subdued hubbub in the lobby was pierced by the harsh tones of the alarm siren followed, some seconds later by the voice warning to evacuate the hotel. The voice, in spite of the distorted tone imposed upon it by the P.A. system, sounded strangely familiar.

What the ...? How on earth did they find out about the bomb – which, by now, would have been defused anyway?

But there was no time to ponder this question – the priority now was to decide what to do in the light of this unexpected development. If Professor Mandelson and Bob Gench left the hotel unharmed, she would have to deal with them as well as the rival hit team. The odds of success on all fronts were now looking slim indeed.

Before long, there would be hordes of people streaming towards the main entrance, making the tracking of individual targets much more difficult. Furthermore, all the emergency exits would now also be in use. The main entrance was probably still the most direct route out of the hotel for people exiting the function room, but there was no telling which exit the rival assassination team might now use. The whole situation was rapidly slipping from her grasp.

As the first wave of guests began to hurry towards the main entrance, it became increasingly difficult to see what was happening at the entrance to the function room. Natasha abandoned all efforts at stealth or concealment and rose to her feet, anxiously scanning the approaching throng for any sign of the professor, or the bitch who had stolen the memory stick.

Finally, Natasha spotted her: the woman in the white dress, and her partner; they had just emerged from a staircase at the far side of the lobby. They had obviously intended to leave by the main entrance, but appeared to be having second thoughts when they saw the crush building up there as more as more people tried to get through. They were conducting some sort of quick-fire conversation, heads turning this way and that, apparently seeking an alternative route. Then Natasha spotted an anxious-looking Professor Mandelson amongst the crowd spilling from the function room. He was clutching his laptop to his chest as if it were a baby.

The situation was becoming almost impossible. It was now necessary to kill the other two assassins, retrieve the memory stick, kill Mandelson, and take or destroy his laptop. If the targets all decided to choose different routes then any last hope of salvaging the mission would be dashed.

Her only hope was that Ethan, having dealt with the bomb, would now show up so that they could divide their resources according to what the multiple targets decided to do.

Where is he for Christ's sake? Surely he's dealt with the bomb by now?

***

Ethan was out of time: even if he decided to abandon the mission and make a run for it, it was doubtful that he'd be able to get far enough away by the time the bomb detonated.

Now oblivious to any concerns about his appearance, he dived to the floor, slipping and sliding in the pool of blood as he thrust his hand back into the jagged gap in the bath panel. He pushed himself forward, groping for the bomb, but now he was disoriented; he had lost his bearings completely, and could not locate the control panel. Panic was now starting to take hold, and his efforts to locate the panel became more and more desperate. But Ethan was a professional: he knew the signs of panic setting in, and he was trained in techniques to control it.

He stopped groping for the bomb and took several long, slow breaths. *OK*, he told himself, *concentrate. Now how, exactly, were you lying? Where, exactly, did you have your arm? Just relax and do what you did before.* He closed his eyes, recreating, in his mind, the precise position he had adopted when he had previously located the control panel.

As he sought to suppress his rising panic and concentrate on recalling exactly how to locate the control panel, he felt the jagged edge of the bath panel once again pressing painfully against the wound he had just treated. He was sure he was reaching for the same place as before, but still his trembling fingers could not find the switches. As he pushed forward to the absolute limit of his reach, he recognised that the pain inflicted by the sharp edge of the broken bath panel was not as agonising as he would have expected. Why?

And then it came to him: it was because of the jacket he was now wearing. The collar was riding up, providing additional padding and protection to the wound. In a flash, though, he realised that this was also why he could not locate the switches; the bulk of the jacket he was now wearing was preventing him from pushing forward that last vital inch.

Letting out a roar of frustration, he withdrew his arm, jumped to his feet, and ripped off the jacket, losing precious seconds in the process. Launching himself back into the gap, he tried once more to find the override switches. *Concentrate*, he told himself, desperately trying to control his ragged breathing, *you can do this.*

He gritted his teeth, pushing through the pain caused as the jagged edge of the broken bath panel cut right through the Band-Aid and sliced into his flesh. Finally, his fingers finally found the switch panel. Taking a deep breath to try to steady his nerves, he felt carefully along the row of switches. One … two … three … They were all in the 'up' position. Feeling for the fourth switch he found it was in the 'down' position. That was the switch which initiated a fixed ten-minute countdown, overriding any previously set time. As he had guessed when he heard that dreaded two-minute warning, he had inadvertently flipped the wrong switch. He moved his hand a little to the left, feeling for the third switch: the one he *should* have flipped before. His fingers found the switch, but—

He was a few hundredths of a second too late. The very last things that Ethan Peterson experienced on this Earth were a blinding white light and a pulverising, percussive blast.

Chapter 38

When the bomb detonated, the last few guests who were leaving the function room were lifted bodily from their feet by the blast, flung forward into the lobby amid a storm of debris. The hot pressure wave hit Natasha like a sledgehammer, almost knocking her from her feet.

Even in the shock of the moment she realised that Ethan was probably dead. She wasted no time on regret or mourning; her main concern was that it was solely down to her now to complete the mission – under the most challenging of circumstances.

She looked towards what was left of the function room. The effects of the blast had been even more devastating than they had planned. Not only had the ceiling above the top table come down, but there was now an enormous hole in the wall dividing the room from the main lobby, through which she could see that practically the entire ceiling had collapsed. Anyone still in that function room would surely now be dead.

But Mandelson was not in there; she could see him standing, dazed and confused, in the centre of the lobby. His previously-dark suit was now completely covered in whitish-grey dust. He continued to hug his laptop to his chest as he sought a means of escape, glancing desperately in all directions. He had evidently decided against joining the panicked scrum at the main entrance and set off across the lobby, making for a corridor on the far side. Now she had a dilemma: should she go after the professor or the other two?

It turned out to be a decision which was not necessary, because the rival team had spotted Mandelson too. As he hurried towards the corridor opposite, they followed him. Clearly, they too had concluded that, as Mandelson had escaped the bomb, they would need to eliminate him and seize or destroy his laptop. In a way, that perhaps made things a little less difficult: assuming they still had the memory stick with them, she could wait until they killed the professor and choose that moment to surprise them, kill them both, and retrieve the memory stick. Maybe she could still pull this off, after all.

Natasha flipped the safety catch of the Glock off, concealed it beneath her wrap, and set off after them. But the rapidly growing throng of humanity streaming towards the main entrance barred her way. Trying to push through it would be impossible. It was clear that she couldn't go through the crowd surging towards her; she would have to go around it. Slipping her heels off, she made her way to the very edge of the lobby, squeezing herself tight against the wall and slowly, painfully edging her way around the bustling throng. By the time she made it to the other side of the lobby, though, her targets were long gone.

She rushed into the corridor she had seen them heading for, following the illuminated, green emergency exit signs; there was nobody to be seen in the corridor. Casting aside her wrap, she bent down, grasping the hem of her dress and ripping it apart, clean up to her thigh. With the constraint of the slim skirt removed, she broke into a full sprint, the Glock in her right hand, ready for action. Natasha was extremely fit, and was now covering ground very quickly indeed. Still following the signs, she rounded a right-hand corner – and there she saw them. Mandelson was about twenty yards from the emergency exit and the other two perhaps ten yards behind him.

She skidded to a halt, diving onto a doorway to ensure that she would not be seen. Fighting to control her ragged breathing, she peeped around the edge of the doorway, checking once again that the safety catch was off.

'Professor Mandelson,' called out the woman in the white dress.

Mandelson spun round, his eyes filled with fear and confusion. 'Who are you? What do you want?'

'I need you to give me your laptop.'

'My laptop? No … you don't understand … it's very important.'

'I believe it's *you* who doesn't understand.' She took several paces towards him, closely followed by her partner. 'You see, this isn't a polite request.'

'No,' he said, clutching the laptop to his chest.

She reached into her handbag. It was not the Gucci evening bag she had stolen from Natasha; this one was a little larger, all white, and devoid of any brand markings. She withdrew a tiny handgun. It looked like a double-barrelled Derringer: not an effective weapon where any significant distance was involved but capable of killing when used at close range. In any event, it was clearly sufficient to terrify the professor, whose eyes bulged wildly as he shook his head violently from side to side.

'Now, then,' she said, her voice low and threatening, '... the laptop.' Their faces were now barely four or five feet apart as her partner stepped past her holding out his hands to receive the machine. She kept the miniature pistol trained firmly on the professor.

'Please,' pleaded Mandelson, 'don't shoot ... I have two children who—'

'Just give it to my friend here, and no-one will get hurt.'

He handed over the machine; the man took it and quickly stepped back a few paces.

'Thank you,' she said. 'Very wise.'

'B-but why ...?' stammered Professor Mandelson.

'Oh, it's a long story ... one which I really don't have time to share right now.'

She stepped forward, levelling the pistol and shooting him in the heart, from a range of just two feet.

He didn't utter a sound as he clutched at his chest before slumping to the ground.

Chapter 39

'OK,' said the assassin's partner, holding out the laptop, 'what shall we do with this?'

'Put it on the ground,' she said.

He laid the machine down.

'Step back.' She pumped a shot through the part of the machine where the hard drive would be located.

With both rounds now fired, the woman set about reloading the diminutive weapon.

This was the perfect time to strike. Natasha stepped out of the doorway, firing a shot over their heads and calling out, 'Hands on heads – NOW!' The two of them froze, slowly raising their hands. 'Now turn around ... very slowly.'

As they turned to face her, Natasha could detect no emotion in either of their faces – she was definitely dealing with a professional hit team here.

'You,' she said, jerking the gun towards the man, 'take off your jacket ... *slowly*.' He did so; there was no shoulder holster. 'Now turn right around and then back to face me again.' There was no weapon tucked into his waistband. 'Let me see your ankles.' He reached down and hoisted up his trouser legs sufficiently to show that there was no ankle holster concealing a small firearm.

She turned her attention to the woman. 'Put the handbag on the floor.' The woman bent down, slowly, and laid the bag down. 'Now pull your dress right up to your waist ... I want to see your thighs.'

'Really, sweetie ... I'd hardly have had you down as a girl who swings both ways.'

A surge of anger rose within Natasha. She clenched the gun a little tighter and lowered it to point at the woman's right leg. 'Just do it, or I'll take your fucking kneecap.' She resolved to make this bitch suffer once she had retrieved the memory stick.

The woman shrugged, reaching down to grasp the hem of her dress, lifting it until her stocking tops, garter belt, and tiny white panties were on full display. As a woman who worked very hard herself to maintain a perfect figure, Natasha could not help but be impressed by this woman's slim, shapely legs and slender figure. They wouldn't help her now, though.

There was no sign of any weapon. 'OK, you can drop the skirt now.'

'You don't want a longer look, darling?' goaded the woman, striking a pose, with hips thrust to one side. Infuriating, but you had to admire her guts when staring death in the face.

Natasha did not react – the bitch would pay for her insolence soon enough.

'OK, which of you has the memory stick?' said Natasha, pointing the gun at each of them in turn.

'Neither of us,' retorted the man. 'We passed it to the third member of our team, and he's already gone.'

Natasha didn't believe it for one moment. 'Nice try, but not good enough.' She raised the Glock, grasping it in both hands and aiming carefully before squeezing the trigger; the bullet grazed the man's cheek before ripping through his left ear, evoking from him a blood-curdling scream. 'Now, before I take the other one, are you going to tell me where it is?' She emphasised the threat by moving the gun to point at his right ear.

'No, don't,' he screamed, holding out both hands in a defensive gesture. 'She has it!'

Natasha smiled as she levelled the gun at the woman in white, who didn't look anywhere near as arrogantly smug now. 'So, where is it?'

She stared back sullenly, but all the bravado had gone; now Natasha could see the cold glint of fear in her eyes.

'OK,' said Natasha, 'you want to do this the hard way? That's just fine by me. Now then … which knee would you like to lose first?' She underlined her intent by lowering the gun and slowly playing it back and forth to cover both of the woman's knees.

That was enough to do it.

'OK, back off … it's here,' she said, slowly lowering one hand to point at her own cleavage.

'Show me.'

No smartass comments this time. She reached down into her cleavage and withdrew the memory stick from a small compartment disguised as a front fastening of her deep-plunge bra. She held the tiny flash drive aloft, offering it to Natasha. Meanwhile, her partner was whimpering like a baby, his hand clamped to the mutilated spot where his ear had been.

'Put it down there … next to the handbag.' The woman knelt down and laid the memory stick on the floor. 'Now step back … both of you.'

As the two of them moved back a couple of paces, Natasha stepped forward, slowly bending down, while all the time keeping her eyes – and the gun – trained on her opponents.

But there had to come a point where she momentarily looked down to pick up the memory stick, and that was the precise moment that the man had been waiting for. He stepped forward, with lightning speed, and launched a vicious, high kick which snapped the ulna bone in her forearm and sent the gun spinning from her hand.

The pain was excruciating, and she was ill-prepared to counter his next move. He grabbed her good hand and spun her around, pinning both hands behind her back and pushing his knee, painfully, into the small of her back. Natasha struggled fiercely, but he was too strong, and the pain from her broken arm was rapidly sapping her strength.

'Grab the gun and finish her off,' he growled. 'Just don't fucking well shoot me in the process.'

But the woman did not pick up the gun; instead she picked up the memory stick, slipping it into her handbag, which she then slung over her shoulder.

'Get on with it!' yelled the man. 'This bitch is livelier than a fucking eel.'

The woman reached into her bag and withdrew a small stiletto – *Natasha's* stiletto. She held it up in front of Natasha's eyes, with one finger resting lightly on the needle-sharp point while slowly twirling it with the other.

'Shame to do this to such a pretty thing,' she crooned, as she brought the tip of the weapon up under Natasha's chin, slowly increasing the pressure she applied.

Natasha felt the sharp point puncture the skin on her neck, but it was still the pain from her shattered arm which overwhelmed her senses. The woman's eyes – just inches from Natasha's – gleamed with a sadistic fervour, as she slowly drove the weapon deeper into Natasha's neck before angling it upwards until it pointed almost vertically. Bit by bit, she began to force it upwards, alongside Natasha's spinal column. Now the pain was utterly agonising.

By the time the tip of the stiletto penetrated the base of Natasha's brain, she had already lost consciousness.

***

Stephen was sprinting along the corridor at full tilt. He had no idea who these two people struggling with Emma were – or now, even who Emma really was – but when he saw the big man holding her, at the mercy of the woman with the knife, he was consumed with a primeval desire to save her. His rational mind told him she was a cold-blooded murderer, but on some subconscious level, she was still his beautiful wife – the love of his life. He propelled himself forward with every ounce of strength he could muster.

He was too late. As he sprinted forward, he saw Emma's head slump forward as the other woman withdrew the weapon, releasing a copious flow of blood which streamed down Emma's neck and the front of her dress.

'Nooo!' he screamed.

At the sound of Stephen's anguished cry, the man let go of Emma and allowed her lifeless body to fall to the ground. He turned to face Stephen, tensing in what looked like a well-practiced martial arts stance.

Stephen launched himself forward, surprising himself at the ease with which he evaded the sharp, jabbing punch which his opponent aimed at his neck. Now, in the heat of combat, all the forgotten skills of his former trade came right back to him. He came around behind the man, encircling his neck in a head lock. He was about to perform the lethal wrench which would snap the man's neck when he saw, out of the corner of his eye, the woman in the white dress – now streaked with blood – advancing with the stiletto thrust forward. He swung around so as to place the man's body between himself and the menacing tip of the weapon. The woman hesitated, feinting this way and that as she sought to find a way past her partner's body. But Stephen matched her every move, using his captive as a human shield. The exertion of hauling the big man back and forth was taking its toll, though; the lactic acid build-up in Stephen's arms was becoming almost unbearable, and his breath came in desperate, ragged gulps. But he kept hanging on. He had to: his life depended on it.

Just when he felt he could last no longer, he detected a change in the woman's facial expression: the intense gleam in her eyes abated and the determined creases in her forehead relaxed a little.

'Sorry, Brett, but the mission comes first,' she said, stepping back and slipping the weapon into her handbag.

The man tried to cry out, but succeeded in producing only a strangled gurgling sound, as the woman turned and strode off towards the emergency exit.

Wrong-footed by this unexpected turn of events, Stephen must have let his grip relax a little, for the man succeeded in delivering a crushing blow with his elbow to Stephen's solar plexus. The wind was driven from him in an agonising rush and he doubled up in pain, dropping to the floor as his captive wriggled free.

By the time Stephen recovered enough to look up, he found himself staring straight into the muzzle of the pistol which had been kicked aside in the struggle.

'Now, you fucker,' growled the man with the gun, his furious scowl rendered all the more menacing by the blood streaming from his ruined ear and down his cheek and neck, 'you're going to the same place as your pretty partner ... but I'm gonna make it slow and painful.'

Stephen's brain went into overdrive as he sought a means – any means – of escape. It took but a second for him to realise there was none.

'Think I'll start with your knees ... one at a time ... then maybe a stomach shot ... let you bleed out slow. Of course, I won't have time to stay and watch – I have to go after my double-crossing partner, you see.'

Stephen was still too winded to speak, and what would be the point, anyway? He looked into his tormenter's eyes, with as much defiance as he could muster but, in truth, Stephen knew that this was the end.

He stared straight into the man's eyes, bracing himself for the excruciating pain which would result when the first bullet shattered his knee. As his executioner lowered the gun to point at Stephen's left knee, a slow, humourless smile spread across the man's face.

Stephen tensed for the impact of the bullet. And then he saw the muzzle flash.

The agonising pain which he had anticipated never came. The bullet tore into the marble floor tiles at least a foot wide of its target. *How could he miss from that range?* Looking up at the man's face, Stephen saw that the malevolent smile had been replaced by an expression of startled surprise. His hand dropped to his side and the gun fell to the floor with a loud clatter. He stood there, unmoving, for what seemed like several seconds, that mask of astonishment fixed on his face. Then his knees buckled and he collapsed to the floor. Behind him stood Carla, holding Derek Schultz's gun in a double-handed grip, the muzzle swaying unsteadily.

Chapter 40

Stephen and Carla had taken a room in the Lago Mar Hotel in Fort Lauderdale, around thirty miles up the Gulf coast from Miami Beach. Although the police had initially assumed the bomb blast at the Palm Grove Hotel was a terrorist attack, their investigations would surely soon reveal that a very different scenario had, in fact, unfolded that fateful evening. Stephen and Carla didn't want to be in Miami when the police really started digging, particularly once Derek Schultz, the security chief, had been interviewed and would have provided detailed descriptions of the two of them.

They sat opposite one another in their hotel room, either side of a glass-topped coffee table.

'So what really *did* happen back there?' mused Carla.

'Hard to say for sure,' said Stephen, his mood sombre, 'but one thing's for sure: that man and woman were a professional assassination team, just like Emma and I were. Just look at the facts.' Stephen laid the forefinger of his right hand on the little finger of his left. 'First off, Emma – I don't know what else to call her – was a trained killer. Only other trained killers would be able to take her out like that.'

'Secondly' – he counted out another finger – 'that woman was prepared to leave her partner to his probable death for the sake of what she called "the mission".'

'And finally,' – he counted out a third finger – 'they shot Professor Mandelson.'

Carla nodded, thoughtfully. 'So, you think it was a rival assassination team, also aiming to steal Professor Mandelson's research and make sure that it never became available to the world at large.'

'I can't think of any other explanation,' replied Stephen, '… and what's more, I think they have succeeded. The fact that they destroyed Mandelson's laptop means it's almost certain that they had a copy of his work. I'd lay bets that woman walked off with it.'

'But who else would want to suppress Professor Mandelson's discovery?'

Stephen shrugged. 'Who knows … maybe a pharmaceutical company which realised its own, relatively ineffective, drug addiction treatments would be rendered obsolete?'

Carla's eyes widened in disbelief. 'A medical drugs company? But surely no reputable company would stoop to such depths?'

Would they? Stephen really didn't know how far the bosses of such companies would go to protect a multi-billion-dollar industry.

'I don't know,' he admitted. 'Maybe it was some other criminal network … perhaps a rival drug cartel, anxious to protect its own illegal trade.'

'Seems more likely,' opined Carla.

Suddenly, a wave of guilt and self-loathing swept over Stephen. 'Oh Christ, Carla, this is all my fault. If Emma and I hadn't taken on this Godforsaken mission in the first place, Doctor Holt and your friend, Sylvia, would still be alive today.' He hung his head in despair. 'And maybe Professor Mandelson would still be alive too. Perhaps his breakthrough would have been released to the world, saving thousands of lives.' He looked up at Carla, gazing intently into her dark brown eyes. 'And now? It's all just totally … fucked.' He paused for a moment, trying to control the tears which threatened to burst forth. 'Just what kind of monster am I, Carla?'

She rose from her chair, skirting around the coffee table to sit beside him, encircling his neck with her arms and pulling him to her. After days spent in the same, unwashed clothes, they had both now enjoyed the luxury of a hot shower and some new clothes. She smelt good, the fragrance of shampoo still lingering in her hair, blending with her own feminine scent. In spite of his dark, morose mood, Stephen felt the stirrings of sexual desire in his loins.

'You can't think like that,' she whispered. 'If you hadn't taken this thing on, they'd have found someone else to do it. Look how they had a replacement lined up when you dropped out.'

He was savouring the closeness of her body, and he felt an almost-overwhelming urge to pull her to him – immerse himself in her completely. But this just wasn't right; he pulled gently away from her, suppressing the desire which had erupted within him.

'But I *did* take it on, Carla,' he whispered.

'OK … you did, but once you realised what was happening, you did everything you could to stop it.'

'But I failed, and what's more I dragged you into the whole goddam mess.'

'You also saved me from being raped,' she reminded him, 'or possibly even killed. You are not the terrible person you believe you are.'

He shook his head, giving a wry smile. 'I was prepared to kill innocent people and deprive the world of a major medical breakthrough which could save countless lives … all just for money. What does that say about what kind of person I am?'

She cupped his chin in her hands, lifting his head until she could look directly into his eyes. 'OK, you made some bad choices … *really* bad choices … but that's in the past. I didn't know you then, but I know you now. You are just *not* that person anymore.'

He appreciated the faith that Carla was placing in him, but he knew he had done terrible things, and no words of condolence could change that. He sank into an even deeper pit of despair.

'You're a lovely person Carla, and I know you really mean what you're saying, but I know what I've done, and what I'm responsible for. Several people are dead because of me, including the most brilliant medical research scientist of modern times, and his discovery is now in the hands of criminals who will use it for their own evil purposes.'

He put his head in his hands and began to weep.

Chapter 41

Responsibility for the bomb blast at the Palm Grove was claimed by ISIS, citing one of their 'soldiers' as the perpetrator. The police refused to either confirm or refute this claim, leading to increased speculation that the explosion was not, in fact, the work of Islamist terrorists, but was somehow linked to Professor Mandelson's death.

The murder of Professor Mandelson made front page news throughout the entire country. Although the police gave no official statement about the motive for the murder, the media lost little time in constructing their own interpretations.

'World Famous Medical Researcher Murdered to Suppress his Ground-Breaking, New Discovery,' proclaimed one headline. The articles beneath the numerous sensational headlines outlined various theories as to who was behind the murder: big pharma, mafia, drug barons – even rival researchers. In truth, though, all such theories were based on nothing more than informed – or, in some cases misinformed – speculation.

Astonishingly, no-one, other than Ethan, had actually died as a result of the blast itself. The evacuation warning had come just in time to get everyone out of the function room before the bomb detonated. Several of the conference attendees had received serious injuries but, mercifully, none of them had proved fatal.

The medical research community showed remarkable resilience and defiance in the face of this vicious attack, and vowed to go ahead with the conference at a later date. It wouldn't be the same without the keynote speaker and his much-anticipated announcement, of course, but there was still plenty of other business to discuss and, moreover, they wanted to demonstrate that the march of medical science could not be halted by such malicious tactics.

And so, just two weeks after the horrendous attack at the Palm Grove, the conference was reconvened, amid much-heightened security, at the nearby Miami Marriott Biscayne Bay Hotel.

***

Bob Gench made the opening address.

'Ladies and Gentlemen, it would hardly be fitting to introduce these proceedings without referring back to the terrible events which curtailed the original conference.

'One can only wonder at the twisted motivation of the people who planted the bomb at the Palm Grove Hotel, but we must thank God that the evacuation warning came in time to save many lives.

'The fact that so many of you are in attendance today testifies to the determination of this community to go on furthering the cause of fighting drug addiction and its devastating impact on so many young people's lives.

'This tremendous turnout also demonstrates that you courageous folk in the scientific community will never, ever, be bowed by the threat of violence – you know that your work is too important to let that happen.'

He paused for a moment to an enthusiastic round of applause from his audience.

When the applause died down, he continued, 'You should all have the new programs, laying out the revised agenda for the conference, but before we embark on the official program, I would like to introduce a special guest.'

He turned to his left and extended his hand to invite his guest onto the stage. 'Ladies and Gentlemen ... Professor Richard Mandelson.'

The room fell into a stunned silence as Gench stood aside to allow the slightly-stooped figure who had shuffled onto the stage to approach the podium. After a few seconds, a solitary handclap in the audience broke the silence, then another, and within a few more seconds the entire room erupted in thunderous applause. It was, indeed, Professor Mandelson.

The professor held up his hand, palm-outward, and patted the air. Gradually the applause died down.

Mandelson cleared his throat, fiddling with the microphone until a faint whistle of feedback had faded away. 'As you can see,' he began, 'I'm not actually dead.'

Another ripple of applause flowed through the room.

'This,' said the professor, reaching into his inside jacket pocket, withdrawing and holding up a small book, 'was what saved my life.' It was his precious diary. 'For those of you nearer the back of the room, here's a better view.'

He tapped a couple of keys on the tablet mounted on the podium and the screen behind him lit up with a closeup image of the diary. Slightly away from the centre of the front cover of the diary was a small, circular hole, blackened around the edges. A collective gasp swept around the room.

'The person who tried to kill me had only a tiny handbag-type gun. I'm told these weapons are not terribly powerful and are only effective at close range. Well the range *was* close … *very* close, but fortunately my diary was in the path of the bullet. The bullet *did* pass right though the diary, as you can see' – he gestured towards the image on the screen – 'but so much of its velocity was sapped by so doing that it only penetrated a relatively short way into my chest. I am still nursing a cracked rib, but the bullet stopped well short of my heart.' He paused and looked up: dead silence, and a sea of stunned-looking faces. 'So, here I am,' he concluded.

A further second or so of silence ensued, followed by a rapturous round of applause.

'I think many of you are aware that I was planning to make an announcement about a very significant discovery at the conference; it seems that certain parties were prepared to go to any lengths to prevent my doing so. They even made sure that they destroyed or deleted all of my research data and every legitimate copy or backup of that data so that, after my supposed death, no other scientists could reproduce that discovery.' He paused for a moment. 'Or at least they thought they had …

'Fortunately, they didn't know about this.' He held up a black, rectangular, plastic object, not much larger than a cigarette packet. 'It's the hard drive which I keep in my own home in order to back up my laptop every evening. I like to have complete control of my data, so I never was entirely happy to rely solely on the backup on the University's main system.'

A stunned silence soon gave way to murmurs of delight.

'My research data is all here,' he said, moving his hand slowly from left to right in order to display the hard drive to all sections of the audience.

Once again, the room was filled with enthusiastic applause.

'The police advised that, until my research findings had been made public, my life was still in danger, so the fact that I survived the attack, and my research had not been destroyed, has been kept secret, until now.

'So now, if you will forgive me for the alteration to the published program, I would like to share with all of you the full details of what I believe is the most effective treatment for cocaine addiction which has ever been developed.'

For the next fifty minutes, Professor Mandelson laid out the details of his research and the addiction cure which it had led to.

'And so,' concluded the professor, as he began to wind up his speech, 'it is my fervent hope, that this new treatment will soon be approved for general usage and will ultimately end this hideous trade in human misery.

'The fact that vested interests in the illegal drugs trade were prepared to commit murder to ensure that such a treatment never became widely available bears testament to just how important it is.

'I seek no personal financial reward for my contribution to the war against this insidious affliction. I just hope that my discovery will save lives that would otherwise have been lost.'

The thunderous applause which greeted his final words said far more than any speech or acknowledgement could ever have done.

Chapter 42

Madison didn't know the name of the man who had contracted her for the assignment; all communication had previously been via intermediaries, and she had never met him face to face. Now though, for the first time, he had arranged to meet her in person. The venue was a seedy-looking office at the back of an out-of-town car workshop. The two men who had brought her there stood either side of, and a little behind her, while the man she had come to see sat opposite her, behind an old and battered wooden desk. He was short, and rather overweight, his swarthy complexion marred by an ugly-looking scar on his left cheek, which ran from the corner of his mouth right up to his eye. The glassy, expressionless stare from said eye left no doubt that it was an artificial replacement. Madison knew this was going to be a difficult meeting, and the intimidating appearance of her employer did little to quell the growing unease in her stomach.

'So,' said the man, his voice a gravelly growl, 'it seems you have not fulfilled the terms of our contract.'

'Look,' said Madison, determined not to be cowed by his menacing manner, 'I'll admit that it didn't go according to plan, but there were mitigating circumstances.'

'And what would they be?' he said, taking a cigar from the box on the desk, twirling it between his fingers as he held it beneath his nose to savour the aroma.

'We thought the original guy on the Colombian team was dead,' replied Madison. 'How were we to know he would show up out of the blue? And he was damned good ... managed to get the drop on my partner for Christ's sake.'

The man did not immediately reply: he cut a small piece off one end of the cigar and placed it between his lips, lighting up and taking several deep draws, causing the tip to glow brightly. He turned his face upwards, expelling a plume of smoke, illuminated by a shaft of sunlight from the single, grubby window in the room. Still he did not speak. Madison was already getting irritated by the man's theatrics – she wanted to get down to business. She was about to elaborate on her explanation when the man finally responded.

'But you were supposed to be professionals ... able to deal with a few unexpected glitches.'

A surge of anger flared within her, but she didn't let it show; she kept her voice calm and level as she replied. 'I'd say that the sounding of the evacuation alarm before the bomb detonated was more than a "glitch". And having to leave my partner to die was rather more than a glitch, too. I did the best I could under the circumstances.'

The man took another deep draw from his cigar, holding the smoke for several seconds before turning his head to the side to exhale. 'The fact remains that Mandelson is alive and his discovery has been announced to the world. For the amount we were paying you that is hardly a satisfactory outcome ...wouldn't you agree?'

Madison knew that there was no point in persisting with trying to justify the failure of the mission. Since the man had brought up the subject of the fee, this seemed like the right moment to press ahead with her prepared negotiating strategy.

'OK, so we failed to suppress Mandelson's research data, but before it can result in a freely available medication, there will have to be extensive trials, FDA approval ... the whole nine yards. That will take years. You have the entire research details in your possession – your experts can produce a drug in a fraction of that time, with no need for all that testing and certification. You have a window of opportunity when *you* are the only ones who will be able to supply the new drug. That's got to be worth a truckload of money.'

The Mexican laid his cigar in an ashtray and leaned forward, placing both elbows on the desk and steepling his hands. 'And why are you telling me something which I obviously already know?'

This clearly wasn't going to be easy, but then Madison hadn't expected it to be.

'Just making sure we're on the same page,' she said. 'So ... we're agreed that, although I have been unable to give you everything you wanted from this project, what I *have* provided still has considerable value.'

'Ah ... so you wish to negotiate.'

It wasn't a question, and Madison did not waste time answering in the affirmative.

'Look,' she said, 'the originally-agreed fee was twenty million dollars. My partner, whose share would have been ten million, is now, unfortunately, dead; I'm not expecting to get any of his share of the money.'

'Very generous of you,' said the man, his tone dripping with sarcasm.

She ignored the barbed comment. 'I also accept that I did not deliver everything we were contracted to, although as you have already agreed, what I *have* delivered has very considerable value to you.'

The man picked up and inspected his cigar, which looked to be in danger of going out. He placed it between his lips and took a long, slow drag, restoring the tip to a bright glow. He held the smoke for several seconds – all the time keeping his eyes locked on hers – before expelling it to the side.

'So, what are you proposing?'

Madison was tensed for this very moment. She did her best to sound calm and confident. 'I believe five million would be a fair figure.'

His response was to dissolve into a coughing fit. She couldn't figure out whether it was due to inhaling too much cigar smoke or a reaction to her demand. It soon became clear that it was the latter. He laid his cigar – now almost finished – in the ashtray and leaned forward, piercing her with a stare like a gimlet.

'Obviously you cannot be serious. You have manifestly failed to fulfil the objectives of the mission, yet you still expect to be paid half of the original fee.'

'Actually, a quarter,' she said, trying to sound much more confident than she felt.

He let out a gravelly chuckle. 'Well your dead partner can't spend his half, can he?'

She did not respond to the rhetorical question. 'Look, in order to keep things civil and avoid any unpleasantness, I'd be prepared to accept four million.'

He shook his head, casting his gaze downward. After a few seconds, he looked up and held her eyes. 'I'll tell you what *I* think is a reasonable figure … zilch, zero, nothing.'

She sprang to her feet, placing both hands, palm downwards, on the desk. 'Why you—'

Before she could even begin to remonstrate, one of the goons behind her had his hands on her shoulders, gently but forcefully encouraging her to sit back down.

'Furthermore,' the man continued, 'I have grave concerns that, following this discussion – the outcome of which I imagine you are not entirely happy with – you might seek to undermine what little advantage we are able to glean from your feeble offering. Perhaps you might even be considering some act of revenge?'

With a sickening certainty, she knew where this was going. She had come completely unarmed; she knew she would be frisked before the meeting anyway, and she hadn't wanted to give the impression that she had come prepared for a showdown. She was, however, expert in unarmed combat, so when the Mexican looked past her and gave an almost-imperceptible nod to the man behind her, she was ready.

She whirled around to confront the man, who was still only halfway towards levelling his gun. A lightning-fast, high kick knocked the weapon from his grasp and the sharp, jabbing punch she delivered to his throat sent him reeling.

Before she could spin around to face the other man, however, she felt a cold, hard force, biting into her neck; in an instant, she realised the other man had slung a garrotte around her neck. The chances of escaping such a hold were slim indeed, but staring death in the face, all her survival instincts kicked in. She drove her elbow back into the man's stomach with all the force she could muster. His grip slackened for a moment, sufficient to allow her to get the fingers of her right hand between the wire and her neck. Desperately, she sought to pull the lethal wire away, but the man had only been temporarily disabled; now he tightened his grip once more, trapping her fingers against her neck. As he pulled, harder and harder, she felt the wire begin to bite into her fingers. She felt the warm flow of blood down her hand, and then, unimaginable pain as the wire found the joints in the bones of her fingers. Still her instinct to survive forced her to fight back … until suddenly she had nothing to pull against. Her hand fell away as the wire sliced clean through all four fingers.

The last thing that Madison ever saw was her own hand, held before her, spurting blood freely from the four severed stumps.

Mercifully, she lost consciousness before the wire sliced fully into her throat.

Chapter 43

Kelly Malone turned up for her late shift at 2 p.m. As she walked through the front entrance of the hospital, she gave her customary greeting to the girl on the reception desk.

'Hi Suzie – how's it going?'

'Good … you?'

'Yeah, OK, I guess.'

'Hey,' said the girl on the desk, a sparkle of mirth in her eyes, 'you got a new guy after you?'

She laughed. 'Not that I know of. Why?'

'You sure? You're not two-timing Rick, are you?'

Kelly tilted her head to one side, drawing her eyebrows together in a disbelieving frown. 'Rick and I are rock solid … you know that. What are you on about, anyway?'

'This guy came in earlier, asking after you. Big guy … quite a hunk actually, but probably a bit older than your usual type.'

Kelly's eyes widened and her mouth flew open. 'What do you mean, "my usual type"? Cheeky bitch!'

The banter between them was good-humoured; both knew each other well enough not to take offence at anything the other said.

'Anyway,' said Suzie, 'he left something for you.' She reached below the counter and retrieved a bulky, brown, padded envelope.

'Weird … did he give his name?'

'No … just said he was a friend. Oh, come on … the suspense is killing me. Just open it, will you?'

Kelly ripped open the envelope. Her jaw dropped as she withdrew the contents: two wads of banknotes; the sleeve on each bore the handwritten label '$10,000'.

'What the …?' murmured Suzie.

'I … I have no idea,' whispered Kelly.

'Wait … there's a note,' breathed Suzie, handing it to Kelly.

She began to read, out loud.

241

Kelly,

I just wanted to thank you for everything you have done for me. I can't begin to explain everything that's happened but I know who I am now, and I have to go far from here to make a new life. I won't ever see you again, but I'll be eternally grateful for your care and your friendship. The first $10,000 is to help you and Rick get started in your new home. The second $10,000 is for Doctor Holt's family, if indeed he has one – we never spoke about such things. If he doesn't have next of kin, then the whole $20,000 is yours.

Please don't ever try to contact me. I can't explain – it's complicated – but I have to disappear completely.

Thanks again.

'Stephen'

The two women looked at each other in wide-eyed disbelief.

'Who the hell is this guy?' breathed Suzie.

'He's ... well, he was a patient of mine.'

'But why the cloak and dagger stuff ... was he involved in Doctor Holt's murder?'

'No, of course not ... he was just ...' Her voice tailed off.

'And why does he sign his name in inverted commas?'

Kelly sighed. 'Like he says ... "it's complicated".'

***

Kyle Richards gazed at the sparkling stone which graced the ring in the small presentation box which he held open on his lap. It wasn't a real diamond – he could never afford something like that. But Sylvia would have loved it; he could imagine how proudly she would have shown it to the other girls in the club and, of course, to her best friend, Carla. A tear welled forth and trickled down his cheek as he struggled to come to terms with the fact that Sylvia was gone, that all his dreams of building a new life with her as his wife were now in tatters.

What made it even more agonising was that there was no reason, no possible explanation as to why his beautiful girlfriend had been so savagely gunned down. The police had no answers, either – they could establish no motive, and no-one had been arrested in connection with this senseless murder. He knew that Sylvia had become involved with some pretty undesirable people, but that was by accident, not design. He could not bring himself to believe that she had actually done anything to warrant such dire retribution.

It had been his intention, when they got married, to take her away from Miami, and the whole shady gang scene – to start a new life far away. That dream was now in shreds; nothing could bring her back. But now, he craved *answers* – some explanation, some way to make sense of it all.

His introspective reflection was interrupted by the strident trill of his doorbell. He let out a deep sigh, closed the ring box, and laid it on the table in front of him. Wiping the dampness away from his cheek with the back of his hand, he went to open the front door. He was confronted by a rather scruffy-looking young boy – probably no more than ten or eleven years old.

'You Kyle Richards?' asked the boy.

'Yeah … and who would you be?'

'Got a parcel for you,' said the boy producing, from behind his back, a fat, brown, padded envelope.

'What's this all about? You ain't UPS or DHL – who gave you—?'

But the boy had dropped the envelope at Kyle's feet and was now sprinting away as fast as his skinny legs would carry him. Kyle picked up the package, which bore his name, handwritten. The envelope felt firm and quite heavy but, as he probed it with his fingers, he could detect no hard edges: it felt as though it contained only papers. He shook his head in bewilderment, closed the door, and made his way back to the couch where he had been previously sitting.

Tearing open the package he was astonished to find two wads of banknotes, each enclosed in a paper sleeve with the handwritten inscription '$10,000'.

'What the heck—?' he breathed out loud.

He looked inside the envelope and saw a single sheet of paper, which he withdrew. It was a typed note … at the bottom was Carla's signature.

Kyle,

I can't tell you how devastated I am by what happened to Sylvia. I can't imagine what you must be going through right now. The fact that Sylvia's funeral has had to be delayed while the authorities carry out an autopsy must have made things even worse – if that is possible.

For reasons which are too complicated to explain, I have to leave Miami for good. Before I go, though, I need to tell you something – I know what happened to her.

You know full well that she – and I – got involved with some pretty bad people, but she never did anything to cross them and that's not why she died. Sadly she was just in the wrong place at the wrong time and became an innocent victim of something else entirely.

I wish I could explain more, but really, I can't. To do so might put other lives in danger, so all I can say is that she did nothing to deserve such a fate.

I know money can't begin to compensate for the loss of such a wonderful person, but I'd like you to be able to at least give her a fitting send-off, so use as much of the $20,000 as you need for this. Whatever is left over is for you to use as you wish.

You're probably wondering how I have come by that sort of money. I'm afraid that's another part of a very complicated story which I just can't tell you, except to say it wasn't through my doing anything criminal.

Sadly, I won't be able to attend the funeral of my very best friend. In fact, I can't ever come back to Miami, and you will never see me again. You know, though, that my thoughts and prayers will always be with you – and Sylvia.

All my love, Carla x

He re-read the note several times. In some ways it raised more questions than answers. He desperately wanted to see Carla, to talk to her, to *understand*. But he knew her well, for she and Sylvia had been like sisters. He knew that she wouldn't take off like that, or leave such a cryptic explanation, unless she absolutely had to.

At least he now knew for sure that Sylvia had done nothing to bring this terrible fate upon herself. That was some small comfort. But the fact that she had lost her life for absolutely no reason was just … such a waste … so utterly senseless. He didn't know what to think – his emotions were in utter turmoil. He needed time to digest what he had learned … to try to make some sense of it all.

He put his head in his hands and began to weep.

Chapter 44

'James Connolly,' said Carla as she gazed at Stephen's new Canadian passport. 'I like it.'

'You think I look like a "James" then?'

She tilted her head as she looked at him, appraisingly. 'Yeah ... and the new haircut suits you, too. Not sure about the beard though.'

They were sitting in the departure lounge at Miami International Airport waiting to board an Air Canada flight to Toronto. They had laid low in Fort Lauderdale for a few weeks before attempting the potentially hazardous manoeuvre of exiting the USA. Stephen's new 'buzz cut' and neatly trimmed beard had radically altered his appearance and, although he was a bundle of nerves as he passed through passport control, it had all gone without a hitch.

Carla, too, had a new identity and a new look. Her hair was shorter, and coloured a medium blonde tone, with contrasting lowlights – perhaps a little unusual for a Latina, but by no means exceptional

Stephen studied her new passport – also Canadian. '"Juanita Sanchez Ruiz",' he read out. 'Pretty.'

She smiled. 'Thanks ... actually, I kind of like it too.'

Stephen – or James, as he kept reminding himself – placed his hand on top of hers. 'Just one more hurdle – when we go through immigration in Toronto – and then we're home and dry.'

She nodded, absently, her eyes drifting off to some faraway place.

'What will you do when we get there?' he said, gently pulling her back to the here and now.

'Oh, I don't know. I don't have any living family, and the few friends I have ... or had ... all live in Miami. Obviously, I can't come back here.' She looked into his eyes. 'I guess I'm starting from scratch.'

The mention of her friends stirred in him a pang of remorse. He squeezed her hand gently. 'I'm so sorry about your friend, Sylvia. Are you sure there's nothing else we can do … no-one we can help?'

'She had no living family either and, as far as I know, I was her only close girlfriend. I think helping Kyle with the funeral expenses was all we could really do … though it seems little enough.' A tear welled over and began to trickle down her cheek. She grabbed a tissue from her handbag and wiped it away.

He paused for a moment before whispering, 'Too many innocent people died over this thing.'

She nodded, 'But at least Professor Mandelson survived, and his discovery will save many more lives.'

They both sat in silence for a few seconds, reflecting on that thought.

'Anyway,' she added, 'we've done all we can now. It's time for us to disappear. What about you? What will you do when we get to Canada?'

He shrugged. 'Everything I thought I knew about my previous life was a lie. It all seemed so *real*, though, especially Emma … she was …' His voice tailed off as he fought to contain the emotion which threatened to burst forth. After a couple of seconds, he continued. 'As for my *actual* previous life, I'm not sure I really want to learn more.' He fell silent once more; she placed a reassuring hand on his arm. At length, he added, 'As far as I know, I have no family or friends to consider, so I guess – like you – I'm starting from scratch.'

'Well,' she said, her eyes holding his now, 'if we're both starting from scratch, what about starting from scratch together? I mean … we could give that a try, couldn't we? You know, sort of see how it goes?'

Even her olive complexion could not hide the flush in her cheeks.

'You know?' he said. 'I'd like that … I'd like that very much.'

__Epilogue__

One year later

Stephen and Carla – or James and Juanita as they were now known – were settling into their new, and quieter, life in Toronto.

Juanita was fulfilling her dream of becoming an artist. She wasn't making huge amounts of money from it: most of her paintings – which, typically, took several weeks, or even months, to complete – sold for around two or three thousand dollars. But she was happy – *really* happy – to have left her former life behind and be making a living, however modest, from doing what she loved, and to be sharing her life with a man who, whatever his previous transgressions, was a caring and compassionate companion.

Much of James's memory had returned, particularly of his earlier career when he had trained to be a doctor, but some of the darker corners of his subsequent life as a paid assassin remained a closed book. It was probably better that way.

He would have liked to rebuild a career as a doctor, but to do so would have involved training and qualifying anew, and there would be a significant risk of his true identity emerging. Instead, he took a job as a security guard with a company delivering cash payrolls in armoured trucks to various companies. These people didn't ask too many questions about one's former life and the pay wasn't too bad.

Strangely enough, he still had no recollection of his real name, but, in the end, did that really matter? He was just happy to be making an honest living and to be with the woman with whom he had now fallen deeply in love.

***

It was Saturday evening. The two of them had settled down to watch TV with a home-delivered pizza and a bottle of Chardonnay. They planned to watch a pay-per-view movie, but decided first to catch up on the latest news.

Most of the news was, as usual, pretty depressing: continuing unrest in the Middle East, another terrorist attack in Europe, hurricanes in the Caribbean, an earthquake in Mexico and—

The next item made James freeze, the slice of pizza halfway to his mouth. As he absorbed the details of the story, he laid the food down: he no longer had any appetite.

A junior reporter for the New York Times, Julia Turner – just twenty-four years old – had been found murdered in Central Park. Now, murders in New York City weren't exactly unusual, but it was the *manner* of the killing which had caught his attention. While the police had, apparently, been pretty tight-lipped about the details, the TV station had learned from 'its exclusive sources' that the victim had been shot once in the chest and once through her ear.

Now, it wouldn't be especially unusual for a murderer who brought his victim down with a body shot to finish the job with a head shot ... but through the *ear*?' He knew of only one person whose M.O. matched that, and he was one of, if not *the,* most highly-paid and highly-feared professional assassins in the world. That person – a former associate of his – could command a fee running into tens of millions of dollars for a single hit. Why would anyone pay that sort of money to eliminate a rookie reporter? Unless of course that reporter was onto something big ... *very* big.

He looked across at Juanita, who showed no reaction at all to the story. Why should she? As he regarded her pretty profile he was suddenly wracked with indecision. Should he just push this news item to the back of his mind and continue to enjoy his comfortable new life in Canada, or should he try to find out what was behind this disturbing report?

THE END.

Author's Note

Most of the action in this book takes place in and around the closely-linked cities of Miami, Florida and nearby Miami Beach. Many of the locations which feature in the book are real: for example, Loews Hotel, the Delano Hotel, the Lago Mar Hotel, and the Miami Marriott Biscayne Bay Hotel. However, I have also created a number of fictitious establishments: The Palm Grove Hotel, Eduardo's Restaurant, El Refugio Motel, La Mariposa restaurant, and the Marsden Medical School. I did so because the plot required some pretty unpleasant events to unfold in some of these locations – I had no wish to besmirch the reputations of genuine establishments!

The medical phenomena described in the book may, or may not, be possible in real life. Who knows? As Doctor Holt says in the book, '… the human brain is an extremely complex organ, about which there is much we still don't understand'.

Ray Green

www.ingramcontent.com/pod-product-compliance
Lightning Source LLC
Chambersburg PA
CBHW020358210626
46816CB00006BB/2023